SHADOW HARVEST

SYDNEY RYE MYSTERIES
BOOK 7

EMILY KIMELMAN

Shadow Harvest
Sydney Rye Mysteries, Book 7
Copyright © 2015 by Emily Kimelman

Heading illustration: Autumn Whitehurst
Cover Design: Christian Bentulan
Formatting: Jamie Davis

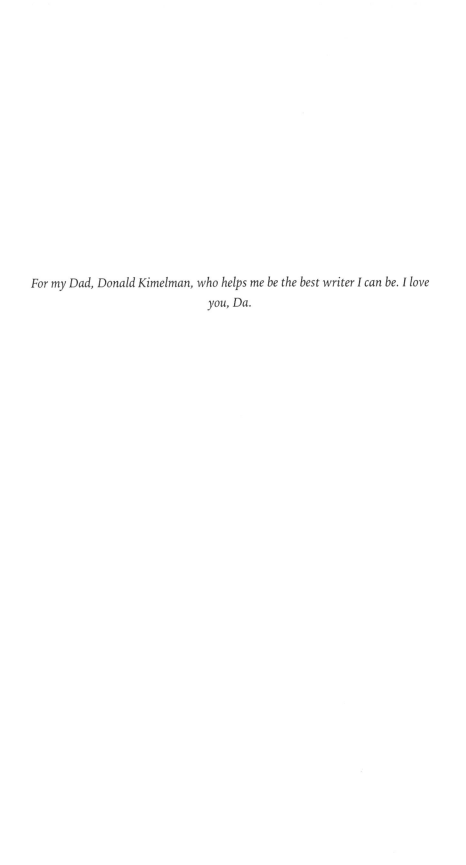

For my Dad, Donald Kimelman, who helps me be the best writer I can be. I love you, Da.

CHAPTER ONE
OUT OF THE FIRE

The plane was small and my mind was full. Full of memories, plans, plots, and worries. Anxiety—a creeping menace slithering across my skin, preying on my nerves, forcing my mind to bend to its will, to hide from the truth and stare at lies. I shook myself, letting my short hair fall over my face in an attempt to banish it all.

The hair tickled the scars around my left eye. My bangs brushed the fainter of the two, which ran just above my eyebrow and disappeared into my hairline. The tips of my chin-length locks grazed the thicker of the two. A deep pink line, it puckered the soft flesh under my left eye, following the arch of my cheekbone. My scars were a reminder of what mad men will do if you don't stop them.

My dog, Blue, raised his head from where it had been resting on my knee. looking at me with his mismatched blue and brown eyes and raising his brows in question. "Everything is okay," I said, resting my hand on the top of his head. Blue closed his eyes, the dark lashes forming a stark outline against the white fur of his muzzle.

A giant of a dog, Blue was a mutt I'd adopted over four years ago. As tall as a Great Dane with the body of a wolf, markings of a Siberian Husky, long elegant muzzle of a Collie and instincts of a German Shepherd, Blue was my rock. Without him I was just a drifting mess of a woman.

Blue had saved my life countless times. I depended on him. A spike of anxiety stabbed through me again as I thought about his age, his inevitable death. I pushed the thought away, breathing in through my nose and slowly out of my mouth.

Blue rested his head on my knee again. I could feel his warm breath through the light linen pants. I'd been traveling for almost twenty-four hours, leaving my clothing wrinkled. My body, used to physical activity, felt tightly coiled. All this sitting in planes was probably partly responsible for the anxiety coursing through my veins.

I looked out the window. Nothing but clouds beneath us. White and undulating, like a whipped cream pie. There were eight seats on the plane, but I had the passenger area to myself. I could see the captain and co-pilot. The co-pilot's hair was jet black while the captain's showed sprays of gray. I didn't know either of the men personally but they were members of Joyful Justice, the vigilante network named after me, inspired by a lie.

The two pilots, the people I was on my way to see, all of the recruits of Joyful Justice around the world, thought I'd killed my brother's murderer. That when the police and politicians made it clear there wouldn't be justice I proved them all wrong. But I didn't. I arrived too late. When I got to Kurt Jessup's office in New York City's mayoral mansion he was dead. I shot his corpse, left my fingerprints, did everything stupid a killer could do. I set myself up. That's why I'd run away and changed my name from Joy Humbolt to Sydney Rye, transforming my life in the process.

"Ms. Rye," came the captain's voice over the PA system. I could see his jaw muscles moving. "We'll be starting our descent now. We'll have you down in about twenty minutes."

I nodded even though neither of them was looking at me. I stared out the window as we descended into the soft white swirls. The small plane shook, bumping along through the rough air. I breathed in through my nose, out through my mouth.

Blue scooted closer, offering his weight as a comfort. I played with one of his velvety ears as we came out of the clouds. The waters of the South Pacific appeared below us, aquamarine over white sand. I could see the island ahead of us. It looked unpopulated, just a jungle of green. The volcano, dipped in the center where thousands of years ago molten lava had burst from the sea, was dormant now. It was comforting to think that such violence had created this peaceful looking place. Did all peace bloom from mayhem?

I let my mind wander to Dan as we circled the runway, a strip of black in a field of green. A founding member of Joyful Justice and a computer genius, Dan was a man I thought I had loved. Whom I imagined I could be happy with if I wasn't so fucked up. A sweet smile, broad shoulders and tapered waist, Dan looked at me like I was some kind of hero, someone he would die for.

But I doubted all that now. I suspected he'd betrayed me. That he'd been telling my secrets for years to the one person I'd tried to hide them from, Robert Maxim. Bobby to his friends. And now, weirdly enough, I could count myself as a friend of Bobby Maxim. After years of hating him, of blaming him for taking my revenge from me. After knowing, for sure, for absolute sure, that Robert Maxim was the worst kind of man, I had now let him join Joyful Justice. I'd decided to trust him.

So Dan had betrayed me to Robert Maxim, but I'd found out after I'd decided to trust Robert Maxim. So how pissed should I be? I laughed out loud. Blue raised his head and checked my face, letting his tail tap against the floor. I smiled down at him and scratched under his chin. He tapped his tail louder. "What do you think?" I asked him. "What should I do about this betrayal?"

As usual Blue did not have a response.

Wind battered the plane. I could hear it whistling around the small vessel and see the pilot's forearms strain to hold the plane steady. As we neared the ground one wing dipped for a moment. Then we touched down with a jolt that knocked all other anxiety out of my mind, sharpening my vision and pumping me full of adrenaline. The wind continued to push against the plane, but we were down. We were safe.

When the plane came to a stop, I stood, grabbed my small bag from the seat next to me, and waited as the co-pilot opened the door. The stairs unfolded and met the tarmac as an open-topped Jeep Wrangler pulled alongside the plane. Dan was at the wheel. His hair was longer than the last time I'd seen him. It covered his ears and brushed the neckline of his worn cotton green T-shirt. His beard was shaggy, bleached from the sun and wild-looking. Dan smiled as he looked up at me. I couldn't help but return the grin.

Dan jumped out of the Jeep. Blue and I made our way down the steps. Dan embraced me. He smelled like sunscreen, salty sea, and a whiff of coconut. Blue tapped his feet next to us, waiting impatiently for his own greeting. I wrapped my arms around Dan's neck and pushed my face into his chest, breathing in his intoxicating scents Enjoying this moment before I exploded our relationship.

Blue, patience all used up, pushed his muzzle between us and we broke apart laughing. Dan knelt down and gave Blue a good scratching while my dog closed his eyes and made noises expressing his gratitude. Dan stood up and took my bag. "It's good to see you, Sydney, you look well."

I nodded. "I'm great," I said. Dan had reason to worry about me. It had been less than six months since he found me in the Everglades, out of my mind after being dosed with the hallucinogen Datura. I was lucky to survive. I had lingering effects, sometimes I saw lightning that wasn't there and heard thunder that did not exist. But I'd learned to see those things for the hallucinations they were. It was possible I'd have to live with them for the rest of my life, or they may just fade away.

Dan threw my bag into the back seat and Blue jumped in next to it. I went around to the passenger side and climbed in, clicking my seatbelt into place. Dan turned us around and headed back down the runway. At the end of the strip of pavement we entered a dirt track that wound through the thick foliage. I held onto the side of the Jeep as we bumped along. "I'm excited to show you around," Dan said. "We've been hard at work. I'm so glad you've decided to join the council."

He was referring to the Joyful Justice council. It consisted of the founding members of the organization with one new addition. The original members included: Dan, Mulberry, a police detective I'd met in New York and convinced to help me escape the city and exact my revenge;

Merl, a martial arts trainer Mulberry sent to me when I was drinking my life away on a beach in Mexico, a man who convinced me to fight, to live for something; and Anita, a former reporter whose life I saved in India and who'd introduced me to the terrifying and seemingly unconquerable world of human trafficking.

Then there was Malina. I'd met her in Mexico right after Merl started training me. We had a friend in common who was brutally murdered like so many women on that treacherous border. Malina had been gunned down a couple of months earlier in Costa Rica. I saw it happen and the memory ripped at my soul, it split the calluses I'd formed over emotions that were best kept under wraps. They made me weak.

Malina was in charge of recruiting spies, assets as she called them. When Malina was killed, her friend, Lenox Gold, took over. He was a gigolo originally from Senegal who now ran an international operation of male escorts. Like Malina, he abhorred the human trafficking in his industry and was willing to spend his fortune and risk his life to stop it.

Then there was me. I wasn't a founding member of Joyful Justice. I found the whole idea of an organized vigilante network absurd. Especially the idea that I was the impetus for it. That I'd inspired these amazing people to take on the biggest, most intractable problems in this big bad world, was hard for me to take on. But after spending months recovering and denying my place in this organization, I'd embraced it. Now I had come to this island to understand the scope of our operations. At least that's what Dan thought. I was also here to make sure I could still trust him. I wasn't sure yet how I'd figure that out.

The path came to an abrupt end. A steep hillside covered in vines of small, shiny and dark green leaves rose before us. Dan hopped out. I went to follow, but he waved for me to stay in the Jeep. Dan pushed aside the vines, revealing a keypad hidden in the foliage, and entered a code. The vines separated like curtains on a stage to reveal a metal door that was rolling up into the rocks above.

"Very cool," I said as Dan got back behind the wheel. He looked over at me and grinned, proud and cute.

"I thought you'd like that," he said as we pulled forward into a cement hall wide enough for two cars to fit in side by side. The metal door closed behind us with a clunk that echoed in the long cement chamber. Fluorescent tubes hung from the ceiling and the space smelled of gas and tires. Brown muddy tracks showed where vehicles had gone before us.

We drove for a few minutes through the subterranean passage before Dan pulled into a wider space that served as a parking lot. There was another Jeep, two vans with off-road tires, and a mud splattered quad.

We climbed out of our ride. Blue hopped down to the ground and stretched before falling in line at my hip. Dan led the way to a metal door with another keypad next to it. "A lot of security," I said.

"You can never be too safe."

I smiled at the irony and nodded my head even though Dan was not looking at me. I watched as he entered the code and committed it to memory. "How many people are here?" I asked.

"Twenty-five right now," Dan said as he pushed through the door. "I'll show you to your room. Do you want a shower or anything before we begin? Are you hungry?"

I shook my head. "I'd like to get to work."

CHAPTER TWO

INTO THE FLAMES

We entered a cement hall, this one narrower, made for humans instead of vehicles. When we came to a door with another keypad Dan entered a different code then led us through to what looked like a hotel lobby. A woman with long blonde hair pulled back into a low braid smiled at us from behind a bamboo counter.

Wicker chairs with floral-patterned cushions faced each other around the room, seating areas for departing and arriving guests. Muzak played low through speakers mounted in the walls. "Welcome," the woman said, her accent Australian.

I smiled at her as we crossed the room. "Hi Bella," Dan said. She nodded and returned the greeting. "Ms. Rye is going to come straight down to control with me. Please arrange to have her bag taken to her room."

"Yes, sir," she said, smiling over at me. Bella was about twenty-five, tan, pretty, wearing a white button-down shirt with a crisp collar and a simple gold chain around her neck, the pendant disappearing into the collar of her blouse.

"Thanks," I said, pushing the bag onto the counter.

"Are you hungry? Thirsty?" she asked.

"Water please," I said. "And a bowl for Blue."

Bella ducked down behind the counter for a moment and returned with a bottle of water. Then she picked up the phone and requested a bowl of water be brought down to the control room for Blue. We headed to the elevators and Dan pushed the "down" button as I scanned the lobby. "This is kind of strange," I said to Dan, keeping my voice low enough that Bella would not overhear.

Dan smiled. "I know, but it works."

The elevator arrived and we entered the small space. Blue sat between us, his tail tapping rhythmically on the carpeted floor as we descended another five stories. "What was this place?" I asked.

"A billionaire's lair."

"Excuse me?"

"A corn mogul with serious fears about . He lived in Ohio and built this place as an ultimate refuge after falling in love with the island. He died before it was complete so we got it cheap."

The doors opened and we were in a large, curved room twice the size of the lobby. It was buzzing with activity. A large screen curved along one wall. It was broken up into sections: a jerky video stream from somewhere in a desert, aerial footage of a village surrounded by thick forests, maps with colored dots moving across them. In front of the screen men and women sat in tiered rows of workstations wearing head-phones and typing away on computers. "Welcome to the control center," Dan said, his face lighting up.

"Wow," I said. "This place is amazing,"

"Thanks, I'm so excited to be sharing it with you. Come into my office and I'll explain what we're doing here." Dan turned to his left and started up a flight of spiral steps to an office that looked down on the control center. He pushed open the glass door and held it for Blue and me. The office was large. A wide glass table covered in computer equip-ment faced the floor below. Beyond it lay a couch and two chairs and, between them, a coffee table covered in files and empty coffee mugs.

Dan passed me and started to tidy up, his cheeks growing rosy for a moment. "Dan, I know you're kind of a slob," I said with a smile.

He stopped and smiled, pushing hair off his forehead. "It's gotten worse," he said.

"Guess you don't find much time for gardening these days," I said. When we'd lived in Goa, Dan had nurtured a patch of vegetables behind our hut. He'd smoked hash and weeded while I read crinkled paperbacks, enjoying the sun and the soft sounds of the river that ran by the property. Now look at us, I thought, underground, surrounded by industrious people armed with the latest technology, fighting for a cause. What a change.

"Not much time, no," Dan said, his smile softer, tinged with sadness. That life seemed almost like a mirage now. "Here, sit," Dan said, grabbing up some papers off the couch. I took the place he offered and Blue laid down on the floor next to me. "So," Dan said, "where should we start?"

"At the beginning," I said. "Explain how we find out about bad guys and how we decide what to do about them."

Dan nodded. "We use the Joyful Justice website as a beginning to everything."

I nodded, anxiety curling up my throat. While I knew about the website, and had even met Dan through it, the idea of the site still made me uncomfortable.

Dan sat down in one of the chairs across from me. "As you know the site was started by Jacquelyn Saperstein." Jacquelyn's husband, Joseph Saperstein, was killed by Mayor Kurt Jessup, the same monster who shot my brother, James, in front of me. I flashed back to the blood on James's cheeks, the color draining from his skin, his gray eyes, so like my own, like my mother's, staring up at me, his lips saying goodbye.

I swallowed, pushing the memories away, bringing my mind back to Jacquelyn Saperstein. She was arrested for her husband's murder. When I exposed Kurt Jessup as the killer, her freedom was secured. In her gratitude she turned me into a folk hero. Not the gift I would have asked for, but in life we so rarely get to choose. "Jackie wanted a place for people to come together and defend you as well as share their own stories of injustice," Dan continued.

"Does she know what we've become?"

"No, she is not as involved in the site. Got remarried, has a kid."

I raised my eyebrows remembering the thin, devastated widow. I was glad to hear she'd found happiness in the four years since I'd seen her.

"Okay, so, it started as a gathering place, but people were sharing their stories and others were trying to help. The whole vigilante thing was starting before we even got involved."

"What do you mean?"

"Well, you know I was a member," he smiled and raised his eyebrows, "that's how we met after all."

When I'd gotten myself into a situation where I needed help I'd turned to Joyful Justice members. Dan was one of the people I recruited. But my motives were almost entirely selfish. I had not been looking to start a movement, just get myself out of danger.

"Yes, I know," I said.

There was a knock at the door. A young man, wearing shorts and a worn T-shirt, held a bowl of water. Dan motioned for him to enter.

The man was a little shorter than Dan at about six feet. His hair was dark brown with highlights from the sun and his eyes a sparkling blue. He smiled as he greeted Blue, putting down the bowl of water. "Beautiful dog," he said, looking up at me with those shiny eyes. The skin around them was unlined, no shadows underneath. I wondered if he could even distinguish his role here from playing an exciting computer game. With eyes like that he couldn't possibly understand the dangers and moral dilemmas that members of Joyful Justice were facing every day.

"Thanks," I said, extending my hand. "I'm Sydney."

"Mitchel," he said, shaking my hand. His was calloused across the palm. Obviously he didn't spend all his time in front of the computer. "Can I get you anything?"

"I'm good, thanks," I said, holding up my water bottle. He turned to Dan.

"Anything for you?"

"No, thanks Mitchel. I'm glad you two got a chance to meet," Dan said, looking at me. "Mitchel is a brilliant hacker, he's doing a lot of great work here."

Mitchel blushed and I smiled at him. "Thanks," I said.

He nodded. "Happy to be here." He looked at me for a moment and his eyes narrowed slightly. "You have the most incredible eyes," he said. "I've never seen that color gray before."

I flicked my gaze away from him, embarrassed. "Thanks," I said, looking over at Dan who smiled at me, a glint of something in his grape-green eyes.

"You want to go out later?" Mitchel asked Dan.

"Don't think I'll have time today. Tomorrow morning?" Dan answered.

"Sounds good."

Mitchel turned and left. As the door closed I asked Dan what "going out" was.

"Stand-up paddle boarding. We do it most days."

"You and Mitchel."

"Most everyone here. I insist on some kind of above-ground activity. As computer nerds, we're susceptible to all kinds of illness: carpal tunnel, back problems, eye fatigue, turning into total dorks," he said with a smile. "So, I make everyone go outside. Also helps them social-ize." He smiled. "Supposed to keep them from random compliments that make girls blush."

I raised my eyebrows. "I'm not blushing," I said.

Dan shrugged. "Maybe just a little." I laughed. "There is a great jogging route, too. I can show you later if you want."

I nodded. "Yeah, I'll probably want a run before bed. But let's get back to Joyful Justice."

"Right, so as I was saying, as more members of the forum posted requests for help and more people responded we created deeper sub-areas of the forum where only invited members could go." Dan leaned forward, placing his elbows on his knees. "We vetted people before inviting them to be a part of the conversation about starting Joyful Justice as we know it today."

"How did you vet them?"

Dan smiled. "Well, tracking their IP addresses. Making sure they were who they said they were. Pretty basic stuff back then. Now we are a lot more careful. I'm not interested in ending up in a black ops prison, are you?"

I shook my head thinking about how close I'd come back in Costa Rica. If it weren't for Bobby Maxim I'd probably be in one right now. "No," I said, taking a deep breath.

"You got pretty close, huh?" Dan asked.

"Yeah, Mulberry told you?"

"Not all the details but yeah, some guy named Declan Doyle has a real hard on for catching you."

I coughed a laugh. "Something like that. He knew me in New York. Actually, he was the one who introduced me to Robert Maxim."

"He was a cop then, right? He's with Homeland Security now."

"Yeah, he was a mounted police officer. When I found Joseph Saperstein's body..." Dan nodded, he knew the story of how on my first day as a dog walker I'd lost control of a Golden Retriever who'd run down an alley where Saperstein's corpse had been waiting to be discovered. "Declan was the first officer on site. He interviewed me and after I figured out it was Kurt Jessup, he was the first person I told."

"You two were close then?"

I shrugged. "We were something. But he told me to keep my mouth shut, that there was nothing I could do. That I'd get myself killed."

"Wow," Dan said. "I guess you proved him wrong."

I shrugged. "After Kurt was killed Declan was assigned to the case, a big promotion, I always assumed Maxim had something to do with it. He thought Doyle was under his control."

"I guess Declan proved Maxim wrong."

"Lots of wrong in that story," I said, trying to keep the bitterness out of my voice. "I guess he never stopped looking for me, even after Robert helped me fake Joy Humbolt's death."

"So, he didn't fall in line with Maxim?"

"No, I guess not. When Robert and I were in the jungle," I looked at Dan, searching his face, there was nothing there but interest, attention; he was listening. "We were at an abandoned hotel Robert owned," I thought I saw something flicker in Dan's eyes but couldn't be sure.

"Declan ambushed us with a platoon. It was totally illegal, violating Costa Rica's sovereignty. He must be desperate to catch me."

My hand wandered to a wound on my leg, tightly stitched and bandaged it would heal with no problem, but Declan had cut me before I knocked him out. My gun was on him, I could have killed him, and he cut me anyway, he knew I wouldn't pull the trigger. The same way I'd known he wouldn't pull the trigger on me. There was still something between us. Something that stopped us from murdering each other. How romantic.

"But, to answer your question, no Dan, I do not want to end up in a black ops prison. I don't want to end up in any kind of prison. But I guess that's just one of the many risks I'm willing to take. Please go on about deeper sub-forums."

Dan nodded and sat back in his chair. "Right, so we follow discussions of people looking for help. Vet that it's a real issue, something we might be able to help with, invite the person to a deeper level, continue the discussion. Once I've established it's someone we can trust and an issue we can do something about, I present the case to the council. Lenox does further research, gathering more intelligence. If it all checks out we come up with a plan of attack. As you know, the first step is the demand for change."

We offered each offender a way out. A document explaining what they were doing wrong and how to change in order to avoid our wrath.

"Sounds so simple."

"In a way it is."

I looked out at the screen beyond the glass wall of his office. "So what's all that?"

Dan turned in the direction of the screens. "Some are live missions we are providing backup for. We use drones, satellite feeds, internet activity, cell phone interceptions, all sorts of tools to help ongoing investigations and missions. Then others are just background." He pointed at the aerial footage of the village in the wooded area. "That's Norway," he said. "We're watching this town, actually, this one guy, who might be at the center of a trafficking scheme moving women into Norway. Which is really unusual and something we could easily wipe out, working with local law enforcement."

"How's that?"

"We have a lot of members who are with the police. We also can just feed information to trustworthy police departments who aren't connected to us. It's easier to let countries and communities that have the infrastructure to keep their citizens safe do it themselves rather than us doing it for them. Whereas that," he pointed to the desert footage. "That's a village in Nigeria. We're looking for those girls. You know the ones that went missing?"

"Of course," I said. It was a huge international story. One hundred school girls taken from their classrooms by armed warriors of Boko Haram. They'd been missing for months. "We're working on that?"

"Of course," Dan said, turning back to me. "Why wouldn't we?"

"I guess I didn't realize we could."

"Well, we're doing what we can. If we find them we don't have the manpower to get them out but we don't need to do that part. Here," Dan said, standing up. "You brought your computer, right?"

"Sure," I said. "It's in my bag, Bella had it taken up to my room."

Dan smiled. "You are not normal, Sydney Rye."

"What do you mean?"

"Most people keep their computers with them." I shrugged. "You're practically computer illiterate," he said, grabbing a laptop off his desk. "I was thinking you'd want to go over all our current missions, our upcoming missions, and our demands that are out."

"A lot of that is on hold," I said.

"I know," Dan said, sitting back down across from me. "Until Fortress Global goes public." His voice quieted. "So you decided to let Robert Maxim join Joyful Justice."

"In exchange for not destroying his clients until after the IPO, a shit ton of money, and all the inside information we could ever dream of."

"And you think he'll stick to his side of the bargain?"

"Don't you?"

"I don't know him as well as you," Dan said, opening up the laptop.

"Don't you?" I asked.

Dan went still, his eyes slowly rising to mine. "What do you mean?"

"Are you trying to play with me?"

Dan sat back in his chair, his eyes glued to mine. "I don't know what you're talking about."

"Dan," I leaned forward and touched his knee. He looked down at the connection. "I know," I said. "I know you were feeding him information."

Dan just stared at my hand for a long moment. "That's not true," he finally said, his voice quiet and hurt. "I'd never do that."

"Then what was it, Dan? What did he have over you?"

Dan's eyes jumped to mine. "Nothing," he said.

"Please, don't lie to me. Not anymore."

"I've never lied to you." I hiccuped a laugh that sounded almost like a sob. "I might have kept Joyful Justice from you but I never lied."

"Omitting isn't the same as lying, you're right. I've never asked you if you were betraying me to Bobby Maxim."

"I would never betray you."

"Then what was it, Dan? How could you buy property from him? How could he know where our camp was? How could he do any of that without you?"

"What did he tell you?"

"Nothing. I figured it out on my own."

"You're making it up. You're paranoid."

I moved back, breaking our connection. "I don't think so. I was prepared to trust you again if you were willing to be honest. I thought you'd come clean."

"Come clean! I didn't do anything, Sydney. All I've ever wanted was the best for you. That's all I've ever wanted."

"What you think is best for me, you mean."

"Well, what do you think is best for you?"

"I don't think you should have been talking to Bobby Maxim behind my back."

"I wasn't!" Dan stood up, his voice angry. Blue stood, watching Dan as he paced across the room and laid his hands against the glass looking down at the busy room below. "You think I would risk this? For what?"

"I don't know."

"It doesn't make any sense. Just think about it. Why would I do that?"

"Money, blackmail, misplaced good will."

Dan laughed, his shirt rising and falling as his shoulders shook. "You are almost impossible to love, Sydney Rye," he said turning back to me. "And yet, I can't stop. But you just want it to be impossible, don't you? You want us to be impossible?"

"Way to change the subject."

"Don't you see what you're doing?"

"Now who's paranoid?"

"You're trying to put something so big between us that we'll never have a chance at happiness."

I stood up, anger suddenly bursting through my veins. "You betrayed me to Bobby Maxim. You told him where our training camp was. And you think this is about us dating?"

"Dating? That's what you're calling it?"

"Whatever we were, Dan. It's over. It's been over."

"Because you're afraid of it."

"No, Dan, because we can't trust each other."

"Because you won't let us."

"I can't believe you are turning this into a conversation about our relationship."

"Isn't it? Even if you're not talking about something romantic. I've been your friend for years, Sydney. Years!" He stepped closer to me. "And you're accusing me of risking not just your life but Merl's," he ticked off on his fingers, "Mulberry's, every single recruit at that training camp. I would rather die than risk those lives."

"Then why did you buy the training center from Bobby Maxim? You're telling me you didn't know? You didn't do the research? That's not like you, Dan." I pointed out the window. "Look at that. You've got a drone flying over a village in Norway to check on reports of a human trafficking ring and you wouldn't do a simple search as to who you were buying land from? Bullshit!"

"Bullshit is right, Sydney!" Dan stepped closer. Blue moved between us.

"Sit," I told him. Blue did as I said, lowering his butt but keeping a steady eye on Dan.

"You're so—" Dan threw his hands up in the air. "You just can't trust anyone."

"I can't trust you."

"Because of something Robert Maxim said."

"Because he owned the abandoned hotel that you bought to turn into Joyful Justice's training camp. Because he saluted me, the way you used to."

Dan shook his head. "How do you know he owned it?"

"When we went to negotiate our deal he took me to another failed property he owned. Told me he had invested in the hotel business in Costa Rica prematurely and badly. We ended up in the security room of that hotel and it looked just like the one we had at the compound."

"That's it?"

"And the saluting."

"And you assumed that I betrayed you on that evidence."

"It's enough."

"For you." Dan turned toward the door.

"Where are you going?"

"Away from you."

The door *whished* closed behind him, and I was alone with Blue and the mess of computers and files. "Well that didn't go well," I said to Blue. He cocked his head. "Should have been more subtle?" Blue sighed and laid down. Maybe it was time for that jog, I thought before following Dan out the door. When I got down the steps he was leaning over a man who was pointing at something on his screen. I got back in the elevator and rode up to the lobby.

CHAPTER THREE
RUN TO REST

Bella was still behind the desk in the lobby. She smiled as I came out of the elevator with Blue. "Can you tell me how to get to my room?" I asked.

"Of course," she said. Bella passed me a key and then pulled out a map. "We're here," she said, circling a square marked 'Lobby.' "Take the elevator up to the tenth floor, and you're number 1007." She moved her pen and circled another square.

"Dan mentioned a running route," I said.

"Sure," she put her pen back to paper. "You can exit through the lobby here, go back the way you and Dan came in but instead of heading to the parking lot, take this exit." She circled a door. "And that will lead you outside. There is a dirt path that winds around the volcano. The full route is over thirty miles so most people run out and back."

"Sounds good, thanks," I said, taking the map from her and folding it up before sticking it in my back pocket. "Can you send up some dog food to my room?"

"There is already some waiting for Blue."

"Great. And...where is Dan's room?"

"He's right next door to you. 1009." She smiled bright and cheery.

I returned to the elevator and went up to the tenth floor. It looked like any number of hotels in the world. Patterned carpet that would easily cover stains, cream-colored walls, numbered doors. Why would a billionaire want his house/bunker to look like a hotel? I wondered. But then again, maybe this was all our renovations.

I should have kept my mouth shut about Dan and just learned everything I could. Having him pissed at me didn't help. And he really sounded like he didn't betray me. Maybe I was wrong. But there was a sense in my gut. An instinct telling me to stay wary. I almost laughed out loud trying to remember the last time I hadn't felt that sense of impending danger creeping up my spine.

I let myself into my room and stopped short as I pushed the door open. To my delight, given the fortress-like nature of the lower floors, it had windows and the view was magnificent. The building was built into the mountain side, tapering as it rose higher. The slope of the volcano, coated in thick vegetation, curved down to the ocean. Waves bashed against black rock, sending up dramatic sprays of white. I realized how hard it would be for anyone to scale those slopes to get to the windows, which looked to be made of tinted, bullet-proof glass.

Blue lowered his head and, ears swiveling, began to investigate the new space. We were in a small sitting room with a kitchenette. There were two dog bowls on the floor, one filled with water. When I checked the fridge I found beer, cheese, and grapes. On the counter was a fresh baguette, suggesting a bakery somewhere below. A handwritten note welcomed me from the "team". Blue's dog food was under the sink and there were several rawhide bones lined up next to the bag.

Blue lapped at the water and left a trail of drips from his chin as he moved toward the bedroom. It had the same spectacular views and a king size bed facing a large flat screen TV. The room was almost as big as the sitting area next door with an attached bathroom. White marble and stainless steel showed off the wealth of the owner.

There was a closet and next to it another door. It was locked. Probably led into Dan's room, I thought. I could deadbolt it from my side. And I did. Not that I expected him to come bursting into my room, but that nagging sensation of impending doom kept me on high alert.

Blue, satisfied with the safety of the room, laid down in a patch of sun and began to snore. My small bag was waiting on a luggage rack by the closet and I unpacked my few belongings. An extra pair of pants, two T-shirts, a couple of button downs, a sweatshirt, bras, underwear, a pair of jogging shorts, and running shoes.

I peeled off my wrinkled clothing and left it on the floor as I went into the bathroom. Removing the bandage from the cut on my leg I inspected the incision. It was light pink, no signs of infection. Pulling open my ditty kit I found disinfectant cream and slathered it on before taping on another patch of sterile gauze. It would soon be just another scar, joining many others on my body.

I changed into my jogging clothing. Blue sat up as I tied my sneakers, his tail thunking against the carpeting. "Ready for a run?" He stood up and came over to me, pushing his face against my leg. I ruffled the top of his head. "Me too."

When I made by way back through the tunnels and stepped outside, the sun was beginning to set, the dirt path shaded and dusty. I walked for a few minutes, stretching my legs. I raised my arms above my head and took turns stretching one side and then the other. Looking back I noted with satisfaction that Joyful Justice's headquarters was virtually invisible, the tinted glass of the upper floors blending into the rock and vegetation. Blue tapped his nose to my hip, a reminder that he was there.

As the sky grew darker my pace increased. I didn't have much time. It was going to be real dark out here soon and I didn't know this path, though it was nicely cleared. I could see other footsteps in the soft dirt. Branches and brush were pruned back giving enough space for two people to pass each other. I broke into a sprint as the ocean came into view. The path curved around the side of the mountain growing narrower as one side dropped down to the sea while the other rose up toward the top of the mountain.

My heart was pounding hard, calves burning, but I pushed forward, desperate to escape my own thoughts, Dan's words, my doubts; everything needed to be wiped away. I pushed harder, my feet pounding on the soft path. Blue ran alongside me, his tongue lolling out of his head.

I had to slow down, my lungs burning. The path narrowed further.

My legs felt wobbly as the trail climbed higher. A breeze blew off the ocean, cooling the sweat that clung to me. I kept my eyes straight, not wanting to see how far a drop it was to the turbulent waters below.

It was Merl who had taught me to love running. After Mulberry and I fled the United States I ended up in Mexico where I was slowly drinking myself to death, wallowing in grief over my brother, slain on my account. Mulberry sent Merl to me and he pulled me out of that pit of despair. He taught me how to communicate with Blue, how to under-stand my own body, how to ease the panic and craziness that invaded my mind. But even Merl I didn't fully trust. I hadn't spoken to him about my suspicions that Dan had betrayed me. I hadn't told anyone. I'd kept that secret just like so many others.

The sun was hovering at the horizon when I turned back. An orange globe, liquid fire, casting its light long and low across the ocean toward me. The sea was a deep blue in the setting sun. The clouds, wisps of condensation hovering at the horizon, caught its light and reflected pink and purple with hints of powder blue on their undersides.

We re-entered the forest and the sun winked out behind us. The sky grew steadily darker as I jogged back toward the entrance of the compound. As the night air turned colder my thoughts returned to Dan. Should I just trust him? Did our history warrant that? Would he trust me now that I'd shown him my hand? And why did I do that? Because deep down I trusted him? And his ridiculous accusation that it was all a ruse to keep him at arm's length. I didn't need a ruse for that. I could do that all on my own.

Blue tapped his nose against my hip, reminding me that we were running, that this was not a time to question everything but to let go of it all. I picked up my pace, throwing in one last sprint before my run came to an end.

EK

There was a knock on the connecting door to my bedroom as I was taking off my sneakers. Blue let out a low growl and I stood to open it.

Dan was on the other side. He avoided eye contact, holding out a memory stick. "Here," he said. "It's got our most recent file on it. Thought you'd want to look it over."

"Thanks," I said, taking it from him.

"You know how to use it?" he asked, looking at my bare feet.

"Yeah."

"Good," he said before turning back into his own room.

I followed him, taking a tentative step into his space. Blue stood and followed, staying close to my hip. "Dan, about earlier..."

He turned around quickly, suddenly close to me.

"Isn't it more likely that the man who you've considered your enemy for the last four years is tricking you rather than the man who has loved you since before he even met you is betraying you? Which is more likely, Sydney?"

Dan ran a hand through his long hair, pushing it away from his eyes. Staring at me, accusing me, pleading with me.

"I don't know," I said quietly, feeling like I couldn't breathe.

"You really mistrust me that much?"

"I think you do things you think are best, and that you don't always do what I think is best."

He shook his head and turned toward the large windows, staring out at the glittering sea and dark sky, opening the space between us. "I don't always do what you want is what you mean?" I didn't answer. Blue sighed and laid down. Used to us fighting now. Knowing it wouldn't turn violent. "The messed up thing is I still love you."

My heart picked up its pace, sending blood rushing through my veins, heating my cheeks, filling my ears with its powerful whoosh. "I'm sorry," I said. And it wasn't because I had accused him of betraying me. It was because I couldn't love him back. My love was a death sentence and I didn't want Dan to die. Even if he did lie to me, if he did tell my secrets to Bobby Maxim, I wanted Dan alive. The world was better with him in it.

Dan turned to me. The only light filtered from my room next door. "I never meant for you to fall in love with me," I said, a pathetic excuse. I could hear the weakness in my voice, What good were intentions? I'd slept with him. I'd laid in the sun with him. I'd let him fall for me, and it healed me, it made me whole. I felt tears prick my eyes and hoped that he couldn't see them in the semi-darkness.

Dan shook his head. "I know."

"You deserve better."

He stepped closer and I shook my head. Dan's empty hands closed into tight fists but he didn't speak. "Thanks for this," I said, holding up the memory stick.

"Tell me that you trust me. At least do that, Sydney," his voice was tight, face shadowed.

"I don't trust anyone, Dan. I'm sorry," I said before turning toward my room. Blue stood and led the way into the lit space. Dan didn't try to stop me as I closed the door. Slipping the deadlock into place I felt tears slide down my cheeks.

I climbed into the shower and tried to rinse away the fight. I pushed the images from my mind, letting the sting of fresh water against my wound focus me. I forced myself to concentrate on what I was here to do: learn. Wrapping myself in a big fluffy robe that I found hanging in the closet I went into the kitchen and fed Blue. Then I grabbed my computer and climbed onto the big bed. While waiting for it to boot up I looked out the window.

The moon was beginning to rise and it cast white-blue light around the horizon, but the ocean in front of the mountain stayed black, shadowed by the volcano.

I scrolled through the files on the memory stick and stopped when I saw "On Hold due to IPO". This was the deal I'd struck with Bobby Maxim. He was taking his company, Fortress Global, public and in order to make it work he needed us to back off on a number of his clients. We were giving him ten days, then going after them harder than ever. With his help. At least that was the plan. So I had ten days to get up to date on everything.

When I'd gone into the Costa Rican jungle to negotiate with Maxim I wasn't fully aware of all Joyful Justice's operations for multiple reasons. Firstly, I didn't want to be. I was still in denial about my place in this organization. Secondly, it felt safer not to know in case it was all a trick and the information was forced from me.

But by the end of three days in the jungle with Robert Maxim I realized that there was no winning this war we were waging. This was not some fight between nations that would eventually produce a victor. It was just an unending series of battles--a philosophical fight about the basic rights of human beings and how we should go about protecting them. We needed money to wage this war and Robert Maxim had a lot of that. And in ten days he'd have even more.

I opened the first file. A chemical company in Peru had been dumping residue in the rain forest for decades, causing cancer and death. Joyful Justice had left a warning on the CEO's desk outlining the changes we wanted to see and warning of dire consequences. So far they'd changed nothing. And probably because Fortress Global told them they didn't need to. That they could contain any threat from Joyful Justice.

There were schematics of the CEO's three homes in the file, as well as information on all the board members. Additionally, there was an attack plan for the actual dumping facility. The plan called for no casualties. A simple, peaceful ending of the business dealings there.

When the company sent in troops was when we'd go to the board members' houses. Take the men from their beds. And what? The file didn't cover that. I thought to knock on Dan's door and ask but decided that was a bad idea.

I felt my eyelids getting heavy. It had been a long couple of days and I closed the computer, pushing it over to the side of the big bed as I climbed under the covers. My head on the soft pillow, cozy under the quilt, looking out at the calm ocean, I thought about the lives we were trying to change. Those children suffering from cancer. They'd never seen a bed like this, a room with such a view. Did they have any idea that Joyful Justice was fighting for them? Did it matter? Would it give them hope? My eyes slipped closed and I fell into a deep and dreamless sleep.

CHAPTER FOUR
A PROBLEM

Blue woke me in the morning. My stomach grumbled as I realized I had not eaten dinner the night before. I'd fed Blue his kibble but after my fight with Dan I didn't have an appetite. Blue whined and paced in front of the bed. I glanced out the window and realized it must be pretty late. I checked the bedside table clock. It was already 10 am.

Blue tapped his nose to my hip as I dressed in jeans and a T-shirt before grabbing a hunk of baguette and heading out the door. The hall was empty and I assumed everyone was at work. Sleeping until 10 am was a great way to show leadership qualities, I thought, as the elevator brought us down to the lobby.

There was a different person behind the desk, a man in his forties with graying temples and deep green eyes. He smiled at me. "Good morning," I said. He returned the greeting. Blue and I made our way out to the jogging trail. Blue left the path, rustling through the underbrush to do his business.

I chewed on the piece of baguette and enjoyed the fresh air, my mind still fogged from sleep. I didn't really know what I was doing today and figured I'd have a cup of coffee before deciding. It was strange to have this respite, this break from action. Maybe that's why I was sensing impending doom. I didn't do well without a hands-on job.

That was one of the other reasons I'd refused to join the Joyful Justice council for so long. As important decision makers with intimate knowledge of Joyful Justice's confidential workings, we weren't supposed to put ourselves in harm's way. But I sucked as a pencil pusher and when I'd agreed to join I'd made it clear I was not going to spend the rest of my days behind a desk. I was going to pick a mission and I was going to go out and make something right in this world, using a gun, my brain, and Blue.

Blue and I headed back inside. The man at the front desk, whose name turned out to be Bruce, directed me to the "breakfast room" which looked out over the ocean and had seating for about fifty. The tables were all empty. I was late for breakfast, I guessed. But there was still coffee set out on one of the long tables. I filled a cup before returning to my room.

I gave Blue his kibble and ate some of the cheese from the fridge before opening my computer again. For the next three hours I poured through files. From the active missions to the open concerns. Requests from forum members: missing family, out of control gangs, unsolved murders, the list went on. There was so much suffering and loss in this world. My heart ached by the time there was a knock at my door.

Blue looked over at me as he glided toward the entrance. Standing up, I stretched, feeling the pain of having hunched so long over a computer. I checked the peephole and saw Dan. He smiled when I opened the door. I was pretty sure we were going to pretend like last night never happened. "How you doing?" he asked.

"Good, I'm just going over everything. Kind of depressing," I said.

Dan cocked his head. "What do you mean?"

"So many people. So many requests."

"Right, but we're helping them."

"No, I know. It just feels, I don't know, so big. So...I want to get out there and help." Dan nodded, and gave me a half smile. "Come on in," I said, pushing the door open wider. He stepped into the small sitting room and kitchen, then made his way over to my computer.

"You have any questions?"

"A few. Like what is the plan for the board members and CEO from that chemical plant?"

"Remind me."

I sat down in front of the computer and Dan joined me on the small couch, our knees almost touching. Pulling the computer onto my lap I opened the file. "We've got their house schematics and clearly we plan on going after them if they try to prevent us from shutting down the plant. But what are we going to do to them?"

Dan looked over my shoulder, leaning into my space. "I'm not sure," he said. "Doesn't look like we have a plan yet. Any suggestions?"

"We don't have a plan yet?"

Dan laughed. "Yeah, Sydney. We don't have everything figured out."

"No, of course not," I said.

"Any ideas?" he asked.

I pictured duct-taped wrists, glinting blades, frightened eyes. "I'll think about it," I said, not wanting to admit the dark direction of my thoughts. Joyful Justice didn't torture people. Unless there was a hell of a good reason, I thought, looking down at the picture of a young boy with a tumor growing out of his shoulder, lumpy and deadly. The child was smiling though. I closed the window and turned to Dan. He sat back into the couch.

"Anything else?"

"Have you heard from Merl?" I asked. He'd left Costa Rica at the same time as me on his way to China. A friend of his, Mo-Ping, the woman who taught him Tai Chi and helped him get clean over a decade ago, was not responding to his messages. At first he'd thought it was because he'd expressed to her that his feelings had deepened into something romantic but when she continued to ignore his messages Merl became concerned. I realized that since I'd made it to the island, he must be in Shanghai by now.

Dan nodded. "Yup, he checked in yesterday afternoon. Called when he landed in Shanghai. So we should hear from him again in the next couple of hours for an update."

"Good, I hope he finds her and everything's okay."

Dan smiled. "So cute to think of him in love right?"

"Totally," I laughed.

"He's so controlled."

"I know, I can't wait to meet this lady."

"You want to get some lunch?"

My stomach growled in response and we both laughed. "I guess so. Just give me a minute."

I shut down my computer and stepped into my bedroom quickly to brush my hair when my phone rang. It was a blocked number but when I answered it I instantly recognized Robert Maxim's smooth voice. "Sydney," he said.

"Robert," I tried to keep my voice steady. The man always put me on edge.

"I've been missing you."

"It's been like two days," I said.

"Yes, and I've been so bored."

"Taking a company public isn't exciting?"

"Not as exciting as spending time with you."

"Okay," I wanted to keep this short. Robert had a way of getting under my skin and I just didn't need it.

"How's it going?" he asked.

"Fine. I've got to go actually, why are you calling?"

"Can't a friend just call to say hello?"

"Not you."

"You're always assuming things about me, Sydney. I just wanted to check in on you."

"Well, now you have. I'm fine. Like I said. I have to go."

I hung up the phone and returned the living room. "Ready," I said to Dan. He held the door for me and Blue. As we walked down the hall toward the elevator I tried to forget the syrupy tone of Robert Maxim's voice but it was floating through my brain, putting me even more on edge. I needed a job. A tough one.

EK

After lunch I called Merl. I glanced over at Blue while I listened to the phone ring. Merl had three Doberman Pinschers of his own and spent years as a dog trainer before joining Joyful Justice. I'd looked over the mission notes Merl left. His plan started with him visiting an old friend in Shanghai who knew Mo-Ping and might be able to provide insight into why she was not responding. I wanted to know what he'd learned so far. but Merl didn't pick up his phone.

I chewed on my lower lip as I looked down at the mobile device. "Everything okay?" Dan asked.

We were in his office. The control room below us was starting to fill back in after lunch. "Yeah, I'm sure it's nothing, just Merl didn't pick up his phone."

Dan was sitting at his desk and turned to his keyboard. "I'll track him," he said.

"Of course, I should have just asked you from the beginning."

Dan smiled, the blue of his screen casting an eerie light over his tan skin. His face slowly shifted, the edges of his mouth turning down and his eyes narrowing. "What is it?" I asked.

"He's probably just in the mountains," he said.

"What do you mean?"

"I'm not getting a signal, but that could be because he is out of satellite range."

"Is that normal?"

Dan shrugged. "Can be. I'm going to check where I last had him." More typing and a bigger frown. "Shanghai," he said. "That doesn't make any sense."

"What are you tracking, his phone?"

"Yes, and a beacon in Chula's collar," Dan said, referring to Merl's youngest dog.

"Couldn't he still be in Shanghai?"

"Sure, but neither beacon has moved or updated in hours."

I walked around the desk and leaned over his chair looking at a map of Shanghai on the screen. It looked like the chaos of veins in a body. A small red dot sat motionless in the center of the screen.

"So, Merl would have had to remove the device from Chula and smash his phone?"

"Basically. Or he went underground."

"Underground?"

"Yes, the beacons can't signal if they are too deep under the earth."

"Is that possible in Shanghai?"

"Sure, it's possible anywhere."

"Should I be worried?" I asked, already feeling worried.

"Not yet. Let's give it a day. Maybe there is something weird going on. But if we have not heard from him by tomorrow I'll start to worry."

"I'm going to call Mulberry and see if he's heard from him."

"Good idea."

Mulberry picked up right away. "Sydney," he said, his voice sounded like he was smiling.

"Hey, have you heard from Merl?"

"He checked in yesterday, didn't he?" Mulberry said, his voice turning serious, reacting to my own.

"Yes, but I just tried calling him and he didn't pick up. Plus, his beacons don't appear to be working."

"Strange," Mulberry said, his voice low.

"If we don't hear from him tomorrow I'm going after him."

Mulberry was quiet for a second. I could hear howler monkeys in the background, roaring at the setting sun in Costa Rica. "Okay," he said. "But I don't want you going alone."

"I can move faster on my own."

"You can die faster, too," Mulberry said, his voice harsh. "We don't need two members of the council disappearing in one city. I want to send you some men."

"That will take time."

Dan was watching me, he cocked his head. "Mulberry doesn't want me going alone," I said to Dan, putting Mulberry on speaker and holding the phone out so Dan could join the conversation.

"I agree," he said.

"You think we should leave Merl out there for longer while we wait for reinforcements to arrive from Costa Rica?"

"No, but I can send a tech guy with you and let's call Lenox, see who he has on the ground."

"Smart thinking," Mulberry said. "Sydney?"

"That's fine," I said.

"Dan, what do you think the chances are that Merl's in some kind of trouble? Couldn't this just be a malfunction?"

"Of two devices? Unlikely."

"Shit. Merl's not an easy man to take down," Mulberry said.

"I'll call Lenox," I said.

"Fine," both Mulberry and Dan said at the same time, their voices edged with tension.

"We'll call you tomorrow," I said to Mulberry before hanging up.

I put the phone down on the desk next to a pile of folders and stared at the screen, at the overlapping red dots in the center of that big mess of a city. "Give me everything Merl left us about his route."

Dan turned to his computer and began to type.

We went over it together. Merl's friend, Mo, was a tai chi instructor at a training center in a small village in Yang Shuo, Guaxgxi about 18 hours from Shanghai. The training center was closer to Hong Kong but Merl had a friend in Shanghai, Xiu Sing, who he wanted to see before heading out there. Sing knew Mo and Merl hoped to confirm that there was really something wrong before he showed up on Mo-Ping's doorstep. It was possible she was just ignoring him.

Sing was a sword maker, one of the last in China. At the age of 82 he still worked every day. Merl had tried to speak to him on the phone—Sing didn't use email--but Sing told him to come to Shanghai. Dan tried the number in Merl's notes. It rang over twenty times before he gave up. We tried the tai chi center's number but as Merl had noted it had been disconnected for months.

I left Lenox a message and hoped that he would get back to me soon. I didn't know exactly where in the world he was or what time it was there...or who he was with, so I guessed it could be some time before Lenox responded.

I returned my attention to Merl's notes. If encouraged to do so by Sing, Merl planned on traveling by private plane to Yang Shuo. A man with three Doberman Pinschers can't exactly just hop on a train. The village was isolated and surrounded by mountains, which is why Dan thought it was possible we'd just lost his signal for a short period of time.

But I had that uneasy sense that was growing stronger with every moment. "Merl doesn't say anything about what he thinks might have happened to her," Dan said.

"I don't think he had any ideas. As far as he knew the tai chi center was perfectly safe. But he was worried."

"Worried enough to go all the way to China."

"He loves her," I said, not taking my eyes off the documents in front of me.

I felt Dan turn his head to look at my profile. "I guess people do crazy things for love."

"It's not that crazy to go to China," I said, my lips quirking into a smile as I glanced up at him. "After all I'm about to go there for Merl, and I'm not in love with him."

"But you love him, don't you?"

"He's one of my best friends."

"Do you trust him?"

"As much as anyone," I said, returning my gaze to the papers in front of me.

"You trust him more than me?"

"We have a less complicated history," I answered. My phone rang, interrupting the conversation.

Lenox's smooth, accented voice came over the line clear and familiar. "Sydney," he said my name like he enjoyed it, playing with the syllables, making me close my eyes and imagine his strong hands, sculpted shoulders, and deep kisses.

"Lenox, nice to hear your voice," I said, moving away from Dan and walking toward the couch.

"Always a pleasure to talk with you. Is everything well?" I could picture his thick lips forming the words. I wasn't sure where Lenox was but I imagined him in the sunshine, wearing a white linen shirt that made his dark skin look that much blacker. The thin gold chain around his neck glittering in the light. The memory of the smell of him as he leaned in for a kiss made me smile despite my troubles.

"I have not heard from Merl," I said. "Dan and I tracked him. He's not answering his phone and his beacon has stopped updating since soon after he arrived in Shanghai. I'm planning on heading there to look for him and was wondering if you had any contacts who could help me."

"Of course, I have an apartment there."

"Right," I said with a little laugh.

"My head of operations, Loki Falk, can look after you. He is a very good man."

"If he works for you I'm sure he is."

"I'll call him now. Send me your travel plans, he'll meet you at the airport."

"He can get me weapons, maybe a couple of men for back up?"

"Send me a list. Guns are difficult in China, but we will see what we can do."

"Thank you."

"Any time. And Sydney?"

"Yes."

"Be brave."

"You too, Lenox."

CHAPTER FIVE
ANOTHER JOURNEY

We didn't hear from Merl and so I was back on a plane, heading west over the Pacific toward China. Dan sent Mitchel, the young man who I'd met in his office, along with me. While I worried that he was young and inexperienced Dan told me Mitchel was the best. It was his first field experience with Joyful Justice but according to Dan, Mitchel had been hacking since he was ten. And I could trust him. Eager to be on my way I didn't argue.

Mitchel was excited and bounced his leg as we descended into Shanghai. Blue was at my knee. I was wearing my jeans, a long sleeve cotton top and a leather jacket. I'd worn it in India and totally forgotten about it, but Dan had been carrying it around apparently. It had a hidden pocket where I'd kept a lead pipe after Blue and I were attacked by a pack of wild dogs. The pipe was gone now, but the pocket was still there.

I assumed that even if Loki couldn't get me a gun there were plenty of other weapons, and I was happy to have a jacket to hide one in. There was also space in the lining for currency, always useful to have in a foreign nation.

Entering China was not a simple process, but Merl had managed to get himself and his three dogs through this very airport days earlier. I hoped we wouldn't have any problems. Blue's papers were in order and this was a "no quarantine" entry point. Mitchel had brought his laptop with him, but was going to pick up more equipment once on the ground. "Some of the equipment would look suspicious," he told me. "But we may need it."

I didn't question him.

It was a cloudy day and I couldn't see anything as we descended to the small private airport. One minute we were in the smog and the next the runway loomed up at us. The landing was smooth and we taxied over to a hangar where we were met by customs agents and Lenox's man, Loki.

Loki was tall with black hair and dark eyes. He was handsome, not surprising considering his profession. It helped that he was dressed in a tailored black suit that followed the elegant lines of his body perfectly and a crisp white shirt with gold cuff links.

Loki did the talking while the stern-looking customs agent inspected our paperwork. Loki's voice was smooth, low and deferential. The customs agent, wearing a green uniform and a sour expression, eyed Blue with distaste but agreed that everything was in order and let us go.

Loki had brought two cars. "Mitchel, I believe you have business in the city you wish to attend to immediately."

Mitchel nodded, "Yes, thanks."

"This is your driver, Chang. He will take you where you need to go."

"Great, thanks," Mitchel said, turning to the small man standing behind Loki who wore a traditional chauffeur uniform, dark suit, narrow tie, white shirt, and cap. Mitchel threw his bags into the backseat of the dark Mercedes and climbed in after them, waving at me. "See you at the house."

"Sure," I said, turning to Loki.

"This way," he said, pointing to another dark sedan.

EK

The air was thick with smog, the sun glowed blood orange through the wavering mist. The sounds of vehicle traffic and the tinkle of bicycles filled the air. Blue tapped his nose against my hip as Loki unlocked the door to the apartment building. It was four-stories tall and European in style. Probably built by the British a century or more ago. I wasn't surprised Lenox kept his apartment in the Bund, the older part of town, across the river from Pudong and its glittering lights.

I liked this street. There was a fruit stand steps away, and as a breeze blew down the block it brought the sticky sweet scent of lychees and mangosteens with it. Loki got the door open and he stepped back, holding his arm out for me to go ahead. Taller than me by about six inches, his dark eyes caught mine for only a moment before dropping to the ground. A subservient stance. I wondered what Lenox had told him about me.

As I passed by him, our bodies close, I paused. "Loki?"

"Yes, Ms. Rye?"

"What did Lenox say about me?"

"He said to help you in any way you needed." His eyes stayed down.

"What does that mean?"

"You tell me."

I smiled slightly, letting my eyes wander over him. Loki's hair was jet black, shiny and straight, curling just a touch at the base of his neck. His shoulders were broad and strong. He had a cat-like elegance to him and moved like a fighter. That was the kind of thing I could see now. How a man moved, where he placed his eyes when I spoke to him, told me so much. "Loki," I said his name again, quietly.

"Yes, Ms. Rye?"

"Look at me."

His eyes came up, slowly, not unsure but careful. "What do you do for Lenox?"

"Whatever he needs."

I smiled fully this time. Enjoying his coyness. Coming from a man who looked like Loki it was funny. He didn't look coy, he looked danger-ous. I turned and entered the building, passing through a small vestibule to a narrow hall. There was a door to my left that appeared to enter a ground floor apartment. "Second floor," Loki told me as he closed and locked the door behind us.

Blue went first, his nails clicking on the hardwood. I ran my hand along the smooth bannister as we climbed. The steps were worn in their centers, the building felt well used and well cared for. The walls were freshly painted, the wood glossy and dust free.

Loki passed me on the landing of the second floor to open the apartment door. He entered first, Blue and I following as he flicked on lights. The curtains were drawn against the waning light of day. Track lighting illuminated a modern space with old world details. Large windows that could have been in a Paris apartment, prominent mouldings and original wood floors contrasted with the white walls, modern paintings, and clean-lined furniture.

I could picture Lenox here, sitting on the heather gray couch, in front of the art book-laden coffee table, holding a glass of wine, enjoying the abstract landscape hanging above the fireplace. Loki walked behind me, moving into the kitchen, which was open to the living room and a dining area. "Would you like a drink?" he asked.

"Yes, and a bowl of water for Blue please."

Loki nodded and began to fill an elegant white ceramic dish with water from a large container on the counter. "Red wine?" he asked me.

"Just seltzer if you have it."

He nodded. "Bedrooms are upstairs," he said as he placed the water on the ground for Blue. I motioned for Blue to drink and he padded across the floor, crossing over an intricate, hand-woven rug on his way to the kitchen. As Blue lapped at the water Loki brought me a blue bottle of seltzer from the fridge. "Would you like to get settled?"

"Yes, a shower would be nice."

Loki led the way upstairs, Blue close behind me. Loki opened one of three doors leading off the landing. The room was of a similar style to downstairs, grays and whites, large windows, antique details. A chandelier hung from the ceiling, and when Loki turned it on the room was bathed in yellow light.

I opened the curtains, letting the opaque light of late afternoon filter in. "The bathroom is through there," Loki said, and I turned to see him pointing to his right where a door stood ajar, darkness beyond it. "Is there anything else that you need?"

"No, thank you, I'll meet you downstairs."

"Your friend..."

"Mitchel."

"Yes, he will be here soon. Do you share a room?"

I laughed. "No, no we do not."

"Will you be needing company tonight then?" Loki kept his eyes on the ground. I felt my face grow hot.

"No, I'll be fine."

"Very well." Loki turned and left, closing the door behind him. I listened to his soft footfalls as he walked back downstairs before heading to the bathroom.

The shower was big enough for two with excellent water pressure. I spent time under the hot spray letting my muscles relax after the long flight. I wanted to take a jog but first needed to touch base with Mitchel. The spot where Merl's red dot disappeared was close to Lenox's place, in the Bund.

I thought about the modern skyscrapers across the river and what Loki had told me about the rapid growth of the city as we'd driven here from the airport. It amazed me what humans could do when they put their minds to it. This was my first time in China and I sensed how different it was. Despite the familiar architectural details of this apartment, of the corporations' names that glowed on the facades of the skyscrapers, this was not like the Western world. There was some of the madness of India on the streets, the pollution, but there was something else. Communism and Confucianism left a mark of order on this place, an attempt at organization that you didn't feel in India.

I found a white quilted robe hanging on the back of the bathroom door and slipped it on before returning to my bedroom. I then dressed quickly in my jeans and a button-down navy blue cotton shirt that had wrinkled a bit in my suitcase but was still wearable and wandered barefoot downstairs. Loki was in the kitchen and the scents of ginger and lemongrass wafted through the house.

"That smells great," I said.

"I figured you would be hungry," Loki said.

I slipped onto a barstool and watched him work. A rice cooker bubbled on the counter. Loki added raw chicken to a smoking hot wok and it sizzled loudly as he stirred it, the metal of his spoon clanging against the pan.

"What are you making?"

"A simple stir fry, it will be good for you after your journey."

I didn't answer, just sipped at my seltzer bottle and watched him work. His concentration was complete as he added a sauce from a small bowl. Smoke rose from the wok as the liquid instantly began to boil.

Blue pushed his nose against my elbow, reminding me that he'd like his dinner as well.

"There's dog food?" I asked.

Loki nodded, "I'll get it."

"Don't worry, I can do it," I said, coming around the bar and entering the cooking space.

"Under the sink," he said.

I found the bag of dog food and a bowl. Blue pranced in front of me, his nails clicking on the floor with anticipation. I put the bowl down away from the cooking area and he waited for me to command him to eat. When I did he descended upon the food like it had been days since he'd eaten rather than hours.

After washing my hands I returned to my seat. Loki was just finishing the stir fry and began to move it to a serving tray. A sprinkle of chopped scallions on top and he placed it on the bar before moving to the rice cooker and spooning mounds of fluffy white rice into a bowl. He placed it next to the stir fry and then provided me with a plate and silverware from the cabinet.

"Aren't you joining me?" I asked.

"No, thank you," he said. "I have a dinner obligation this evening."

I wondered if it was with a client. Did Loki just run Lenox's business here or was he also a gigolo? I wondered if he'd been offering his own company this evening or if he would have brought someone in for me. I didn't judge people who sold their bodies. But I'd never paid for pleasure. Lenox explained it to me once as a game of pretend that both parties enjoyed. Like actors, they knew the passion wasn't real, but that didn't make the feelings they evoked invalid.

The stir fry was delicious, subtly flavored with a touch of heat. "So good," I told Loki.

His smile was small but genuine. As I ate he cleaned up the kitchen. While he dried the last dish I finished my first helping, and was eyeing the still almost full platter of stir fry. Blue rose from where he'd been sleeping at my feet and moved quickly to the door, a low growl rising from his throat.

"Someone is here," I said, putting down my silverware and stepping off the barstool.

Loki moved quickly to the door just as the bell rang. "It's probably Mitchel and Chang," he said. By the entrance was a screen and buzzer. Loki confirmed his suspicions before buzzing them in.

Mitchel looked disheveled. He was carrying two laptop bags over his shoulder and a metal case. Chang came in behind him carrying a large duffel bag. Blue sat by my side, watching me, making sure these guests were invited.

"Get everything you needed?" I asked.

"Yup," he grinned. "Where should I set up?"

Loki escorted him upstairs, Chang following with the duffel bag.

Loki and Chang returned moments later. "We will leave you for the evening," Loki said with a small bow. "The first floor apartment is mine. Chang will stay there until I return this evening. If you need anything at all use the intercom." Loki pointed to a panel in the wall by the door.

"Okay, tomorrow I'd like to get an early start," I said, antsy to begin looking for Merl.

"Of course," Loki agreed with a small nod.

Mitchel came down as the two men were leaving. "Thanks again," he called as the door closed.

"You hungry?" I asked.

"Starving," Mitchel answered, moving toward the bar.

"I'll get you a plate." Grabbing my own empty dish, I put it in the sink before pulling out a clean one for Mitchel. I pushed it across the bar to him before finding the silverware.

"Any chopsticks?" he asked.

I returned to the drawer and, replacing the knife and fork, pulled out a pair of chopsticks. They were black and smooth, thick and square at one end, round and narrow at the other. Mitchel had already spooned stir fry and rice onto his plate. He took the chopsticks and began to skillfully shovel food into his face. I watched him for a moment before turning to wash my dishes.

"How'd you get so good with chopsticks?" I asked.

"I've spent a lot of time traveling in China and Southeast Asia," Mitchel said, his words muffled by the food in his mouth.

"When was that?"

"Right after high school."

"Wow, that's brave," I said, glancing up at the young man.

He shrugged. "I'm an army brat so I'm used to travel. I love it. Do you travel much?" he asked.

"Not for pleasure," I admitted. "I'm not really a vacation kind of person."

"No?"

"I always seem to find trouble," I answered, drying my plate and putting it back into the cabinet.

Mitchel laughed. "Yeah, I think Dan said something like that. You guys went to India together, right?"

I nodded, turning back to him. "Dan told you that, are you two close?"

Mitchel nodded. "Oh yeah, he's taught me almost everything I know. The guy's a genius."

"That's what he said about you." Mitchel grinned as his cheeks flushed with pride. "I'm gonna go for a jog."

"Cool, I'll get the computers set up."

After I'd changed into my jogging clothing Blue and I stepped back out onto the street. The sun was setting, casting a pink glow over the city. The buildings threw long shadows, covering the sidewalks in shade. The fruit stand was shutting down as we walked past. The streets were still crowded with cars and thick with bicycle traffic.

I picked up my pace to an easy jog once my legs were warmed up a bit. I didn't know the neighborhood but had looked at a map before leaving my room, trying to memorize how to get to the spot where Merl's red dot last appeared. The streets grew narrower as we neared our destination. We came around a corner and I almost collided with a man pulling an empty wooden cart. He stopped short and glared at me. "Sorry," I said, side stepping out of his way and hurrying down the block.

Merchants were closing up their stores while restaurants turned on their lights. I reached Sing's block. It was lined with stores, their gates being pulled down for the night. I slowed my pace to a walk and counted the storefronts until I found where I thought I was supposed to be. The shop was already closed, the big glass windows coated in dust, as though the store had not been open for years. I didn't stop in front of it, just let my eyes glide over the abandoned-looking space before continuing down the block.

The buildings were all four stories with apartments above and the storefronts below. Maybe Merl had gone up into one of the apartments. I picked up my pace and ran a couple of blocks before doubling back and walking down the other side of the street. There were lights on in the third floor apartment over the abandoned store. On the second floor the curtains were drawn, but I could see the dim glow of a TV. Blue tapped my hip as I slowed even further, reminding me to keep walking.

We returned to Lenox's apartment and I took another quick shower before finding Mitchel in an office space on the third floor. He sat behind a large, burnished-metal desk, two laptops surrounding a large monitor. He smiled when he looked up at me. "How's it going?" I asked.

"Pull up a chair."

I grabbed one of two leather chairs that faced the desk and brought it around next to Mitchel. "No sign of Merl's beacon but I did find out about the building it sent its last signal from. It's owned by Sing, Merl's friend. He's the sword maker, right?"

"Right."

"Well, there is no mention of that, he is listed as a businessman which is vague enough. He rents out two of the apartments and lives in the third."

"What about the storefront?"

"No sign of a tenant."

"Agreed."

Mitchel glanced over at me but I didn't elaborate.

"So," Mitchel said, returning his gaze to the computer. "I guess he went to see his friend and got into trouble there. Sing and Mo were friends, right?"

"Yes."

"So, maybe they were in the same kind of trouble. But you have no idea what that trouble would be?"

"No, Merl didn't either."

Mitchel leaned back in his chair. "Maybe they got mixed up with a triad."

"Organized crime. Why would they go after a geriatric sword maker and a tai chi instructor?"

"Government corruption?"

I sat back in my chair. "We just don't have enough to go on right now. We need to get into that building."

"We're going over there with Loki tomorrow, right?"

"Yes, it's smart to go with backup," I answered, as much for myself as Mitchel. I wanted to just go back there now, break in, and check it out. But I wasn't going to do that. "Do you think you'll be able to find the device?"

"If it's still in the building."

"There is no way it could just be out of satellite range?"

"Unless there are secret underground passageways under the building, which, hey, I'm not ruling out."

"No, never rule out secret underground passages," I said with a smile.

"You laugh but you'd be surprised by how many underground passageways there are."

I laughed. "Trust me, I believe you. Is there anything else you can do tonight?"

"I'm going to continue to look for info about the tai chi school and Sing to see if I can find any connections."

"Get some sleep, though," I warned, guessing that Mitchel, like Dan, could become so wrapped up in his work that he forgot to rest. "I need you alert tomorrow."

"Yes, ma'am," Mitchel said.

"Don't call me that," I warned. "I might be older than you, but I'm not *that much* older than you."

Mitchel grinned. "Sure."

"All right," I said, standing up. "I'll leave you to it."

Back in my room I changed into sweat pants and a T-shirt before climbing into bed. Blue hopped up and circled twice before settling at my feet. I thought about Merl and wondered how anyone could get to him. He was so careful and capable. Had he walked into a trap? But who would even know to lay one? How could they guess that he was coming to see Sing? What did it have to do with Mo? I rolled over, bunching the sheets around me in frustration. Blue raised his head and looked at me, his mismatched eyes glowing green in the dark room. "Sorry," I said. He sighed before returning his head to the mattress and closing his eyes. He was snoring within seconds.

I envied Blue and his easy discipline. He didn't have trouble falling asleep, eating balanced meals, and exercising. Blue wasn't staying up nights worrying about friends. Dogs lived in the moment—something I needed to learn from him. Something Merl had tried to teach me. Tai chi, the discipline that Mo had taught Merl that helped him conquer his addiction to heroin, was a moving meditation, a practice of staying focused on the moment at hand. I'd never been any good at tai chi. It was slow and deliberate, I preferred fast and deadly. But as I lay there, tying the sheets in knots, I recognized that I needed meditation in my life. Climbing out of the bed I stood and moved to the center of the room.

Blue woke with my movements and hopped off the bed. "Go back to sleep," I said. He cocked his head. "Down," I commanded. He lowered himself to the ground. I took a cleansing breath and closed my eyes, feeling the air move through me. I went through the fifteen movements of the sun style. After I was done I felt calmer and, climbing back into bed, fell asleep.

CHAPTER SIX
GETTING IN TROUBLE

I woke the next morning with a start. Blue was by the door, his ears perked forward. I listened over the sound of my heart pounding and heard a shower going in another room. I quickly dressed in my jeans, a cotton T-shirt, and a pair of lace-up black boots, then grabbed my leather jacket and headed downstairs. There was a pot of coffee waiting, Loki must have set up the machine to start automatically. As I poured milk into my cup I heard steps on the stairs. Mitchel joined me, his hair still wet, eyes bright.

"Find anything?" I asked.

He shook his head. "No, I crashed soon after you."

"Hopefully we will come up with something when we head over there," I said, glancing at the clock on the stove. It was 8 am. Loki had said we could leave at 9. Mitchel poured himself a coffee and then turned to the fridge, opening it. "Anything in there for breakfast?" I asked.

"There's eggs, you want?"

"Sure," I said, even though I wasn't really hungry. I wanted to get the day going. To go check out Sing's property. To stop this pussyfooting around.

After feeding Blue and then eating the eggs Mitchel made for me, I did the dishes. Loki knocked on our door at 8:45 and, without waiting for a reply, entered. He smiled when he saw us both in the kitchen. "You found everything you needed?"

"Yes, thanks," I answered. "I'm ready to go whenever you are."

"I'll grab my stuff," Mitchel said, hurrying out of the room.

"A car is waiting downstairs."

"Great." I put a leash on Blue and slipped into my jacket.

"Lenox told me you wanted weapons. As you may know, the gun laws here are very strict. I carry a pistol but was not able to obtain one for you. However, I was able to get you this," Loki said, holding out a slim black pipe. I took it in my hand, feeling the weight. "It extends," Loki said.

"Yes," I said, noticing the seams in the metal. I stepped back and whipped it out, the foot long pole became almost three feet.

"There is a button there," Loki said, stepping forward and showing me the small impression in the side of the weapon. "For retraction."

I pressed down the button and, pressing the tip against my leg, shrank the pipe back down to size. Slipping it into my jacket I smiled at Loki. "Thank you," I said, the weight of the weapon bringing me comfort.

Mitchel returned and we headed down to the street. It was busy with people hustling to work. A black sedan waited at the curb. The driver was broad with a flattened nose that looked like it had gotten that way through punishment rather than genetics. Loki held the door for Blue, Mitchel, and me to climb into the back seat, then took the front. It was a short drive to the building and when we pulled up in front it looked as abandoned as it had the evening before.

I got out of the car, Blue with me. Loki and Mitchel joined us on the sidewalk. Loki nodded and looking down the block I saw another dark sedan idling at the curb. "They're with us?" I asked.

"Just in case," Loki answered.

"I like the way you think."

Loki rang the bell of Sing's apartment, and when there was no answer he pulled out a small lock-picking kit and deftly opened the door. It creaked on its hinges. The hall was dusty. The steps had the same worn out centers as Lenox's place, but the walls were not freshly painted and the wood hadn't been polished in years, possibly decades.

Loki checked the door to the commercial space and found it locked. He used his tools again and soon we were inside. The space was separated into multiple rooms. A small anteroom faced the street, as dusty and abandoned-looking as the hall. But when Loki picked the lock into the back room we were surprised to find an immaculate studio.

At the back of the room was a furnace, turned off now, but the ashes in its hearth showed it had recently been used. The furnace vented out the back of the building. In front of it were several anvils. Rows of hammers fanned out from them, all within easy reach. In the front of the room were racks with swords on them. I picked one up. It was lighter than I thought. Grasping the handle, which looked like it was made from bone, I pulled the blade from its sheath. It caught the low light in the room and shone bright silver on the edge, while the rest of the blade was matte.

Loki looked over my shoulder. "A beautiful weapon," he said.

"Yes," I agreed.

Mitchel picked up another and Loki narrowed his eyes. "Be careful," he warned. Mitchel put it back, his cheeks flushing with color.

"This place is clean, I mean, it looks recently used," I said.

"Yes," Loki agreed, approaching the furnace.

Mitchel pulled a hand-held device out of his bag and turned it on. He began running it over the space. "Checking for listening devices."

"Okay, Loki, let's you and I go upstairs," I said. "See if there is anybody home."

Loki nodded and after replacing the sword on its holder we headed back to the steps, leaving Mitchel in the studio. On the second floor landing we stopped to listen at the door. I could hear a TV on, canned laughter floated through the wooden door. We continued up to the third floor. It was quiet. A knock brought no one to the door.

We continued to the top floor. Loki knocked. I watched Blue's ears but there didn't seem to be any movement inside. Loki pulled out his lock pick kit again and went to work on the door. It opened into an apartment that smelled like home-cooked meals but nothing fresh. We walked into a living room with a couch and two chairs. The walls were lined with books. A hardback sat open on one of the chairs as if someone had gotten up from reading it and come to the door. A half-finished cup of tea sat on the side table next to the chair. There was a ring where the liquid had initially sat, the evaporated surface was now covered with a layer of dust.

Blue, nose to the ground, investigated the living room, his ears swiveling. I started through a door to our left and found the kitchen. The sink was clean, dishes all put away. There was an eerie stillness to the place, more than just an unoccupied home. Blue ran out ahead of me, checking under the counters and around the fridge. I opened the door. Leftovers in a bowl covered in plastic wrap had not gone bad. Maybe he'd left this morning, maybe several days ago but not long.

"What do you think?" I asked.

"Doesn't look like a struggle."

"He locked the door behind him."

"Yes."

We checked the rest of the apartment. Found the bed made, the bathroom clean, medication lining the sink, toothbrush in its holder. There was nothing to suggest that this man was not due home any minute. Except there was a staleness to the air. The windows were all closed, curtains drawn. Not that any of it meant anything. Maybe I was creating signs of trouble where there wasn't any.

"Let's knock on some doors. See if anyone heard anything."

"Okay."

"Let's check the first apartment, I heard their TV on."

Loki led the way downstairs. When he knocked on the door the TV played on, no other sounds joining it.

"You think no one's home or no one's alive?" I asked.

Loki frowned. "Perhaps they just left the TV on."

"Want to find out?"

Loki picked the lock and called out a greeting as he slowly opened the door. The thick scent of rotting food hit us as we entered. Blue followed his nose toward the kitchen. The living room had a couch facing a TV. Loki crossed the room and turned it off. Three empty plates, with old food crusted onto them sat on the coffee table facing the TV. Loki and I followed Blue into the kitchen slowly, our knees bent, hands loose at our sides, ready for an attack, ready for anything.

The apartment had the same layout as the one above it but the kitchen was not the neat and simple abode of a bachelor. There was food scattered across the counter. An open window carried the smell of rot toward us as the wind blew in. The sink was full of dishes. Several pots crowded the stove and a rice cooker crusted with rice sat on the counter.

In the bedroom we found three single beds and men's clothing, all large sizes. "What do you think?" I asked Loki.

"Apprentices?" Loki suggested.

"Big ones," I said, holding up a shirt that I could fit into twice. "Who left in a hurry days ago."

"Or are just total slobs," Loki suggested.

"Sydney," I heard Mitchel's voice coming from the hall. He was standing in the living room when we came out of the bedroom. "Smells terrible in here," he said.

"What did you find downstairs?"

"Nothing. The place was clean."

"Check this apartment." Turning to Loki I continued, "Let's see what's going on in the middle apartment." He nodded.

We left Mitchel and returned to the one apartment we hadn't checked. Again we knocked and I watched Blue's ears but there didn't appear to be anyone home. Loki picked the lock and we entered another living room. This one also had a TV but it was off. A worn leather couch faced it. Other than that the living room was bare. The kitchen was clean, fridge empty. In the bedroom we found a double bed, stripped, mattress bare, new looking.

Loki opened the closet and found just a few empty hangers. "I guess no one lives here."

"There was a light on in here last night," I said.

Loki turned to me, his brows raised. "How do you know?"

"I took a run. Checked out the place."

Loki nodded looking over at the drawn curtains. "Did you see any movement?"

"No, but there is no light on in here now." I stepped over to the switch by the door. A single dome in the ceiling flickered and then slowly glowed to life. "Someone turned off this light when they left." I glanced around the bare space. "I wonder what they were looking for."

"None of the other apartments looked like they'd been searched," Loki said.

"No," I agreed.

Blue, who'd been investigating the apartment, came into the bedroom and trotted around the edge, sniffing. "What is he looking for?" Loki asked.

"Anything and everything," I answered.

Blue stopped at the closet and pushed his way in. His tail wagged as he sniffed around the floor of the small space. He came back out and continued along the perimeter until he reached the bed. He lowered himself down and checked under it, his sniffing loud in the barren, silent room.

When he was done Blue came and sat by my side. I chewed on my lip. "Any thoughts?" I asked Loki.

"I have no idea," he answered.

EK

Loki was standing at the end of the bed. I was near the head, Blue leaning against my right side, my hand resting on his head when I felt his ears perk. Then he was gone, like a shot, bolting through the bedroom door. I followed, my instincts carrying me as quickly as my feet. I saw the tip of his tail disappearing out the apartment door and ran after him. Loki was right behind me. We sprinted down the steps, returning to the apartment below.

Blue barked from the kitchen and we ran through the living room. Mitchel was standing there, his hands up, pushed back against the sink, Blue was in front of him, hackles raised, a deep growl emanating from his chest. "Whoa," Mitchel said. "What the hell?"

Mitchel still held his bug-tracking device. It was emanating a low beep. Behind him a partially open window looked out onto a fire escape

54

and another building beyond it. "Shh, Blue," I said, thinking I heard something out there.

Blue quieted but his hackles remained raised, ears forward, body filled with tension. "Mitchel," I said, "come to me."

"He won't bite me?"

"Not unless I tell him to."

Mitchel slowly inched to the side, moving around Blue. I stepped up to the sink and smelled the putrid scent of still water left in a dirty sink for days. I leaned forward, trying to see onto the fire escape. I heard a rustle. A bird? Blue growled behind me, one short, low-pitched warning. There was a person out there. Turning around I motioned to Loki, then pointed out the window. His eyebrows pulled together in question. I pursed my lips and pointed again, raising my eyebrows. He nodded and pulled a black pistol from inside his black blazer. I reached my hand out for it. He looked at my waiting palm and thought for just a moment before handing over the weapon.

I moved dishes over so that I could climb onto the countertop and, crouching next to the open window, tried to see out again. The glass was smeared with grease and dirt. From my angle I could only see the metal landing of the fire escape right outside the window and a few empty steps leading up. Keeping my body back, gun in my right hand, I used my left to open the window further. It rose easily and quietly.

I pushed it as high as it would go, a space big enough for me but not much larger. Not wanting to stick my head out and get it shot off I grabbed a pot soaking in the sink and shaking off the brown water pushed it outside, watching the reflection in the bottom on it. In the blurry image I saw a small figure crouched on the steps. When it saw the pot it turned and began to run up the fire escape, headed for the roof.

I dropped the pot and dove out the window. I heard Blue's nails as he scrambled up onto the counter and followed. One hand on the railing, the other holding my gun, I ran up the fire escape, unconcerned by the loud clanging my weight made on the old metal structure. The figure was a flight ahead of me. Clad all in black, lithe and fast, it was pulling away.

When I reached the roof I saw it running across the open space and took after it. The roof was old. Made of tar, it was dappled by depressions filled with water. I splashed through a puddle, water spraying up my leg. "Stop!" I yelled but the figure kept going. Blue streaked past me, his ears flat to his head, legs pumping hard underneath him.

The person looked back, a female face. I saw just a flash of flesh as she glanced over her shoulder, a brief expression of horror crossing her features before she faced forward and hit a new level of speed. But she was not faster than Blue. He leapt onto her back. They flew forward onto the roof. I heard a scream of fear and pain and then silence.

Blue had her face down, his paws on her shoulders, jaws around her neck. I ran up to them, gun in both hands extended out. "Come," I said. Blue retreated to my side. The figure lay motionless. "Roll over," I said. She didn't move. Loki joined us then. "Tell her to roll over, slowly," I said.

Loki spoke and the figure rolled onto her back. She had jet black hair, straight and chin-length framing a beautiful face. "Who are you?" I asked.

Loki translated. The girl, who couldn't have been much more than seventeen, licked her lips. She had a smear of dirt across her forehead from the roof. Her palms were black with soot. She narrowed her eyes at Loki, rage emanating from her dark irises. When she spoke the words were tight, sounding almost like a curse. "She is Sing's granddaughter," Loki translated.

"Does she know Merl?" Loki began to translate.

"You know Merl?" she said, interrupting us, now in English. The girl looked over at Blue and seemed to relax. "You are friends of Merl"?

"Yes," I said. "You know him?"

"Yes, he is in grave danger."

"Tell me, where is he?"

She began to sit up and then an almost silent thwap raced through the air. She crumpled back to the roof, her head twisting, face down, her hair fanning out in a small arch as she dropped. Loki and I both knew that sound and crouched down, our heads swiveling, looking for the shooter.

There was one building higher than us. And there was one open window. A black hole in a checkerboard of glass. "Move," I said, but there was no reason, Loki was already zig-zagging across the roof. With Blue close to me, I followed, keeping my body upright and narrow, while making fast, jerking movements. But nobody fired. We dove back down the fire escape and reentered the kitchen. Loki was on a walkie talkie barking commands. I heard commotion from the street as engines roared, doors slammed. Those men we'd brought were going after the shooter. But he or she had a head start and a big building to hide in.

I looked around the kitchen, my heart beating hard in my chest, my mind ticking slowly over what I'd just seen, when I realized that Mitchel was not here. "Blue," he was right next to me. "Search," I said. He lowered his nose to the ground and began to search the apartment. Moments later he barked to let me know the apartment was empty.

I walked out into the hall. There were men coming in the front door. I looked down the stairs and recognized our driver. "Did you see Mitchel?" I called down to him. He looked up at me and shook his head.

"Search," I said again to Blue, motioning upstairs. He started up the steps and I followed slowly. I held my gun up, muzzle pointing toward the ceiling. Blue gave another bark. He'd found him. "Mitchel?" I called. But no answer came. The door of the top floor apartment was open just wide enough for Blue to fit through. I kicked it open all the way. It bounced against the wall with a small thunk. Sing's living room looked the same; undisturbed and abandoned.

Blue barked again from the bedroom. "Mitchel," I called again.

"In here," he answered. "I found something."

I let out a breath but kept my gun up until I walked into the bedroom and confirmed that he was alone. Mitchel was standing in front of the closet. "Look," he said, motioning me over. I stepped up next to him. He'd pushed away the hanging clothing and pried open a panel in the back of the small space. A series of switches with lights glowing next to them. "What is it?" I asked.

"A ridiculously sophisticated signal blocking system," he said.

"What do you mean?"

"I think this thing disabled Merl's beacons. It's possible he's fine and his phone is just out of service. You couldn't sneak a listening device or tracking device past this thing. Not in a million years."

Mitchel looked over at me then and his brows furrowed. "What's wrong?"

"That was Sing's granddaughter we chased onto the roof."

"You grabbed her?"

"She's dead."

His face went white. "How?"

"Shot in the head."

"Why?"

"No idea. But I'd guess that Merl is not just out of cell range."

Mitchel turned back to the device in the wall. "Sing must have been involved in something pretty serious."

"Or his granddaughter was," I said. "Does that look like something an 80-year old would set up or a teenager?"

"Teenager," Mitchel answered.

EK

"This thing is still working?" I asked.

"Yes."

"Turn it off."

"It will take a little while," Mitchel said. "And I'll need my laptop."

"Okay."

I turned to go find Loki when I heard him in the living room.

"Sydney?"

"In here."

Loki came in. "Did you find the shooter?" I asked.

"Not yet but we are still looking." His walkie talkie crackled and a voice spoke in Mandarin, a language I had zero familiarity with. Loki responded and then returned his attention to me. "I'd like to get you back to the apartment."

"Why?"

"Security reasons."

I laughed and began to walk by him. "Loki, I'm not in danger."

He followed me. "You are very important to Mr. Lenox and he insisted that my priority must be your safety."

I turned and faced him. "I thought you were supposed to do whatever I needed."

He looked pained. "Yes."

"Well, what I need is to go take a look at that girl's body. See if she has any ID. If you want to be helpful you can come with me. And..." A photograph on a shelf behind Loki caught my attention and I stopped speaking. I walked past him and picked up the silver framed image. The girl on the roof, the crumpled body, was alive and younger in the photo, smiling under a blossoming cherry tree. She was with a puppy, a Doberman Pinscher.

"We've got to find the girl's apartment," I said. "Mitchel," I called.

"Yeah," he answered from the other room, sounding distracted.

"We need to know where Sing's granddaughter lives."

He came into the room. "I should be able to figure that out. But it's going to take a while to shut this thing down."

I turned to Loki. "Mitchel needs a ride back to the apartment, he needs his laptop." Loki spoke into his walkie talkie again. "Mitch, I'll call you if we find ID on the girl—otherwise I want you to find her place first."

"Okay."

"I can find out the girl's address," Loki said. "More than likely she lives with her parents. If she is unmarried."

"Right," I said, nodding my head.

Loki's walkie talkie crackled. "The car is ready for you," Loki told Mitchel.

Mitchel left the apartment and Loki and I went through Sing's kitchen and climbed onto the fire escape, returning to the roof. The girl's body was where we had left it. The sun was high in the sky, shining down onto her black outfit. Her hair covered her face. Loki pulled out his phone and took pictures while Blue and I stood by. I looked up at the tall building and saw movement behind the open window. "It's an apartment up there?" I asked.

"Offices," Loki answered me as he kneeled down next to the girl. He ran his hand lightly over her pants, reaching into her pockets and pulling some folded cash. In her other pocket was a key. But no ID.

"Will you call the police?" I asked.

"I've already spoken with the authorities," Loki answered.

"What does that mean?"

Loki looked up at me, the sun was in his eyes and he squinted. "It does not need to concern you."

I let it go. "Okay, let's go talk to some neighbors."

Loki stood, looking down at the girl. A breeze blew across the roof pushing some of her hair off her face. Her head rested in a pool of blood. "She was pretty," he said.

I turned away. Mourning for girls I didn't know wasn't something my heart had room for anymore. "Don't worry," I said. "We'll find who did this." I looked back up at the open window the shooter had fired from. "Why do you think they let us live?"

"I suppose the reason for killing her would answer that," Loki said. He pulled out his cell phone as we headed across the roof. I glanced back at the girl—she looked small. Her black clothing blended with the roof. Camouflaged. Did she know there was a threat against her life? Loki was speaking into his cell phone. His voice sounded hard, professional, almost threatening. He hung up. "I should have her address within the hour."

"Good."

My phone rang, it was Mitchel. "Just a heads up," he said. "Your beacons were disabled. So don't do anything crazy."

I laughed. "Good to know," I said.

"I'll be able to reboot them though."

"Okay."

I returned Loki's gun and he slipped it under his jacket before we headed down to the street. His men were still searching the area and Loki suggested we get some lunch. "I'd rather talk to neighbors," I said, eyeing the shops around us. It was midday now so most were open. "They must have seen something."

"They will not want to talk to you," Loki said.

I raised my eyebrows. "Because I'm a woman?"

"A foreigner. A woman. An outsider. Young. I could go on."

"So who will they talk to?"

"My men will make inquiries. It must be done in a respectful manner."

"Sure, I understand. But don't you think they are going to want to help catch the person who killed their neighbor's granddaughter?"

"It is best not to get involved in matters like this," Loki said. "It will have to be done with—" he paused looking for the right word. "With elegance."

"Elegance," I said with a smile. "Okay, I'll leave that to you. But I can't just sit around with nothing to do."

"Soon we will have the girl's address, we can go there together. But first we should eat."

"You're kind of obsessed with feeding me."

"Lenox asked that I take good care of you."

CHAPTER SEVEN
GRIEF

Loki took me to lunch at a small place with plastic tables and fluorescent lighting. There was a sink by the entrance where we washed our hands. The proprietor, a woman with her hair pushed away from a broad and handsome face, eyed Blue with suspicion. But a few words from Loki and Blue was allowed to settle under our table.

I let Loki order, trusting his taste. "I'm not picky," I promised him.

He smiled, something shy and somehow knowing, as if that might be true about my eating habits but not about other things. The woman brought us bottled water and then disappeared into the back. A moment later the door to the back burst open as a yell rang out. Three cats, white, skinny, tails high, eyes wide, clearly on the run, skittered through the open door. Blue growled from under the table but I shushed him, this was not our fight. I could feel his breath vibrating with tension. Blue wanted to chase those cats.

They broke for the exit to the crowded street but a man wearing a stained white apron, jeans, and a tank top blocked their way and shooed them back into the kitchen. I watched him close the doors tightly and then turned to Loki.

"To keep the mice away," he said.

"Right."

"You've never visited Shanghai before, or any part of China?"

"No, closest I've ever been is India. Which is very different."

"They do not eat much meat."

"Not in a lot of the country. But in Goa, where I spent most of my time, it's pretty international, they eat everything."

"Yes, the cuisine there is fantastic. The Portuguese influence is wonderful."

"You've been?"

"Yes, I enjoyed my time there."

"Was that working for Lenox?"

"Yes," Loki answered.

The proprietor returned with a bamboo tray, the lid still secured. She placed it between us and then removed the top. A puff of steam rose, revealing six buns resting on a bed of lettuce. She smiled at Loki, who said something complimentary. I smiled and nodded.

"These look great," I said.

Loki passed me a pair of chopsticks from a plastic cup on his side of the table. "Pork and shrimp," he said.

"How long have you lived in Shanghai?" I asked, holding the chopsticks, watching Loki, waiting to see what he did before attempting to use the two sticks to the get the small fist-size bun to my mouth. I'd never been good with chopsticks.

"Off and on about 10 years," he answered, reaching forward and grabbing one of the buns, making it look easy. He dipped it into a bowl of sauce and then put the whole thing in his mouth.

I didn't know if it would fit in mine but was game to try. When Loki saw me staring at the chopsticks in my hand he reached forward and adjusted them, then nodded, smiling, as he continued to chew. Reaching forward I managed to get the sticks on either side of the bun but when it came to lifting if from the bed of lettuce things went sideways and the bun flipped upside down, landing back on the leaf.

"Try again," Loki said. "This time, don't squeeze so hard."

I placed a chopstick on either side, keeping the pressure gentle and got halfway to my mouth before it flopped onto my lap and then bounced onto the ground, right in front of Blue's nose. He sat up, his eyes on my face. I nodded and he gobbled it up in one bite. No need for chopsticks.

"If I use my fingers will I embarrass myself?" I asked.

Loki smiled. "More than you just did?"

"Yeah, okay," I grabbed one of the dumplings between my trusty thumb and fingers, dipped it in the sauce, and took a bite. The mix of pork, shrimp, and spices with the steamed dough and vinegary dipping sauce was heavenly.

"That is really good," I said.

"I'm glad you like it."

I finished off the bun and then wiped my hand on a thin paper napkin I pulled from a holder in the center of the table. "You seem very calm," I said.

"What do you mean?" Loki asked, reaching for another bun.

"You just saw a girl get murdered and yet you're sitting here eating steamed buns."

Loki was in the middle of chewing and finished before answering. "So are you."

"Yes," I leaned forward. "But I'm cold and heartless, calloused against death."

"What makes you think I'm not?"

"Are you?"

The proprietor returned with another bowl of steaming food and a bowl of white rice. Behind her the man in the apron followed with two more bowls, a soup and a noodle dish. "Thank you," I said, staring at the bounty.

Loki expressed my gratitude and his own. Blue touched his nose to my shin, hoping for more dumplings.

After they'd returned to the kitchen Loki served me a plateful of food. Roasted pork with vegetables, sesame noodles with ground tofu, and a small bowl of fish soup. I started with the soup, it was buttery at first and then a burning sensation rose up my throat. "Whoa, spicy," I said.

"Yes," Loki answered, slurping at his own soup. "The soup will cool it."

He was right, more of the buttery soup cooled the spice but then as soon as I was done sipping the heat began to rise again. "It's really good but how do you stop eating it?"

Loki smiled. "The chef would prefer you didn't."

I laughed. Lenox had chosen a good partner for me. Loki was not afraid or affected by death, and under all the professional seriousness he had a sense of humor.

Loki's phone rang and I listened to him speak in Mandarin while I continued to consume the soup. I was getting close to the bottom of my bowl and was wondering if I should try eating some rice or just go for a second bowl when he hung up. "We found neighbors who saw Merl enter the building."

"You did?" I put down my spoon. "Did they see him come out?"

"No, and they say they were in their store all day. They remember him because of the dogs."

"So, there is another way out."

"It would appear so."

"I mean, we know there is the fire escape, but why would Merl do that?"

"There must be someone watching the building."

I took a long sip of water feeling my mouth was on fire. "Do you think they are still watching?"

"I imagine it could be the same person who shot the girl."

"Anything on that?"

"Not yet."

"What about her address?"

"We should have it soon."

"Okay," I said, returning my attention to the meal.

Loki was as good as his word. He got a text soon after I'd managed to move onto the roast pork after calming the fire in my mouth with big bites of white rice. "It is not far from here," he said. "Her name was Bai."

I put down my chopsticks. "I'm ready to go." Loki nodded and called for the check.

Our black car slid through slow-moving traffic, bikes and rickshaws squeezing in around us. "Is the traffic always like this?" I asked.

"Not very late at night."

"Right," I said with a smile. A moment of silence passed between us. I thought about the girl on the roof. "It's normal to live with your parents as an adult?" I asked.

"Yes, until marriage, very common," Loki said. "There is a housing shortage in the city. And it is very expensive."

"So why don't you live with your parents?"

Loki shook his head. "My parents are no longer alive."

"Oh, I'm sorry," I said, feeling like an ass.

"Besides, I left China for a long time during my youth."

"Where did you go?"

"Australia."

"Really? How did you end up there?"

"My brother was an educated youth. Do you know what that is?"

"No."

"During the cultural revolution it was thought that people from the city, educated youths, age around sixteen, should go to the countryside to be reeducated by the peasants. That they should learn farming, hard work. At the time, triads were struggling. Most had existed for hundreds of years but Mao was cracking down. My brother learned about them in the village he was sent to. He joined the triad in order to flee. He wanted to go to America. He did not get the chance for over 15 years. By then, his mother had died, my father had remarried, and I was born. Despite our age difference my brother was very attached to me. He offered to take me with him and my parents felt that I'd have better opportunities abroad."

"Wow. So you went to the States first?"

"No, our ship did not make the crossing of the South China Sea. My brother drowned."

"I'm sorry," I said, watching his profile.

Loki turned to me, his eyes dark and empty. "It taught me many things. The most important being how to survive. An Australian ship picked me up."

"Were there other survivors?"

"Two women. They both died on the Australian ship. They were sick already. I think they died for me. They gave me the best parts of the fish we caught."

"How long were you at sea?"

He shrugged. "I'm not sure. At least six weeks."

"How old were you?"

"Five."

"Amazing."

"Yes, the Australian captain adopted me. His wife could not bear children and was overjoyed to have me. They thought I was lucky. Which," he smiled, just a slight twitch of the lips, "of course, I was. I've kept their name. Falk."

"What was your parents' name?"

"I do not remember," he said, turning away from me.

"Are the Falks still alive?"

He shook his head. "They were older, already in their sixties when they adopted me." We pulled up in front of an apartment building. The dilapidated cement structure was about ten stories tall. I recognized the communist era architecture, ugly, utilitarian. Loki climbed out of the car, horns blew behind us as we blocked traffic. I followed him, Blue behind me. The car pulled away. "He will come back for us," Loki said as he led the way toward the entrance.

There were two doors. One pane of glass was cracked. It looked like a rock had hit it, the glass splitting from the central impact point in a snowflake of cracks. The other door's glass was gone, replaced by a piece of plywood. It looked soaked, as though it had been through numerous storms.

The lobby was bare, just a wall of mailboxes and a cement bench built into the wall. No one manned the folding table and chair by the front door. "This is government housing," Loki told me. "These apartments are handed down through generations."

"I don't understand. Sing owns a whole building. Why would his granddaughter be living here with her parents?"

"That is something we can ask them," he said, starting up the dark stairs.

"Wait, they are going to be there?"

"Her mother works nights so should be home."

I grabbed his arm, stopping him. "Then I think we need a plan."

"I will do the talking," he said.

"What are you going to say?"

"I'm going to tell her that her daughter was killed. That the authorities will come and tell her it was an accident but that is not true. That we are her only hope for justice so she should share with us everything we need to know."

"Oh, I guess that's pretty good. Do you think it will work?"

"Only one way to find out."

Blue and I followed Loki up to the sixth floor. By the time we reached the apartment door my heart was beating hard and not just from the climb. I did not want to see this mother's grief. I was cold but not that cold. The ice I'd built around my heart, around the feeling part of myself, could be cracked, just like the front door of this building. With a hard enough whack from the right stone I might remember my own losses.

EK

When Loki knocked on the door it rattled on its hinges, sounding cheap and easy to break down. Blue sat by my side, pressing his weight against my leg, sensing my discomfort and doing his best to alleviate it. When there was no answer Loki knocked again, harder this time. "Maybe no one is home," I suggested.

"She is sleeping."

Blue's ears perked forward and I heard shuffling footsteps. A woman spoke, she sounded tired, her voice thick with sleep. Loki responded and a lock turned before the door opened just enough for her to peer through. The woman had bags under her eyes and gray running through her hair. Loki spoke quietly to the woman, his voice soft, almost a hum. He sounded trustworthy.

The woman looked over at me, her eyes narrowing. I gave her a weak smile. Loki looked at me and then returned his attention to the woman, apparently explaining who I was. I wondered how that was going. The woman's eyes wandered down to Blue and she opened the door a little in surprise.

Loki took a step forward and she retreated into the apartment, letting the door slip open as she did so. The apartment smelled like cooked food, like a home. The room we walked into had a mat on the floor with scrunched bedding, as if the woman had just risen from it. There was also a plastic table with three stools around it. A small kitchen occupied a corner behind the table. Windows, clean on the inside but dust ridden on the outside, let anemic yellow light into the small space.

There was another mat on the floor and I wondered if it was the girl's. How could she be so involved with computers and live in this small apartment with her parents? Unless all her equipment was at her grandfather's house. The woman went into the kitchen, holding a robe tight around herself. Her feet were bare and looked as old and worn as the linoleum she walked upon.

"She will make us tea," Loki told me.

"What did you tell her?"

"That I had to talk to her. I promised her money."

"Okay, I have some cash on me."

"Don't worry, I have it." He took a wallet out of his pocket and placed some bills onto the table. The woman looked over from the stove at the money. Her eyes glowed for a moment before she returned her attention to the tea kettle. Loki spoke to her and the woman offered a one-word answer. He waited until she'd poured the tea and sat down at the table with us before he spoke again.

I looked down into my chipped tea cup. It was green tea, the smell familiar and soothing in this strange place. I was tense, waiting for Loki to break the news. The horrifying news that this woman's only child was dead. The apartment was making the girl more real, slipping under my skin. The memory of her spinning from the shot, the elegant arch of her neck, the way her hair swirled. Looking up at the two of them again I saw Loki pushing the money across the table and the woman taking it, disappearing it into the folds of her robe.

Loki reached out and took the woman's hand. She went to pull away but he was speaking again and her face was crumpling. She shook her head, refusing to believe the news. He squeezed her hand. Blue pushed in close to me, sensing the emotion in the room.

Tears ran down her face as she shook her head, at once knowing the truth and refusing to acknowledge it. I felt tears prick at my eyes and looked back down at the tea again. The leaves had tinted the water now, the subtle green of American money.

The woman stood up suddenly and yelled at Loki, pointing at the door. But he stayed seated, talking calmly. The woman collapsed back onto the stool and held her face in her hands, sobbing. A lump sat in my throat, the air thick with grief, almost suffocating. Loki's face remained impassive, compassionate but not overwhelmed. He continued speaking until the woman nodded her head and began to talk. Loki was quiet then, listening, his face gentle, understanding, the face of a therapist, of a grief counselor, of one who understood the pain of loss, and the hole it left, as well as what it took to survive it.

I sipped the tea and listened to the woman's words. They meant nothing to me but the tone in which she spoke them made it obvious she was speaking about someone she loved. Her voice sounded so different from the tired one that answered the door. She was talking about her daughter and as she spoke the tears continued to flow. I wanted to know what she was saying but there was no time for translation. It was clear to me then, quite suddenly, how out of depth I was here. With no language skills or cultural understanding I'd never be able to find Merl without Loki's help.

Then I heard Merl's name. Loki was asking about him. The woman looked over at me. She nodded her head and spoke, looking at Blue. She knew Merl, I was sure of it. Loki sipped at his tea while the woman spoke. She was calmer now, her tone changing again, slipping back to that tired voice, but it was not just fatigue bringing her down now.

Loki poured her more tea despite the fact that she'd only taken one sip. She reached forward and drank, licking her lips and began to cry again. Loki held her hand, his eyes sympathetic. He seemed to be making her promises. I hoped they were promises we could keep.

CHAPTER EIGHT
RETURNING TO THE SCENE OF THE CRIME

Back on the street over an hour later I breathed in the air thick with pollution. It was fresh compared to the stifling apartment. "You were amazing in there," I said.

"Thank you."

"How did you know how to do that? I mean, have you done police work?"

Loki looked down at me, his expression unreadable. "Grief is like any other emotion. We must listen and care. That is all it takes to communicate."

I nodded and looked away, somehow uncomfortable with his honesty, or perhaps with that particular truth.

"She knew Merl," I said after a moment.

"Yes, but only because her daughter mentioned him. Sing is her husband's father. Father and son do not speak. But she knew that her daughter saw Sing. Her husband does not know."

"I didn't see any computer equipment in the apartment."

"No, they do not have any extra income. I think the girl must have been keeping it at Sing's."

"Or a friend's."

The black car pulled up in front of us. "What makes you think that?" Loki asked as we walked toward the back door.

"From what I know of hackers they often learn from friends. I mean, she could be totally self-taught or learned from people online, but it's also possible that she has friends in town. Maybe kids she met online who she then became real world friends with, but that's where her equipment could be."

Loki opened the door for me and I climbed in followed by Blue who sat at my feet, making himself small and pretending to be a lap dog as he rested his head on my knee. Loki slipped in next to me and spoke to the driver, who pulled back into traffic.

"I asked about Bai's friends but her mother said she did not know. The girl was withdrawn. Hated living with her and her husband."

"I'd have hated living in a room that small with my parents when I was her age."

Loki did not respond.

"But why wouldn't she live with her grandfather?"

"He would never let her move in without her parents' permission. No matter how much they did not get along."

"But he would have a relationship with her?"

"He had her mother's permission and may have thought her father approved."

"Why weren't they speaking?"

"She wouldn't go into it."

"Weird."

"It is not that strange."

"I don't know, you let two people you've never seen into your apartment who tell you your daughter is dead and that it's no accident. You tell them about how your husband didn't speak to his father and that your daughter did but you won't say why the two men fought."

Loki nodded. "Perhaps there are some things too private to share, even for a good sum of money."

We rode in silence the rest of the way to Sing's building. Mitchel was in the living room of the top floor apartment. "Almost done," he said when we walked in, glancing up with a smile. "How did it go at the girl's place?" he asked, his voice turning serious.

"Okay," I said. "Did you find any computer equipment? We didn't find anything at her apartment. She didn't look like she could afford a tablet, let alone the kind of stuff you found in the closet."

"No, but I have not done a deep search."

"My men can do that," Loki said, pulling his phone out.

"They never found the shooter?"

Loki shook his head. "No fingerprints, nothing. They were very careful."

"I want to go check out the roof, see what I can see about alternative exits."

"Okay," Loki said, "I will come with you."

After he spoke to someone about searching the apartments we headed back up to the roof. The girl's body was gone, a bloodstain marked where she died. "What happened to her corpse?"

"It was moved."

"Got that part."

"Arrangements have been made."

"Too vague," I said, pushing hair back from my face as a wind blew it into my eyes.

"I have made arrangements with the local police. It is best if her death is considered an accident. So that we may proceed with our investigation without interruption."

"You can do that?"

"Yes."

I left it at that and continued along the roof. It was flat, like the rest of the roofs on the block. They were all connected from one end to the other, an aerial grid pattern defined by the streets below. The only new building, taller than the rest, was the one the shooter had fired from. "That building is offices?" I asked.

"Right."

"When was it built?"

"In the last five years I would guess. It is hard to get permits to build in the Bund. It is historically significant. The city wants to maintain its authenticity. At least on this side of the river," he said with a small smile, expressing the irony considering the mass of skyscrapers on the other side of the Huangpu River.

Walking to the back edge of the roof line, I saw that there were fire escapes on all the buildings. "Merl, Sing, and the dogs could have gone down any one of these fire escapes. But why? What were they up to? Why not use the front door?"

Loki didn't answer me.

"What about the three assistants?"

"What do you mean?"

"Sing and Merl are gone, disappeared into the wind. There were also three guys living in that other apartment. What happened to them? They seem to have left in somewhat of a hurry. I mean, sure they were slobs but who leaves their dinner plates just sitting on the coffee table?"

"Single men."

I shook my head. "You don't really believe that. Can you check and see if any bodies have turned up?" Loki nodded and pulled out his phone. "Thank you," I said. He nodded again.

Blue touched his nose to my hip, reminding me he was there. I placed my hand on his head. "What do you think?" I asked. "What did Merl get caught up in?"

Blue sat down next to me, leaning his weight against my leg. I closed my eyes feeling the sun on my face, a breeze played with my hair, and I tried to clear my mind. There was something here I was missing. Who would want to kill that girl? Did her death mean Merl was dead, too? I didn't think so because there was a part of me that didn't think Merl could die. He was too strong, too smart. The man was infallible. But how could he have been taken, or whatever happened to him?

Unless her death was a coincidence, which seemed impossible. But what if it had nothing to do with Merl? What if Merl and Sing left for the tai chi center? Maybe this girl was mixed up in something else entirely. I wanted to go to the tai chi center. There was nothing I could do here. I didn't speak the language or understand the politics. I needed to be out looking for Merl, and there was one more place to check.

Loki came back to where I stood. "They are checking for the bodies."

"I need to go to Yang Shuo. To a tai chi center there. That is where Merl was heading and I need to make sure he didn't make it."

"Okay, I will escort you."

"I was hoping you'd say that."

"Allow me to make arrangements."

"Can we leave tomorrow?" I asked.

"It may take a day to arrange it. I will start immediately though."

"Fine."

Mitchel was waiting in the kitchen for us, his head popped out the window. "I got it down," he said.

"Great," I said. Mitchel offered me his hand as I climbed back in the window. "Did it give you any info about what beacons it's put out of commission recently?"

"Nothing like that but I want to get us back to the apartment so I can set up new beacons for us both. Right now we are off the radar."

"Okay," I said, a part of me loving that news. It made me want to run off, do something crazy without any of my friends watching. I almost laughed out loud. What would I do?

"The car is waiting for us," Loki said.

EK

Back at the Lenox's apartment Mitchel took Blue's collar and my cell phone and went to work in his office. Loki said he had matters to attend to for us to travel to the tai chi center and left.

I wanted to take a run, to clear my head and get some thinking done but Mitchel begged me to wait until after he'd gotten my tracking device working. I agreed, reluctantly. There was nothing for me to do while Mitchel worked and so I exercised in my room.

Push-ups, sit ups, side bends, squats, no matter how I made my muscles burn I couldn't clear my mind. Where was Merl? Who would want to capture him or kill him? Not that we didn't have enemies. But I didn't think these enemies were ours or I'd have been shot on that roof. This was something else. Something Merl stumbled into. But what would an aging sword maker, a tai chi instructor, and a tech-savvy young girl be involved in that would get them captured or killed?

I wandered into Mitchell's office. He looked up at me and raised his brows. "What's up?"

"You done yet?"

"Almost, these things are really fried."

"Really? I need to go for a run."

Mitchel screwed up his face. "That sounded almost like you were whining."

I laughed. "Sorry," I said, sitting in the chair opposite him.

The phone on the desk rang and we looked at each other. "Should we answer it?"

"I don't know. I mean it could be Loki."

"Wouldn't he just call your cell?" Mitchel asked.

The landline stopped ringing, solving our dilemma. Then Mitchel's cell began to vibrate. He answered. "Loki," he said, "sorry about that, we didn't know if we should answer the phone." He listened for a moment. "That's great news. Okay, I'll be here." He hung up the phone. "They found a laptop at Sing's house. In the studio. They're bringing it here."

"Great. Maybe we will get some answers."

"Let me get back to this," he said.

I returned to my room and flopped onto the bed, annoyed with my lack of action, with having nothing to do.

That night I drank three glasses of red wine, which helped me fall into a nice deep sleep that Mitchel woke me from at around 3 am with a knock on my door. Blue leapt off the bed, a warning growl escaping his broad chest. I sat up, the pipe I'd placed under my pillow in my fist before my eyes were fully open. "Sydney," Mitchel called. "Come here, quickly."

I was wearing a T-shirt and boxer shorts but moved to the door, my pipe up. Mitchel was waiting on the other side, his eyes bulged when he saw the weapon. "Oh, no, everything's fine like that. I mean, I was working on the computer. Just come here, you should see this." He looked down at my loose shirt and then quickly back to my face.

I followed him to the office. Bai's laptop was sitting at the center of his desk, wires lead out of it to an external monitor, Mitchel's laptop and what looked to me like an external hard drive. The screen was black except for the question "Who are you?" in red Helvetica in the top right corner.

"What is it?" I asked.

"Some kind of security, I think. Or it could be a person."

"A friend," I said, sitting down in front of the computer. I typed in *Joyful Justice*.

"Really?" Mitchel said.

"If she is a part of a hacker group they will have heard of us and know that we are not the authorities."

"Where are you?" came an answer.

"In Shanghai."

"How did you get this computer?"

"Your friend is dead."

The whole screen went blank.

"Shit," Mitchel said, leaning over my shoulder and then turning and looking at his own computer. "They wiped it. He was just keeping us talking to wipe it."

"Call Dan," I said.

Mitchel picked up his cell and Dan was on the line moments later. Mitchel explained what happened, then put Dan on speaker so I could hear him. "Interesting," Dan said. "What do you think, Sydney?"

"I have no idea, Dan, this is your department."

I could picture him, sitting on the edge of his bed, hair ruffled from sleep. Bare chest, long strong arms, elbows resting on his knees. "Mitchel any thoughts?"

"Obviously she was a hacker."

"Right. There are a lot of groups in China."

"Yes," Mitchel agreed.

"Let me ask around. I'll get back to you." Dan sounded thoughtful, his mind far away.

"We're leaving the city tomorrow," I said. "Headed to the tai chi center, see if Mo or Merl is there."

"Okay, I'll get on this now. Give me a couple of hours."

"Thanks."

"Of course."

Mitchel hung up and we looked at each other. "Tell me about the Chinese hacking community," I said.

Mitchel laughed. "That's a big question."

"Try to make it simple for me."

He sighed and closed his eyes for a second thinking. "You've heard of the Great Firewall of China."

"I know the government censors the internet."

"Yes, and they can do this because there are only three places that it comes into the country. Everything comes through these checkpoints and is censored right there. The routers automatically check all traffic moving in and out of the country. It's like an online border control. Anything with banned keywords, domains, or IP address are sent back to the user as 'file not found' or a message that there is something wrong with the internet rather than specific content is 'forbidden' or 'blocked'. Average users give up on those sites, deciding they are too slow and annoying to deal with."

"I can understand that," I said, thinking about how quickly I gave up on any site that took more than a few seconds to load.

"Right," Mitchel said. "So that works for any site that is seen as a threat as a whole but there is also a full-time bureaucracy searching the internet for things the Chinese government doesn't want their citizens to know about and blocking those articles and websites. It's so sophisticated that they can block specific articles on websites like the New York Times that they deem subversive or dangerous."

"So people think they have access when they don't."

"Sort of yeah, I mean, I could Google Tiananmen Square right now and we would not be able to find a single reference to the protests and killings that happened there."

I nodded.

"The next level is the '50 cent army'," Mitchel continued. "They post pro-government comments on blogs drowning out any dissenting voices."

"So, what do people do to get around all that?" I asked.

Mitchel frowned and shrugged one shoulder. "There are a lot of different things. People use code words, have you heard of the grass fed mud horse?"

"No," I said with a smile.

"It's all over the Chinese internet. There are comics, videos, you can even get stuffed animals. In English it doesn't sound like anything but if you change the tone in Chinese it means 'fuck your mother'."

I laughed.

"There is a famous Chinese artist, Ai Weiwei, who took a self-portrait of himself jumping naked into the air, just a stuffed grass fed mud horse covering his crotch. With a shift in tone 'grass fed mud horse covers the middle' can mean 'fuck your mother, Communist Party Central Committee.'"

"Wow," I said, smiling. "Inventive."

"Yeah, so there is that kind of thing, using a new language that the censors don't know yet and then of course, there is software to get around the censors."

"Like what?"

"One group, Falun Gong, they're a spiritual movement I guess you could say. They were banned as a subversive group or some such crap at the end of the '90s and have been persecuted in this country ever since. Their leader lives in the US, and they've created a pretty brilliant piece of software that allows the user to fake out the censors. They disguise their browsing by rerouting their traffic using proxy servers. The programmers have to constantly switch the servers, which is a hard and painstaking process but works for now."

"Impressive."

"Yeah, those guys are pretty awesome. They've hacked into TV satellites and switched the programming."

"Sounds like a 1980's movie."

Mitchel laughed. "Yeah, but it's pretty twisted. I mean, Falun Gong is totally peaceful but because the religion became popular the government has been trying to destroy it. It's based in Buddhist principals, from what I understand." Mitchel put up his hands. "I'm really not an expert, I just know about it because of their hacking prowess. But man, being a Falun Gong practitioner is dangerous."

"What do you mean?"

"They get locked up, none of that due process stuff necessary. There are stories of torture, organ harvesting, it's sick."

"Horrible," I said.

"The thing is, there is a big movement of people in China using the internet to try to gain freedoms, not just of speech but from actual bondage. So, the fact that Bai was somehow involved is a great clue, but doesn't get us much closer to a solution. She could also have been involved with an international organization like Anonymous."

"What is Anonymous?" I asked

"It's the biggest hacking group. They are kind of like Joyful Justice in that they work together to bring down evildoers."

"Evildoers," I said. "Yeah."

Mitchel looked up at me. "Yeah," he said, "What would you call them?"

"I don't know. Evildoers just sounds like something out of a fable. Not real life."

"If only evil was contained in fables."

"You're right." I walked over to the shelves behind the desk. They were lined with art books, David LaChapelle, Robert Mapplethorpe, Chagall. Big, expensive, beautifully bound. "Tell me more about Anonymous."

"Their most recent accomplishment is bringing down a pedophilia ring in the UK."

"Wow," I said, turning back to him. Mitchel was disconnecting the wiped computer.

"Yeah, pretty awesome. I think Dan was a member, but it's called Anonymous for a reason."

"So you're not a member?"

Mitchel looked over his shoulder at me and smiled. "Like I said, it's called Anonymous for a reason."

"Okay," I laughed. "So you think she might have been a member."

He shrugged. "No way of knowing. I mean, I'd guess she had the skills considering the level of equipment she had at Sing's place."

"We never found her cell phone, did we?"

"No."

I went and sat in one of the chairs facing the desk. Mitchel's face glowed in the blue light from his computer screens. "That's strange, right?"

"Unless she wasn't using one. They are ridiculously easy to track." I looked at his mobile phone sitting on the desk. "I take precautions," he said. "Why do you think you get a new phone every couple of weeks? Dan is on top of that shit."

"Wouldn't this girl be?"

"Maybe she dumped her last phone and hadn't had time to pick up a new one."

"Because she hurried over to check us out."

"What do you mean?" Mitchel asked, looking up at me.

"You said there was no surveillance equipment in the house."

"That's right. With her equipment in there it would have been insta-fried."

"Insta-fried. How big a range?"

"The whole building, probably into the surrounding buildings by twenty feet give or take, depending on what the walls are made of."

"Okay, so maybe she had cameras set up on the block."

"Sure, that's possible."

I stood up. "Let's check it out."

Mitchel nodded. "Okay."

CHAPTER NINE
A LIVE LEAD

I liked a partner who didn't think it was crazy to head out at three in the morning to check on a hunch. Mitchel was working out just fine.

The streets were pretty empty. We weren't in the party district. And though I knew that the city had a night life to rival any in the world, in this residential neighborhood it was just us and the rats out for a stroll. There was too much light pollution for any stars. The sky seemed low, like a ceiling, right above the buildings.

When we turned onto Sing's block I saw a skinny kid up on a ladder fiddling with something on a building five doors down from Sing's. I broke into a sprint. Blue stayed right at my hip but Mitchel couldn't keep up. I heard him stumble after me for a few steps before I was burning down the block. The kid on the ladder heard me coming and after a quick glance in my direction, hustled down, leaping the last few rungs onto the sidewalk. He glanced over his shoulder for just a second before taking off at a full sprint, throwing up the hood on his black sweatshirt as he went around the corner.

"Blue, go," I commanded. He broke past me, his speed so much greater than mine. As we came around the corner I saw the kid grab onto the ladder of a fire escape and pull himself up. Shit that kid could climb. Blue leapt after him but missed the boy's ankles by mere inches.

The kid didn't even glance down, he kept going up the ladder, his speed incredible.

I took a deep breath as I approached the ladder and leapt, just catching the bottom rung with my right hand. I swung out and caught it with my left before using my arms and the swinging motion I had going to catch the next rung. The boy was climbing onto the roof by the time I had my feet on the ladder.

Scrambling up after him I reached the roof, poking my head up slowly. I scanned the flat space but didn't see him. Light from the low clouds reflected back the city's glow and swathed the roof in a dull luminescence. The parapets between each building tossed short black shadows.

Was he hiding in the dark? Or did he already scamper down another fire escape? My breath was even, heartbeat steady, vision saturated with color, the adrenaline of the chase making me calm and ready for a fight. But it didn't look like I was going to get one.

"I don't want to hurt you," I called into the night. "We want to find Bai's killer," I said, guessing this kid was on her side. They shared a youthful grace and preference for rooftops. "My friend is missing," I yelled. "I need your help."

Nothing. I was walking in the center of the roof, swiveling my gaze, hoping to catch sight of the kid but he was gone. I turned back to the fire escape and was just about to step off the roof when I heard footsteps behind me, quiet and quick. I turned fast, the boy was right there. A knife flashed in the dull light, headed straight for my gut.

I blocked him, the knife slicing across my forearm. The cut didn't hurt, but I felt a warm ooze of blood. The boy came again but I was ready this time and grabbed his wrist, turning my back and twisting so that the knife was in front of me, my back against his chest. His body was light, slim. I pulled back on his thumb and heard it pop from its socket as he screamed into my ear.

The knife dropped to the roof and I raised his arm, twisting again so that I was facing him before putting pressure on the broken thumb. He fell to his knees in front of me.

I knocked off his hood and stared down into a face twisted with pain.

"Who are you?" I demanded. He didn't answer. Tears were streaming down his cheeks. "Answer me," I said, pushing on the dislocated thumb so that he cried out.

The knife was under my foot but I saw his red eyes light on it. "Don't think about it kid, I'm so beyond you. Now tell me your name."

He looked up at me. The boy was young. Maybe not even eighteen. His straight, black hair was cut into a bowl shape, like a little boy. His eyes were dark, black in the night. "Just kill me," he said, his English accented but clear even choked with tears.

I laughed. "I'm not going to kill you. I need you for information." That's when I realized I should get off the roof. The last kid I confronted up here got shot. "We better get down," I said, looking over at the building where the shot came from. "I want you alive, kid."

"You do?"

"Yes. If I let go do you promise not to run?"

He nodded and I dropped his injured hand. He clutched it to his chest. "Come on, don't worry, I can get your thumb back in for you." I picked up the knife and gestured toward the fire escape. He stood, still holding onto his hand. It was slow going down the steps, he was dragging his ass. Afraid? Just a sullen teen? I couldn't tell. Then Blue barked and the boy flinched. "He won't hurt you," I promised. "Unless I tell him to."

When we reached the ladder the boy kicked a latch and the thing dropped to the sidewalk. Blue jumped up onto it, his front paws resting on the fifth bar up, his tongue lolling out of his head. "Down," I called to him. He stepped back and lowered his butt to the sidewalk, but kept his eyes glued on me and the boy as we descended.

EK

Back on the ground I pulled the boy's thumb back into its socket. He went pale and I thought for a second he was going to pass out, but he managed to make it back to Loki's apartment where I gave him a bag of ice to hold against the swollen joint. He sat at the bar in the kitchen, holding the pack against his injured hand and frowning. "You were friends with Sing Bai?" I asked.

He didn't answer. I sighed. Mitchel, who'd been up the ladder pulling down what he told me was a video camera, placed the small device in front of the boy. "Did you put this there? Or was it Bai?"

When he didn't answer I poured him a glass of water and put it in front of him. "My friend is missing."

"Mine's dead," he shot back.

"I understand. I'm hoping mine is still alive. He was last seen going into Sing's building. If you have footage from that video I'd really love to see it."

The boy looked at the small camera but didn't respond.

"Have you seen the footage?" No answer. "My friend, his name is Merl, he has three dogs. Doberman Pinschers." I saw a flicker of recognition on the boy's face but he didn't speak. "Big black dogs, sleek and strong. To take him and his dogs would be a pretty nifty trick."

"What makes you think he was taken?" the boy asked, looking up at me, his eyes clear now, the tears from earlier gone.

"It's either that or he's dead."

"Maybe he doesn't want to be your friend anymore."

"What makes you say that?"

He shrugged. "You don't seem very nice."

"Hey, I didn't stab you," I said. "I coulda stabbed you."

Mitchel elbowed me and I stepped away. "This is sophisticated stuff," Mitchel said. "You set it up yourself. Or was it Bai?"

"We did it together," the kid admitted.

"You were friends?"

"Best friends."

"Did you wipe her computer?"

He looked up at Mitchel. "You have her computer?"

"Yes."

"Give it to me." The boy stood up, his shoulders set into a strong line, tension racing through his body.

"It's gone now," I said.

His eyes jumped to me.

"Someone wiped it."

He titled his chin up and narrowed his eyes.

"You know anything about that?" He didn't answer. "What's your name?" I asked again.

The boy frowned and didn't answer.

I felt impatience zinging through me. This kid knew stuff about Merl. He could very well know where he was and he was acting like a little shit. I took a deep breath and tried to calm down but I wanted to grab the kid by the hair and scream into his face. Instead I smiled at him. "Look, you tell me everything you know about my friend and I'll tell you everything I know about Bai's death. We can share info, be friendly."

"I'm not your friend."

"Well, I don't see why not."

He held up his thumb.

"You came at me with a knife first."

"I thought you killed Bai, for all I know you might have done it."

"Well, I didn't. That was a sharpshooter. I'm a pretty good shot but I'm not a marksman. Besides, I was on the roof with her." The boy sat back down, placing his injured hand on the counter. He reached for the water I'd put in front of him and took a couple of big gulps. "I want to help find her killer," I said. "I don't like seeing innocent people get hurt."

"What makes you think she was innocent?" the boy asked, looking up at me, his eyes hard, angry.

"Wasn't she?"

He tilted his chin up, defiant. "We were fighting for what we believed in."

"So you did work together," Mitch said. "Are there others in your crew?"

"I'm not a rat."

"Fine," I said. "We don't actually care about your crew. What I care about is finding her killer, finding Merl, and that's about the extent of it."

"You don't understand how much bigger this is than that."

"Explain it to me then."

He shook his head. "You couldn't understand."

"Try me."

The boy stood up again. "Am I a captive?"

"Yes," I answered in the same moment that Mitchel answered "No."

"Then I'm leaving."

"It's not safe."

"And you're going to keep me safe? Like you kept Bai safe."

I shook my head. "You want to take this on alone. You don't want my help, here," I threw his knife onto the counter. "Good luck, kid." He went to pick up the knife and I leaned forward quickly, grabbing the front of his shirt and pulling his face close to mine. "But if I find out you know where Merl is, that you had anything to do with his disappearance, dying will be your greatest wish."

His face went a little paler but his mouth set into a grim line. "You don't scare me," he said. "I've seen much worse than you."

"You don't know me, baby face." I pushed him away. He turned to leave and I tried one more time. "I'll pay you." He didn't turn around. "Show me the footage of Merl entering the house. Give me all the info you have and I'll pay you whatever you want."

The boy stopped, looked around the plush apartment. "You can use it for whatever you want. To keep fighting for whatever it is you and Bai were fighting for, to get the hell out of here, go live on an island somewhere."

The boy looked at me. "How would I leave? This is China, you can't just leave."

"Is that what you want?" I asked. "You want to leave? That I can do. In fact, I can probably offer you a job on an island somewhere."

Mitchel looked over at me, his eyebrows raised.

"Really?" the boy asked, taking a step back toward me.

"Mitch, tell him."

"Yeah," he said. "For sure, we can get you out of here. You give us that footage and we'll have you out of the country in no time."

"What about my family?"

"How many people?"

"Just my mother."

"Maybe, I'd have to make some phone calls."

"You're American?" he asked.

"Yes."

He chewed on his lower lip.

"How do I know you're telling the truth?"

"What do you think I'm going to do?"

"Kill me after you get the information."

"I won't. Trust me."

"Who are you?"

"Sydney Rye. We're from Joyful Justice."

His eyes narrowed, as he appraised us anew. "Joyful Justice."

"You've heard of us?"

He nodded.

"Well, you want to come work for us?"

"How do I know you are who you say you are?"

"You don't. The same way I don't know that you aren't actually the person who killed Bai." He opened his mouth to protest but I cut him off. "I don't think that because my gut says you were her friend. What does your gut say? Do I look like I'm working for whoever you're fighting against? Or do I look like I'm one of the leaders of an international vigilante network that helps victims of exploitation?"

His gaze ran over my worn jeans, leather jacket, scarred face, and settled on my gun metal gray eyes.

"Let's talk about my friend Merl," I said.

"I need a computer."

Mitchel went upstairs and came down with a laptop that he put in front of the boy. Typing with his one good hand he began to navigate, Mitchel looking over his shoulder. "Interesting," Mitchel said, nodding.

"What?" I asked.

Mitchel looked up at me and smiled. "Tech stuff."

I put my hands up. "Okay," I said, smiling. "Never mind."

More typing and then the boy motioned me over. "Here, this is your friend."

Looking at the screen I saw a video of Sing's block. Merl was about ten feet past the camera, his back to the lens, but still unmistakable with his long, black ponytail of tight curls. He wore a black T-shirt and pants, which looked dark gray in the black and white cctv footage, that were tucked into his ankle-height boots. They were the same style of boot I had on my feet at that moment.

Merl was flanked by his three dogs. Michael, the largest of his pack was on Merl's right side, Chula, the youngest behind Michael. Lucy, Merl's bitch and the smartest dog he'd ever known, was on his left. They moved as one unit down the block. The people they passed turned to stare after them.

Merl reached Sing's building and knocked on the door leading to the apartments. It opened a moment later and he disappeared inside. "Yes," I said, "that's my friend." I struggled to keep my voice even. A mix of excitement at this breakthrough and a worry in my gut pushed hormones into my system. I stepped away from the computer and paced behind Mitchel and the boy, trying to release some of the energy bundling up inside of me. Blue touched his nose to my hip as I paced, keeping even with my stride, ready to follow me anywhere, even just back and forth across a living room.

"When was that?" I asked.

"Five days ago," the boy said.

"Is there footage of him leaving?"

The boy scrolled through the video, fast forwarding it. The sun set, traffic passed, the stores closed, darkness fell, the street became quiet.

And then the day started over again and the cycle of life on the quiet Shanghai street repeated. No one went in or out of the building through the main entrance until Loki, Mitchel, and I showed up days later.

"Okay, who else was living there?" I asked.

The boy sat back. "Sing, his apprentices."

"Tell me about them."

"They are all good men. Friendly, serious about their work."

"Why would Sing disappear? Why were you surveilling them?"

The boy chewed on his lip. "Bai never really talked about it."

"Well, what were you two working on?"

He stared at me, as if trying to measure my trustworthiness. I held his gaze. He chewed on his lip for a moment and then seemed to make a decision, a small nod of his head, a softening of the eyes. "Organ harvesting," he said, holding my gaze.

I grimaced. "That sounds gruesome."

"It is," the boy said, his eyes flashing with anger. "My father was killed."

"By who?" I asked.

"The government. My father was a dissident. He was taken to a prison camp where he died. My mother was told he died of a heart attack while working, but we never saw the body."

"How do you know what happened to him then?"

"Bai helped me." He looked at the computer "We found a book, one published in the United States, it had evidence that organ harvesting was taking place at the prison camp my father was sent to."

"So, what can be done?"

The boy shook his head. "Bai thought that exposing the truth would help, but—," he shrugged. "It is known, there are books on the topic. The Falun Gong are exposing it at every turn," he looked up at me. "And still it continues."

I thought of Anita and the limited power of the media. She called it compassion fatigue. People could only care so much. And once they were done worrying about their families and their friends—and periodically the victims of headline-grabbing disaster like a major earthquake or tsunami—there wasn't much left for a Chinese dissident whose organs were sold on the black market.

"I'm sorry," I said, the words weak and useless. The boy didn't bother to answer. "Do you know why Bai's father and Sing weren't talking?"

The boy nodded. "Falun Gong," he said.

"What do you mean? What about it?"

"Sing was a practitioner, his son thought it was far too dangerous so wanted nothing to do with him."

"What about Bai, was she very close to her grandfather?"

The boy shook his head. "No, she was not religious. However, she believed strongly in the right of her grandfather to practice his religion without persecution."

I began to pace again. "Okay, so let's think here for a moment. Sing is selling exquisitely-crafted swords, obviously a profitable business."

The boy nodded. "Yes, he did very well."

"But at the same time he's trying to fly under the radar because of his Falun Gong connections. Why the security? He must have been organizing or something, right?" I asked, turning to the boy.

"Bai said she wanted to make sure that her grandfather had protection, in case someone tried to steal from him."

"Did you believe her?"

"I thought maybe there was something more to it."

"She wouldn't tell you."

"Maybe not."

"But you were best friends."

"She might have thought she was protecting me," he ventured, his voice low.

"Okay, so," I paced around the room. "We know Merl went there, we know there was some kind of threat against Sing, something that made Bai want to keep an eye on things." I turned to the boy. "She didn't use the front door on the day we saw her."

"She usually came up the fire escape."

"Why?"

"It was how she always did it."

"Why?"

The boy shrugged. "She said it was more fun."

"But when she was running away from me she went up, not back down."

"She was probably headed for a different fire escape."

I started my pacing again. Blue touched his nose to my hip. I looked down at him and then out the window. It was starting to get light. I needed to get some sleep if I wanted to be functioning properly for my trip to the tai chi center.

"I think we should call it a night," I said. "Since it's morning, you should stay here," I said to the boy.

"My mother will worry."

"You can call her."

He nodded. I looked over at Mitchel. He was sitting on a barstool next to the boy, watching me, waiting for my next move. My phone vibrated in my pocket. Pulling it out I saw Dan was calling and walked out of the room for some privacy.

"Hey," I said. "What did you find out?"

"Not much, I asked around my contacts and no one had heard of Bai but that's not unusual, I mean she would have used an alias."

"Hold on a second." I walked back into the other room. "What was Bai's alias? Her handle?" I asked the boy.

"UglyLlama," he answered.

"Really?"

Mitchel nodded. "That's sounds about right."

"Okay, UglyLlama," I told Dan.

"That's helpful, who told you that?" I left the room again, wandering down the hall as I explained about the boy. "Well, that's a great lead," Dan replied when I was done.

"Yeah, I'm headed out to the tai chi center tomorrow with Loki."

"Be very careful," Dan said. "You know Falun Gong uses Qigong a lot, which is very similar to tai chi. I would be very careful, that center might be under People's Liberation Army rule."

"I didn't know that. Mitchel said it was a form of Buddhism. But he admitted to not being expert."

"Yeah, it's based on Buddhist principles but there is a lot of Qigong, and as Bai's friend told you, the Communist Party of China is not messing around when it comes to ending all trace of Falun Gong."

"I'll be careful."

"I'll get back to you, now that I have Bai's handle I should be able to get a lot more info."

We hung up and I went back into the kitchen area. Mitchel and the boy were both looking very sleepy. "You should stay here," I told the boy. "Mitchel, tomorrow you can work with Dan to get him and his mom out of here."

Mitchel nodded. "I noticed some extra bedding in my room," he said. "I'll grab him sheets for the couch."

I nodded before heading up to my room. Stripping off my clothing I climbed into the bed and tried to quiet my mind. Images of prison camps and of organs, red and bloodied and expensive, roamed through my head.

The light outside continued to brighten, seeping through the curtains and filling the room. I put a pillow over my head, hiding in the darkness it provided. I thought about the video of Merl, his graceful movements, his supreme confidence. Did he just walk in on his friend being kidnapped or were they waiting for him, the way they were waiting for Bai? And what was the connection to the tai chi center over a thousand miles away? There were clues waiting there, something that would help me understand what happened to my friend.

CHAPTER TEN
ON THE ROAD AGAIN

I only got about an hour of sleep but it was better than nothing. Loki was surprised to find the boy on the couch when he came by later in the morning. "We found him last night," I explained, "taking this," I held up the small video camera that had been left on the kitchen counter, "off a building down the block from Sing's."

He nodded and took the camera from me. "What time did you find him?"

"It was about 3 am I guess."

"You went out at three in the morning and did not tell me?"

"Sorry, I didn't want to wake you."

"Sydney, it is very important to me that you remain safe. I cannot protect you if I am not with you and have no idea where you have gone."

"I understand Loki, but just so you know, I can really take care of myself."

"I do not mean to diminish your strength, only to beg that you allow me to assist you to the best of my abilities."

"When you put it like that Loki, I promise to call you next time I get a hunch at 3 am."

"Thank you."

"Are we all ready for the trip today?" I asked.

Loki nodded. He was wearing another suit, this one navy blue, with a light blue tie and another crisp white shirt. His hair was pulled back into a small ponytail at the nape of his neck.

I sipped at my coffee, it was rich and creamy. The caffeine was doing me good.

"We will fly as far as Qiliping and then I have arranged a Jeep to pick us up. We will stay in a small village for tourists and continue on to the tai chi center from there."

"Are the roads bad?"

"Some are not paved. We shall see what condition they are in once we arrive."

"Fair enough, Mitchel is going to stay here with the kid."

Loki looked over at the boy on the couch. "Who is he?"

"A friend of Bai's."

"Why did they have surveillance equipment?"

"He said he didn't know."

"Then why was he taking it down?"

"We didn't really get into it but he wiped her computer too. I'm guessing it was all a part of a protocol that Bai set up," I said, crossing the room toward him. His arm was flung over his face, blocking the light coming in through the curtains. "I think she was trying to protect him."

"From what?"

"Sing was a Falun Gong practitioner."

I felt Loki stiffen and looked back at him. "Our flight is in three hours," Loki said, his face calm.

"How long will it take?"

"Two and a half hours in the air and then another three by Jeep."

"Have you been to the area before?" I asked, walking away from the boy, not wanting to wake him. There was something about his narrow shoulders, the pale skin of his forearm that made me want to let him sleep. My maternal instincts showing up for the first time in my life.

"No, I have made arrangements for a guide."

"Someone we can trust?"

"Not entirely. He is a tourist guide. Someone who we have used before for trips."

"Ah, so we'll be pretending to be a couple."

Loki nodded. "Yes, it is for the best. I have told him you have an interest in tai chi and that you want to see the center, perhaps take a class."

"Sounds like a plan," I said, putting my empty coffee cup into the sink.

Loki nodded. "We should leave in an hour. Traffic can be thick at this time."

EK

The flight was uneventful, the scene below us mostly clouds. The private plane had a rich leather interior and a smiling flight attendant with an elegant scarf tied around her thin neck. A scene I'd grown used to. One I'd never imagined in my youth.

Growing up in Beacon, New York, a small, once-industrious town on the Hudson River that had become an enclave of ugly homes and poverty surrounded by natural beauty, my great dream was to move to New York City and escape that tiny, shabby world. My mother came to mind, not the make-up encased, Jesus-loving freak of the present but the young, lost girl who loved my father and read me stories before I fell asleep.

When my father died, after cancer had sucked his life away leaving just a skeleton draped in yellowing skin, my mother lost it. She lost touch with the world, with the reasons she had to live, and fell hard into alcohol abuse. A tendency I understood. The sweet relief of sedation. I felt that pull too, the urge to dull the effects of a brutal world. And yet here I was, flying over a sea of clouds, on my way to a rural part of China on the hunt for a friend. Because while it was easy to drift beneath the surface of life, to keep the pain of reality at bay with tools like drugs and alcohol, that didn't change a thing. Not really. It just changed you.

My mother escaped her alcoholism through finding God—by way of my stepfather, a preacher, one of the ones you saw on TV asking for money. When I thought about her deep convictions, that my brother was in Hell because he was gay, that I was destined to go there as well because I refused to lay my burden at an imaginary figure's feet, anger crawled up my spine.

Blue pushed his nose against my elbow. I ran my hand down his neck, over his shoulder where under the fur a scar lingered. The scar was a record of the first time Blue saved my life. When my brother's murderer shot him instead of me. Blue leaned into my touch, closing his eyes, the thick black of his lashes contrasting with the white fur around his eyes. My heart filled with love and gratitude for the dog, for his loyalty, his faith, and his companionship. Perhaps he was like my bottle of booze, my religion, my salve against the storm of upset that swirled around me. With Blue by my side I felt invincible.

It had been almost six months now since he'd kept me safe as I wandered, unresponsive, hallucinating through the Everglades after being doused with an almost lethal dose of Datura. A weapon at once sophisticated and barbaric. My arms and legs still showed fine white lines, thin, slowly fading scars from the thick brush that had torn my skin. Blue kept me safe and when Dan and Mulberry came looking for me, he led them to where I slept; curled up in a ball on the ground, the earth turned by Blue's claws into a bed.

I didn't remember it. Flashes came to me now and then. Such as sitting on the trunk of a tree smoking a cigarette. It's a habit I never formed except in the recess of my subconscious. Apparently, it was a well-known hallucination amongst Datura victims. Those who could remember, who survived, often reported smoking in that alternate universe. While in my mind I smoked cigarettes and ran from monsters that tore at my skin and chased me through the dark, fire licking at my flesh, lightning and thunder crashing all around me, on the outside, I was totally compliant. Following the orders of anyone who gave them. Even Blue.

That was why Datura was a popular drug for raping and robbing people in Colombia. Blowing a small dose into a person's face turned them into your own personal slave. The victim would gladly empty their bank account, hand over their most valuable possessions, offer you their body without complaint. Blue saved me from such a fate, keeping me hidden, keeping me safe.

It took twenty-eight days for me to come back to reality. And I still had residual effects, I saw lightning that wasn't there, heard thunder on sunny afternoons. But I could recognize those hallucinations for what they were. It was something Merl and I had argued over. Whether I was ready to return to active duty, to go back out in the field or if I was a danger to myself and others. A part of me knew that I was a danger. Not because of the thunder and lightning but because I was human, fallible, flawed, and afraid. But so was everyone else. I was lucky enough to have Blue, to feel his nose at my hip, hear his growl in my ear, know his strength and speed were mine to command.

The plane descended into a valley surrounded by jutting mountains covered in green. They were beautiful, like something out of a painting, their hard angles, the steepness of their sides, didn't look like they could hold life. But there it was, lush and bursting, clinging to the rocky sides. There was one runway, paved but brown with dirt. The landing was rough, the concrete uneven. I gripped the sides of my chair, my heart leaping for just a moment.

I'd recently overcome my fear of flying—after surviving a near-crash in Costa Rica. Lenox was flying a helicopter and we were in close proximity to a yacht that exploded. The pressure of the blast had pushed us perilously on our side, hurtling toward the ocean below, and as I looked down into the churning sea a calmness came over me. A realization that control was a myth, a fallacy, a joke really. But even with that knowledge gained in the most dire of circumstances, the stiff bump of a small plane injected adrenaline into my system, tensing my muscles and forcing my heart to beat harder, flushing me with the will to live.

Loki glanced over at me and I smiled. "I'm fine," I said.

He just nodded and unbuckled his seat belt as we slowed to a stop. Glancing out the window I saw a man standing next to a Jeep. He was short and broad wearing loose dark green khakis, a dark green colored T-shirt and flip flops stained the same brown as the dirt blowing across the runway. "Our guide?" I said.

Loki leaned over, looking out my window. "Yes, Ming."

I took a deep breath, preparing for our latest deception. Playing another person was as comfortable to me now as playing myself. As we descended the steps a wind pushed my loose pants flat against my body. I was wearing comfortable but expensive clothing. Green silk pants, tight at the ankles and belted at the waist, with a white cotton T-shirt. Along with the outfit Loki had given me a gold necklace and matching bracelet along with a fine leather purse and slip on shoes to match. I needed to look like money, but the kind that liked adventure. Expensive men, expensive trips, but at the same time trying hard to seem down to earth. At first, I hadn't bothered with makeup, which Loki thought unwise. "I've never had a client who didn't wear makeup," he said, handing over mascara and a tube of lipstick.

Ming came forward as we reached the bottom of the steps, offering his hand to me. "Welcome," he said.

"Thank you," I said, taking his hand. It was calloused at the base of his fingers, perhaps from gripping the wheel, maybe from some other work. "I'm glad to be here."

He looked to Blue. "Your dog is very beautiful. Like a wolf."

I laughed. "Yes," I agreed.

"He brings you much luck, I think."

"You're right."

"You are interested in tai chi," he said with a smile, his accent thick but words clear.

"Yes, I practice at home. I find it very meditative."

"It is the best thing for the body," Ming said, leading us to the Jeep. The vehicle was splattered with mud, the wheels large with deep treads. It was painted army green and had a snorkel running up from the engine. Ming saw me eyeing the snorkel. "For the rainy season," he said. "Do not worry, we will not be crossing too many deep rivers on this trip." He grinned at me and I saw a gold tooth flash in the sunlight.

"I don't mind," I said as he opened the back door. "I'm up for some adventure." I motioned for Blue to jump in the back and he did, leaving dusty paw prints on the cracked leather seats. Ming grabbed a towel from the front seat and quickly wiped it down before offering me his hand. The Jeep wasn't high but I put my palm in his and allowed him to help me up.

Loki loaded the luggage into the trunk and then slid in next to me as Ming climbed into the driver's seat. Loki's long arm wrapped around my shoulders and he pointed to one of the nearby mountains. "Have you ever seen anything like it?" he asked.

"No, they are beautiful."

"To the hotel first?" Ming asked, his eyes in the rearview mirror falling on Loki.

"Yes," he said with a smile. "We need some lunch."

I wanted to head straight to the tai chi retreat but knew that would seem strange for a woman on vacation with a handsome man whose company she was paying for.

EK

The Bamboo House Hotel was on the main street of a small village catering to tourists visiting the region to admire those exquisite mountains and the Li River. Our room was in the back of the hotel and looked out onto a rice field. Women bent over their crop, wearing wide straw hats, skirts pulled up around their legs. It made the perfect postcard of rural China. There was one bed, a queen size, with clean sheets and towels folded into the shape of swans.

A watercolor of the Li River, those oval mountains looming right off its banks, hung above the bed. There was a small desk with a chair. On the desk was a phone and a menu for the restaurant downstairs. "Are you hungry?" Loki asked.

"I want to get over to the tai chi center," I said.

"I understand but we must keep up appearances."

"For who?"

"There are always people watching, especially in a village this size." He lowered his voice. "If Falun Gong is involved there will be many eyes on us."

"Okay," I said, nodding my head, willing to follow his lead. "Let's eat." As we walked back downstairs I felt nervous, a tension in my shoulders and jaw. We were so close. "Can we ask about Merl, see if anyone saw him? I mean, an American with three Doberman Pinschers. Someone would remember him."

"Yes," Loki said, stopping and turning to me in the narrow staircase. With him a step below me we were almost the same height, I was just a little taller. "I'm sure he would be remembered. And watched. You are supposed to be here on vacation. Please, allow us to keep up this charade for some more time."

I nodded and he turned around, headed back down the steps.

"Can't I just say my friend recommended the place, was here years ago? That's true."

Loki stopped and turned back to me, a small smile on his lips. "Do you trust me?"

I felt like I was getting that question an awful lot lately. "I'm sorry," I said, "I just wish I knew if he was here."

"I understand your impatience but what I asked is if you trusted me."

I didn't answer, he held my gaze. "I do," I said finally.

Loki smiled. "Come, let's have lunch, the food here is excellent."

We sat on a deck that jutted out over a canal. The air was fresh, especially compared to the smog-filled skies of Shanghai. Loki ordered for me and then held my hand while we waited for the food to arrive. I watched the women in the rice field, their repetitive movements, hunched postures. Was it like meditation or torture?

"There are several activities I'd like to take you on," Loki said.

I nodded but didn't answer, watching those women, fascinated for the moment at the difference in our lives. But weren't our worries the same? Didn't they wish for the same things? Didn't every human on the planet want the same things? The safety and health of our loved ones.

Since losing my brother I'd tried to wall myself off, destroy any chance of getting hurt again. But people like Merl climbed into that empty hole and began to fill it. Losing Malina months earlier had hurt too much for me to even acknowledge. Violence, revenge, these were my solutions to the pain that resided in my chest. But as I watched those women, their slow steady progress across the field, I realized I needed their patience. The bloodshed that I craved, the hate in my center fueled by the love I felt, was a war, a battle I was waging. And nobody cared who won. Nobody but me.

"Sydney?" Loki said, squeezing my hand.

I turned to him and smiled. "Yes, sorry."

"What were you thinking about?"

"I was just enjoying the view. What were you saying?"

"We can go out on the Li River. It is fun, exciting."

"Exciting," I said, smiling, comparing it to the images of bloodshed in my head. I didn't think it could really be that exciting.

"Yes, we will go on a narrow bamboo raft, with a man on the back using just a wooden staff to direct us."

"Exhilarating," I said.

Our food arrived and we talked of other tourist activities in the area as we ate. When we finished Loki paid the bill and took my hand as we walked through the lobby. Ming was waiting for us. "What would you like to do this afternoon?" he asked.

"I want to see the tai chi retreat," I said before Loki could speak.

Ming blushed slightly. "I'm sorry, but I could not arrange a class for you yet. Their phone is out."

"Let's just drive over there then," I suggested, moving toward the back seat. Ming hurried to open the door for me.

"The road is very bad," he said as he opened the door. "And the drive is very long."

Blue jumped in and Ming was ready with the towel this time. "I don't mind," I said. "I like adventure." I got in next to Blue and Loki climbed in after me. Ming nodded, his face red, hands jittery.

"I will try," he said.

Loki leaned over to me as Ming went around to climb into the driver's seat. "I thought you trusted me."

"I do," I said, turning to him so our faces were close. "Now trust me."

Loki smiled, a small laugh escaping on his exhalation, but he nodded and leaned back into the seat, opening the space between us.

Ming climbed into the front seat and we started off.

It did not take long for the road to turn rough. The dusty, cracked cement of the village turned into rutted paths as we drove deeper into the mountains. We bounced on worn shocks, the tires crunching over large rocks. A half hour into our journey we got our first flat tire. Ming apologized profusely as he hurried to change it.

Loki, Blue and I stood on the side of the road while Ming jacked up the Jeep, removed the damaged tire, and replaced it with one from his trunk. Loki spoke to him in Mandarin. "What did you say?" I asked.

"I wanted to know how many spares he had," Loki said.

"How many?"

"There is one more. Perhaps we should turn back."

"Let's not argue Loki," I said, putting my hand on his forearm, the way I imagined a woman who'd hired him to be her companion might.

Ming, dusting off his pants, motioned for us to return to the vehicle and we took off again. The landscape was beautiful. The mountains stunning, the rice fields shimmering in the sunlight. "I worry that we will not make it before dark," Ming said.

"I do not mind driving in the dark," I said. We drove through a large pothole at that moment and I flew up off the seat, hitting my head on the roof.

"Sorry," Ming said, his expression pained as he turned to look at me. "You are okay?"

"I'm fine, all a part of the adventure," I assured him.

He faced forward again, concentrating on the rough road ahead. I snuggled close to Loki, holding onto his arm as much to keep myself from flying around in the back seat as for our cover. As the sun set it dusted the world in a pink glow that turned the mountains soft and edgeless. Their shadows stretched, inching longer, as we continued to maneuver through them. As we followed the road, the landscape lifted up, like the plane of the earth was rising, the mountains set into them moving with it.

Stars twinkled in the darkening sky. A pale half moon shone between two of the mountains, beautiful and almost translucent. I watched it as we bounced forward. With each bump and thump I knew we were getting closer to an answer about Merl, about Mo, about what had happened to my friend and his dogs.

"Do you know the tai chi retreat well?" I asked Ming.

He made eye contact for a moment in the rear view mirror. "Yes," he said. "I bring many customers to there over the years."

"Has it become very popular?"

"Not so much in the last few months," he said. "The phone has not been working."

"Is that normal?"

"It is not rare," he said, his cheeks going pink again.

Loki leaned in close to me, his breath on my ear, sending shivers down my neck. "Giggle," he said. I did as directed, letting out a girlish laugh, like he was whispering something naughty into my ear. A large bump, Loki's arm came around my waist pulling me closer. "It is embarrassing for him that the phone does not work all the time."

I nodded, turning my face toward his. "I understand," I said. He kissed me, lightly, just his lips against mine, nothing dangerous, nothing serious. Surprised, I sucked in my breath, getting a heady whiff of his scent, a mix of incense and soap. Loki's hair, loosened from the rough ride tickled against my face. He palmed my cheek, his lips still close, thumb running along my cheekbone. Loki's long fingers caressed my jaw line for a moment before he sat back.

I felt my cheeks flush as I returned my eyes to the road ahead. Loki's arm around my shoulders had a different texture than a moment ago. I'd pushed from my mind what Loki did for a living, but that kiss and caress were a reminder of what type of professional he truly was.

The sun blasted its final rays of light out in thick lines, hitting the low clouds with a deep orange glow before setting. An hour later the sky was black velvet inset with diamonds of twinkling stars.

A tire exploded, and the Jeep swerved violently. It sent Blue crashing into me, me sliding into Loki, and Loki slamming into the door before we came to an abrupt halt. The moon sat at the top of the mountains and threw a blue glow across the landscape.

Ming twisted around, looking back to us, concern etched onto his face. "I'm fine," I said, reaching for Blue, who was resettling himself, looking a little miffed at the banging about.

"I'm also fine," Loki said.

Ming hopped out to take a look at the tire. Loki and I climbed out as well, Blue following us. He stretched, opening his large jaws in a big yawn, waving his bushy tail back and forth languidly as he enjoyed the night air.

Ming stood next to the rear right wheel, his hands on his hips, elbows pointing back, flip flop clad feet hip width apart. Something had shredded the tire.

I turned to examine the path, Blue by my side. I saw the tacks twinkling in the starlight, sharp and just long enough to do damage, littered along the right side of the road. If you knew they were there you could just drive around them but without that special knowledge you'd blow at least one tire.

"Loki," I said, calling him over. He joined me, Ming following him. "Strange," I said. "They must have fallen off a truck."

"Yes," Loki agreed.

Ming said something in Mandarin that sounded like a curse. He then returned to his Jeep and began to change the tire. "We should head back," Loki said to me quietly.

"Aren't we close?"

"Yes, but we are out of good tires. And," Loki looked over at the tacks, "I think we will not make it with these four."

I chewed on my bottom lip, not wanting to turn back but understanding Loki's logic. "Can we try again tomorrow?"

"If Ming can get new tires."

"Money is no object."

Loki nodded. "I'm aware, but resources are scarce. It may not be a matter of cost." He went over to Ming and began to help the other man, speaking to him in tones I could not hear. I stared down at the tacks. Blue lowered his nose to the sharp metal and sniffed.

I looked around at the black monoliths of the mountains. The night was quiet. No other traffic on this deserted road. No homes nearby. Boulders shrouded in shadow lined the path. If you were planning an ambush this was an excellent place to do it.

Blue sniffed at the air, his ears flat to his head. "There someone out there?" I asked him. Peering into the deep black I saw the green glint of eyes; they weren't human, the iris glowing in the way that dog's did at night. Another pair blinked and then I heard the soft paw falls of an animal as they disappeared. Blue gave no sign of danger. Could they be Merl's dogs I wondered? Was he somewhere out here?

I looked back to the Jeep. Loki was holding a flashlight for Ming as he pulled the ruined tire off the wheel. I felt a pang of guilt. Was I putting Ming in danger? Would this man pay for my sins like so many others?

I missed Merl hard in that moment. I knew he wouldn't push on. Merl was always level-headed. He would have doubled back, resupplied, and gotten a fresh start in the morning. What did I hope to learn? I almost laughed out loud. I hoped to find Merl at the tai chi center, out of cell service. All the madness in Shanghai a strange coincidence.

I wanted to find Merl with his girlfriend, Mo, enjoying a well-deserved rest. But as I stared down at the tacks glimmering in the moon's cold light I knew that was impossible. There was something happening here, something I was ill-suited to address, but was determined to unravel.

Loki called me over to say the tire was changed and we were ready to head back. The ride home was slower but without further incident. Our headlights created beams of bright light in the dark night, illuminating the rough road, showing every rock, ridge, and pothole.

CHAPTER ELEVEN
MAKING PLANS

By the time we returned to the hotel my body ached from bouncing around. Ming and Loki spoke briefly before we said our good nights and Loki and I returned to our room.

"I'd like to shower before dinner if you can wait," Loki said.

"No problem. I'd like to shower too."

"Would you like to join me?"

I smiled, my mind racing over the possibilities for a moment. "No thanks," I said.

"As you wish."

Loki went into the bathroom, leaving the door open just a crack as the shower started. I couldn't figure him out. Did he really want me—or want to please me in that way? Or was he simply determined to make our cover as credible as possible? What had Lenox told him about me?

I decided to make some calls while I had a moment alone. Lenox picked up on the second ring. "Sydney," he said in that voice of his, each syllable sounding like an important note in a melody that I couldn't get out of my head.

"Good to hear your voice," I said.

"How is it going?"

"Not great." I filled him in on the drive, the tacks in the road, and our hunt for new tires.

"What does Loki say?" Lenox asked.

"Not much."

"He is quiet."

"It's a part of his charm."

"Many women agree with you. I hope you will avail yourself of his services, Sydney. I know how important that is to you." Only Lenox Gold would say things like that to me. No judgment, just a fact: I needed to fuck to stay sharp. It wasn't a love thing, it wasn't a feeling thing. It was a recognition that life was not just about survival. There was pleasure too.

"No, I don't think that is a good idea."

Lenox laughed softly and I closed my eyes enjoying the rich tones of it. "You are always trying to punish yourself."

"Is that it?"

"What other reason would there be?"

I didn't have an answer so quickly got off the line, promising to call him again tomorrow. The shower was still going in the bathroom, steam floating through the narrow opening in the door so I made another call. Mulberry didn't answer his phone. A woman did. "Oh, sorry," I said. "Is Mulberry there?"

"Yes," she said. "May I ask who's calling?"

I felt the hairs on the back of my neck rise and looked over at Blue who lay snoring quietly by the door. I took a deep breath and relaxed, trying to unruffle my hackles. "Who's this?" I asked, aiming to keep my voice light.

"I asked first," she said.

I heard Mulberry's voice in the background and then he was on the line. "Hello."

"It's me," I said.

"Hey, how's it going?"

I filled him in, repeating what I'd told Lenox, hoping in the retelling something would occur to me but I was just as confused. "What do you think?" Mulberry asked.

"I think that probably the tai chi center was a place for Falun Gong practitioners. I hope that they are okay but with the phones not working and the fact that Bai was killed, it seems like we could be walking into a real mess. I just need to get there. To see what is going on."

I heard the shower turn off but figured I had a few more minutes before Loki came out.

"I understand," Mulberry said. His voice was reassuring. I closed my eyes and pictured his hazel eyes. Imagined the feel of his arms around me, holding me close, telling me everything was going to be all right.

"I should go," I said.

"Thanks for calling, for reporting in," he said, his voice turning official.

"Yes, sir."

I glanced up as the door to the bathroom pushed open. Loki stood there, his bottom half wrapped in a small white towel, steam billowing around him. His chest and arms were completely covered in tattoos. "I'll call you later," I said to Mulberry.

"You okay?" Mulberry asked, hearing the shift in my voice.

"Yeah, thanks for your help." I hung up the phone without waiting for an answer.

Loki walked into the room, his eyes on my face as my gaze roamed over his chest. The inked patterns were intricate, intertwined, beautifully lined. "I had no idea," I said, realizing it was a stupid thing to say the moment it was out of my mouth. Pulling my eyes off his body I climbed off the bed and went to my suitcase to grab some clothing before heading into the shower.

The water was tepid but fine, the shower stall small and the towel rough, but I was happy to be clean. I changed in the bathroom, putting on a pair of tight black jeans and a gray linen button down shirt that brought out the hints of silver in my eyes. Loki was dressed when I came out, wearing a long sleeved shirt and dress slacks that hugged his narrow hips. "Would you like to get some dinner?" he asked. "It's late and the restaurant will soon close."

"I want to call Mitchel. I'll meet you down there."

"Certainly, may I order you a drink?"

"Sure, red wine."

He smiled and nodded before leaving the room. His hair was still wet, slicked back from his handsome face, showing off his deep brown eyes, black in the half-light of the room. I waited a beat after the door closed, staring at the knob, thinking about his bare chest, the intricate patterns inked across it, before picking up my phone and calling Mitchel.

"How's it going?" he asked.

"We didn't get far," I said, repeating my story quickly. "How's the kid?"

"Seems fine."

"So he hasn't run off yet?"

"Think he wants that ticket to paradise."

"Right, you talked to Dan about it?"

"He's working on it. He asked me to fill you in on what he found out about Bai."

"Great."

"She was involved with Falun Gong. Used their software to evade the censors. She was working with a small group that was hacking into the government computers trying to find evidence of the organ harvesting of prisoners."

"As we suspected."

"Yes. Does it help?"

"I don't know."

"Do you need me to do anything else for you?"

"Just stick by the kid, did you find out his name by the way?" I asked.

"Shi Guang."

"Right, if he gives you any more info let me know. How's my signal by the way?"

"Coming through strong and clear."

"But only because you fixed it, right?"

"Yes, there is no way that Merl's would have worked after stepping into Sing's place."

"What about his phone?"

"The beacon would have been disabled but he still could have made calls."

"So he wouldn't know that his beacon was off."

"Yeah, like I told you, he'd have no idea. Why?"

"Just double checking," I said, not wanting to share my fantasy of finding Merl alive and well at the tai chi center. "I'll talk to you tomorrow."

We hung up and Blue and I headed downstairs to the restaurant in the hotel. Loki waited at the bar. He was leaning against it, sipping on a beer. He smiled when he saw me. "You look beautiful," he said, slipping his arm around my waist and kissing my cheek, the scent of his shampoo filling my sense for a moment.

"You too," I said.

"Shall we sit down or do you want to have your drink first?"

"Let's eat, I'm hungry." And I really wasn't in the mood to play date. There was security in the lobby, a stout man in an ill-fitting suit, his arms folded behind his back, eyes watchful, obviously there to make the tourists feel safe. From what? I didn't know.

The dinner was as good as the lunch, but I barely tasted it. My mind was on those tacks on the road. I wanted to go back and I didn't want a guide, I just wanted Loki and me and Blue and a Jeep with a bunch of tires. I broached this with Loki when we got back to the room. He shook his head. "That would be impossible."

"Why?"

"There are ways that we must behave, Sydney. China is a dangerous place. There are eyes everywhere."

"Are you being watched?"

"Everyone is being watched."

"But you've been here before."

"Yes, with other clients. This area is popular for river cruises. If there is something going on at the tai chi center then the authorities in this village will be involved. They will be curious and worried about a tourist who insists on going there with such," he paused looking for the right word, "gusto."

"Gusto," I said, nodding my head. "Okay, fine, so what do you propose? And who exactly are these authorities?"

"I suggest we go on a river cruise tomorrow while Ming gets new tires. He will suggest you take a tai chi class in town."

"And I will explain that is not what I'm looking for."

"Yes."

"I can't be the first obnoxious American tourist who wants what she wants."

"No," he smiled and looked over at Blue. "But the dog makes you strange, worth watching. Especially if they know about Merl and his dogs. This is why I do not want you to mention him."

"If you think there is someone in this village who knows what's going on then I want to talk to that person."

Loki shook his head. "That's not how it works."

"How it works?" I said, anger rising up my throat. I stepped closer to Loki, he held his ground, his expression passive, eyes calm. "Do you understand why I'm here?"

"To find your friend."

"And Lenox told you to give me what I wanted."

"Yes, and to keep you safe. What you are suggesting is very dangerous. You don't just walk into the office of the local cadre and tell him of your suspicions, ask him for help."

"Why not?"

"Because if, like you suspect, Falun Gong is involved in some way, the local cadre will not take kindly to a foreigner marching in and asking questions."

"How do we find out then?"

"We play along, we pretend to be having a nice time, we listen, we wait, we watch."

"Watch what?"

"The way that people act toward us, to you insisting on the tai chi center. But you must let them put you off."

"I can't do that. I'm not that kind of woman."

"I see."

Loki walked over to his suitcase and pulled out a small knife. "Do you have any black clothing?"

"Yes." I had a pair of black jogging tights and a long sleeve running top.

"Good, we will wait until everyone is asleep and then visit the cadre at his house, in his bedroom. We shall find your answer."

"Really?" I was surprised by his sudden reversal.

"This is the dangerous route."

"But we get answers."

"They will not help us if we are dead or detained."

"Tell me about this cadre."

Loki laid the knife on his side table and sat on the bed. I took the chair by the desk. "His name is Xi Jing. He has been in power for some time, ten years I think. He does not move up because he says that he loves this area but really he has a drinking problem, which prevents him from rising in the ranks. Easily manipulated by the local gangs and government in Beijing he is the perfect leader for this region."

"Tell me about the gangs. The triads."

"There is a long tradition of organized crime in this country. They work closely with the government. It is hard to discern one from another at times."

"You must work with them. In your line of work."

"We pay a price for our operations. To a local triad in Shanghai and to a larger one based in Hong Kong that has dealings all over the country. There is a local triad here but we work with Xi."

"So couldn't we go to him as your friend?"

"He is not my friend. He is friends with Lenox."

"But surely, any friend of Lenox is a friend of yours, of mine."

"That is something you would have to talk to Lenox about."

I picked up my phone and dialed Lenox's number. "Can you set up a meeting for me with Xi Jing?" I asked him when he picked up.

"I don't think that is a good idea. Unless I'm there."

"Why?"

Lenox laughed, a sensual rumble. "Because you are hot-headed and are not good at playing the game necessary for a successful encounter with a cadre leader."

"Loki suggested we just break into his house and hold him at knife point until we get the answers we are looking for."

"That would be dangerous but possibly more effective."

"Really?"

"Yes."

"You surprise me, Lenox."

"You must wear masks. But I suppose you already knew that."

"You seriously think it's a good idea?"

"I've never known Loki to lead me wrong. If he thinks it's the way to go, he is probably right. But I'd suggest, as I'm sure he would, that you leave the area immediately after. Even with masks you'd not be safe. Obviously, don't take Blue."

"If we're leaving..."

"He will hunt you down. You don't want to be hunted in China. Leave Blue behind."

"I'll think about it."

"Is there no other way?"

"I don't know. Loki originally suggested we stay here for a few days and play a game where we pretend to be on vacation."

"I would listen to Loki."

"Okay, thanks."

I hung up and Loki raised his eyebrows, questioning what I wanted to do. "Let's sleep on it," I suggested.

"Certainly. Are you tired? It is still early for sleep."

"Is there anything to do around here?"

"Karaoke."

I laughed. "No way, I'm not a singer."

"Fair enough. There are other bars where tourists frequent."

"Let's just watch TV," I suggested.

We got into pajamas. I had an oversized T-shirt and a pair of boxers. Loki slept in just a pair of loose fitting pants, his inked chest exposed again. At first I tried not to look but after only a few minutes under the flickering glow of the TV I turned to him. "Okay, what's up with the tattoos?"

"They were done when I was much younger."

118

"Who did them?"

He looked down at his chest. "Many different artists."

"They look like the same person did them."

"I drew them all, but then it was others who put them on my body."

"You're an artist?"

"I like to draw."

"You still do it?"

"Yes," he said.

"I have not seen you sketching or anything."

"I've been working."

"Right," I looked down at his arm, a snake curled around his bicep, its scales looking almost real, shadowed in black and gray, shimmering in the glow of the TV. "Do you like working for Lenox?"

"Yes."

I reached out to touch his arm but stopped myself, putting my hand back under the cover. "You can touch me," he said.

"No, I shouldn't. It would be taking advantage." I looked up at him, smiling. "As you said, you're working."

"What if I wanted you to touch me?"

"I'd say that would be a misplaced emotion."

He raised his eyebrows. "Would you?" Loki leaned forward, the images across his chest shifted as he raised his far arm, reaching out and brushing my hair behind my ear. His fingers barely touched my skin but they raised goosebumps across my flesh.

I turned away. "Don't Loki, trust me. You don't want to know me. Not like that. Not at all."

"As you wish."

I rolled over and closed my eyes, trying to sleep but I couldn't find peace. I was surprised by my measured response to the suggestion to break into a man's house and hold him at knife point until he gave me the information I needed. It wasn't like me not to jump at that. Was it because I was unsure of the consequences? And since when had I cared about those? No, there was something in my gut telling me to just get to that tai chi center. Some part of me that didn't want to rush in the wrong direction. I almost laughed out loud thinking it was Merl's voice in my head telling me to stay calm, take it slow. Merl would never break into a man's house, possibly having to kill his guards, if there was any way to avoid it. And there were a lot of ways to avoid it.

I drifted off to sleep thinking about Merl, his voice in my mind, reminding me of my other strengths. I was not just a weapon to wield, I was also a mind to think.

EK

I woke up with my arm around Loki, head on his chest. He was asleep still, his left arm wrapped around me, the right reaching across his body and resting gently on my hip. I rolled away from him slowly, not wanting to wake him. He moved with me, spooning me, his breath warm at the back of my neck, the position intimate and comforting. I stayed that way, letting his body curl around mine, feeling safe and protected while at the same time knowing it was an illusion.

Blue came around to my side of the bed and sat, looking at me, his head cocked in question. I imagined he was judging me but knew that he was really just asking when I planned on getting up. Blue was thinking about his morning walk, breakfast, perhaps a jog. He wasn't worried about who I spooned. That was in my head alone.

Pushing Loki's arm off my body I dressed quietly, but Loki woke as I opened the door. "Where are you going?" he asked.

"For a run."

"Let me come with you," he said, throwing back the covers.

"I'll be fine, I've got Blue."

He stood, his hair slightly disheveled, adorable on a man usually so put together. "I insist," he said. "It will take me only a moment to dress."

"Fine, I'll meet you downstairs." I walked out the door and hurried toward the steps before he could answer. When I got to the lobby I thought about just running off but decided to wait, after all I'd said that I would. The man behind the check-in desk, wearing a suit a little too large, smiled and asked if he could help. "A bottle of water please."

He nodded and went to the restaurant to grab one for me, leaving the lobby empty. Through the glass doors I could see the dusty street. It was light out but just barely. The curtains had been pulled in our room but the clock had read 7:30 am. I didn't usually get up this early but with all the things on my mind it had been impossible to stay asleep. Loki came down right as the desk clerk returned with my water. I took a big swig as we headed out to the road and handed it to him. He took a drink and we started left.

I didn't usually run with other people. I liked to go at my own pace, which usually involved a slow warm up, sprints, followed by breathless slow jogging, and then more sprints while listening to pumping music in headphones. Loki let me pick the pace and as we left the small village, rice fields lining both sides of the road with those impressive mountains right behind them, I ran a bit faster.

As we came to a bend I picked up my speed even more, letting my legs stretch to their capacity, my arms swinging close to my body, pumping hard. Loki stayed right next to me, Blue on my other side. We ran like that, fast and then slow, for a half hour before turning back and doing the same on the way home. An hour of running always made me feel better. Cleared my mind because when I sprinted there was only room for the pain in my legs, the beat of my heart, and the wind in my hair.

We took quick showers, separately, before going down for breakfast. Ming showed up as we finished our meal. He did not have new tires yet and Loki suggested we take a river cruise. I said I wasn't feeling great. That maybe I'd eaten something that wasn't agreeing with me. "Let me lay down for a little while," I suggested.

"I will wait here," Ming promised, pointing to his Jeep parked in front of the hotel.

Loki took me to the room. "Are you really ill?" he asked.

"No, but I can't stand the thought of going river cruising when Merl is missing. It just seems too, I don't know. I can't fake having a good time. Fake being on a date with you right now."

"I understand. Let me speak to Ming about the tires and find out when we can return to the tai chi center."

He left and I laid down on the bed, staring up at the plain white ceiling above. The round, sandblasted lamp in its center was filled with dead bugs, I could see their dark corpses against the light.

The room's phone rang and I rolled over, grabbing it off the cradle. "Sydney Rye?" A woman's voice said. Her accent was thick, turning my name into Schindy Wy?

"Yes, who is this?"

"I have information about your friend."

"Which friend is that?" I sat up, Blue came to my side, his head cocked, recognizing the tone in my voice.

"The man you are traveling with."

"Really?"

"Yes, meet me at the wifi cafe down the block from your hotel. Come alone."

"Why should I trust you? Loki is a friend of mine."

"He is nobody's friend."

"How do you know?"

"Meet me and I will tell you everything. It is not safe to talk over the phone."

The line went dead. Minutes later the door opened and Loki came in. "Ming said we can go tomorrow morning."

"Do you believe him?"

Loki shrugged. "It could go either way. He may put us off tomorrow. He thinks we are staying for four days. He may plan to put us off for all those days."

"And there is no way to rent our own car?"

"Not without looking strange. Wealthy tourists do not drive themselves around."

"Okay, I'm going to go get another bottle of water."

"I will go for you."

"No, I want to."

"But if Ming sees you he will know you are not really sick."

"You're right, you go."

I waited for Loki to close the door behind him and then grabbed my leather jacket out of my suitcase and threw it on, feeling the weight of the pipe. Blue and I took the steps down, pausing at the bottom, just out of sight of the front desk. I peered around the corner and saw Loki talking to the same man who had been on duty this morning. Looking through the glass front doors I saw Ming sitting in the driver's seat of his Jeep talking on his cell phone.

Moving quickly, but not so fast that I'd seem strange, I walked into the restaurant. It was deserted at this hour, just one waitress setting tables, getting ready for the lunch rush. She looked up when Blue and I walked in. I passed her quickly and stepped out onto the deck, which was in part cantilevered over the canal.

The fence was not high and I stepped over it, alighting onto the grassy bank before the woman followed me out. She let out a little cry when she saw Blue jumping over after me. I smiled at her and shrugged. "Didn't realize there wasn't an exit this way."

She didn't appear to understand English but smiled back at me. I moved around the building, following the canal until there was an opening between the buildings to the street. It was narrow and smelled like trash, rotting fish, and old fry oil. It was shadowed and cool. Blue touched his nose to my hip as we reached the end, and I took a final check up and down the block. Ming was still in his Jeep, Loki was nowhere to be seen, and the doors to the hotel remained closed.

The street was busy with tourists, shopping in the stores, driving by in rickshaws, generally have a grand old time on their great Chinese adventure. I slipped out of the narrow alley and hurried down the block until I came to a wifi cafe. The doors were glass but plastered with posters so that I couldn't see inside. I glanced back toward the hotel one more time before pushing open the door.

The cafe consisted of two rows of computers with big monitors, aged and stained yellow. The keyboards had large keys and wires snaked out of them into the computers under the desks. The air was filled with a hum from all the fans keeping the old machines cool.

Three computers were occupied. A tourist couple, young and deeply tanned with almost white blond hair and large dirty backpacks, spoke to each other in a Nordic language as they stared at the screen. A young Chinese woman wearing shorts and a tank top copied a hand-written letter into her email. And a young man, his glasses thick and hair in need of a cut, clicked on his mouse without any expression.

Behind a high counter an older woman sat on a stool. She waved. "No dogs!" she yelled at me. I approached the desk, pulling out my wallet. She frowned, her lips growing thinner with disapproval until I pulled out a big bill.

"You need internet?" she asked. "Or just wifi password?"

"I actually wanted a cup of coffee."

She frowned. "No internet?"

"Just the coffee."

She turned around and poured steaming black coffee into a Styrofoam cup and handed it to me. I paid her with the bill and she did not give me any change. I smiled and then sat down at the one table without a computer on it wondering what I was doing here.

It had been a woman on the phone but I didn't think it was the one behind the counter. The Chinese girl copying the note didn't even glance at me though. I drank my coffee. The young Nordic-looking couple left, hauling their giant packs onto their thin backs. I envied them, they were on an adventure together, an exploration. I'd never done that. Travelled just for the experience. When Dan and I spent time in India it was to run away. To be somewhere no one knew us and we could just enjoy each other's company without worrying about our pasts. Not that it lasted, but that kind of thing never did. Your past came for you, because it was in you.

The young Chinese woman stood up and, folding the piece of paper she'd been typing from, moved toward the point of sale. She paid the woman behind the counter and as she passed me dropped the paper, letting it slip between her fingers. Blue laid down on it, covering the sheet with his body before anyone else noticed. I finished my coffee and reached down, giving Blue a pet on the head before reaching under him and picking up the note. I put it in my pocket as I stood.

Blue and I left the cafe and looking down the block, saw that Ming's Jeep was gone. I started back toward the hotel. I saw a drugstore and figured out a good cover for my absence. I walked in thinking I'd buy some tampons, men always shied away from that kind of talk, but discovered they didn't sell them in China. Only pads. Wow, I thought, as I paid for the sanitary napkins. The poor women of this nation.

EK

When I got to the lobby the man behind the desk sighed with relief. "You are here, miss."

"Yes," I said.

"Your friend, he was looking for you. Very worried."

"No, I'm fine, just needed to run to the store."

When the man saw the plastic bag in my hand he blushed, recognizing the packaging through the thin white plastic. I went up to our room and found Loki on the phone. "She's just walked in," he said. "Yes, I'll tell her." He hung up. "You scared me," he said.

"I needed to go to the store." I held up the bag.

"Why didn't you tell me?"

"It's personal, Loki." I moved toward the bathroom. "Was that Lenox you were on the phone with?"

"Yes."

"What did he want you to tell me?"

"To call him."

"Okay, I'm going to use the bathroom first."

I locked the door behind me and turned on the tap before unfolding the letter. It was written in pencil, the lettering precise and strained. Like the person wasn't comfortable with English.

"The man you are with is a dangerous man. He is tied to the local gangs. He will rob you and leave you for dead. You must be very careful. It is best if you leave this place."

I turned off the tap and sat on the closed lid of the toilet for a moment, thinking. I didn't believe it, obviously. Why would this girl tell me to leave? Who did she think Sydney Rye was? A tourist on vacation with Loki, one of his regular customers who would be scared off by something like this?

I stood up and unlocked the bathroom door. "I've got a clue but I have no idea what it means," I said, handing the note to Loki. He took the paper from me and read the few lines.

"Where did you get this?"

"I lied earlier, I didn't just go out to the store. I got a call in the room from a woman telling me to come to the cafe because the person had information about the man I was traveling with, you."

"And you went without speaking to me?"

"I wanted to see what she had to say."

"Do you believe this note?"

"I believe that you are in some way tied to organized crime. You've admitted as much yourself, and the tattoos covering your body seem to hint at that. I think you're on my side, though." I laughed. "I doubt your plan is to drug and rob me."

"Who gave you the note?"

"A girl, she was in her early twenties, pretty, thin, wearing shorts and a tank top. Long dark hair with bangs."

"I think I know who this is."

"Really? Who?"

"The cadre's daughter."

"Really, that's interesting. Why would she give me this note?"

"She is obviously trying to get you to leave the area."

"A message from her father?"

"In a way, perhaps yes."

"It could also be a test. Any normal tourist would leave, right? But someone here for another reason would stay."

I sat down on the bed and looked at the note in Loki's hands. "We've got to get out to that tai chi center. Obviously, something is going on. Where did Ming go?" I asked. "His Jeep was gone."

"He was driving around looking for you."

"Did you tell him I was back?"

"Yes, Sydney, we must wait until tomorrow to insist on going to the tai chi center. Then you may put on a show of anger if Ming says he cannot drive us. You can demand to rent a car. Make a scene."

I smiled. "I like making scenes."

CHAPTER TWELVE
MAKING SCENES

I woke up in Loki's arms again, our legs intertwined. That's what happens when people sleep in a queen bed together. Loki's eyes were open when I glanced up at his face. Dawn was breaking, gray light creeping through the curtains, making the furniture in the room look translucent. Loki's mouth was turned down in a small frown, his fingers tight on my shoulder, not so hard that they hurt, just an extension of the tension on his face.

"What's wrong?"

He looked over at me. "You're awake."

"Just, you look upset."

"Thinking," he said, returning his gaze to the room. "I'm wondering why someone would send that note to you."

We'd talked about it a lot the night before. Broken down the possibilities: 1. They thought I was like the other women who traveled with Loki and they were trying to mess with his business. 2. They knew I was not like the other women who traveled with Loki and were trying to scare me off or test me. After all, a regular tourist would probably leave after a note like that. She would not continue to insist on going to the tai chi center. She would pack her bags, climb back on her private jet, and boogie on out of there, possibly out of China all together.

By staying, by forcing my way to the tai chi center, I was making it obvious that I was not what I pretended to be. It was all pretend though, wasn't it?

The message in that note wasn't really what they were trying to say. The problem getting to the tai chi center wasn't just a matter of not enough tires. I was ready to play the game, to keep pretending, but Loki and I had agreed that we needed to be ready for a fight.

"I wonder if they will attack before we get to the tai chi center or wait until we arrive," I said.

"Who do you think 'they' are?" Loki asked, his fingers tightening on my shoulder. I sat up, and he let his hand drop.

"I'm looking forward to finding out."

"What makes you think we will make it through? Why would we not meet the same fate as your friend Merl?"

"Are you afraid?" I asked, looking down at him.

He didn't look scared. His tattoos made him look tough. Incredibly tough, like a warrior clad in armor. "Yes," he answered. "You'd be a fool not to be afraid."

"You don't look scared."

He smiled, almost shyly, and I got a glimpse of the child he'd once been. Not for long but at one point in this man's history he'd been a boy, a playful one.

"Practice," he said. "You don't look scared either."

"I'm not afraid of a fight."

"What about your own death?"

"No." I didn't fear my death. I was afraid of the death around me. Of the curse I'd become. Somehow Blue and I always survived. I couldn't say the same for those who joined me in battle. "I'm more worried about you," I said.

He raised his brows. "Really?"

"I'm pretty indestructible."

"Whereas I am a mortal?"

"Something like that."

"What do you mean?"

"I'm a survivor," I said.

He laughed. "And you think I'm not?"

"I have a way of ending other people's streaks of luck."

He sat up and our faces were close. "Sydney, I am the lone survivor of a shipwreck. I have a golden star of my own."

"Good, I think we're going to need it. I wish we had some guns."

"Yes, I agree. That is something I was thinking."

I threw off the covers and climbed out of bed, stretching toward the ceiling, bending one way and then the other. Blue wagged his tail and yowled a good morning then bowed down, joining me in a morning stretch. "Have you ever done any tai chi?" I asked.

Loki nodded.

"You don't practice now?"

"I do."

"I haven't seen you."

"You only believe what you see?"

I laughed. "Sorry, you're right. I just thought real practitioners did it every day."

"You don't."

"I'm not devoted. Merl has been trying to get me into it for years. And I go through phases. But meditation is hard for me."

"That probably means that you need it."

"Sounds like something Merl would say."

"I look forward to meeting him."

I bit my lip. "I hope that happens."

"We will find him."

"I like your confidence."

EK

An hour later, after breakfast and an apology from Ming about not having the tires yet, I was making a scene in the hotel lobby. Wearing big sunglasses, the gold bracelet on my wrist glinting in the sun streaming through the glass lobby doors, I was slowly raising my voice. "I came here for the tai chi," I said, staring at Ming. He kept his gaze cast to the ground. "And if you're telling me that you cannot provide a ride then I will have to get my own car." I turned to the man at the front desk whose cheeks had turned bright red watching me berate the two men working for me.

"Can you hire me a car?" I asked him, my voice hard, loud.

He didn't make eye contact. "That is a very rough road—"

I cut him off. "This is a yes or no answer."

A woman came out from the back wearing a blue suit. Her eyebrows raised and her nails flashed red when she placed her hands on the counter between us. "May I help?" she asked.

"Well, I hope so because no one else seems to be able to. I came here because I heard about the tai chi center. Apparently their phone does not work." I made a kind of disgusted snorting noise I'd heard a lot of rich pissed off ladies make when they were repulsed by the perceived inadequacies of others. "So, fine. I'm willing to drive there unannounced, but—" I pointed around the room, first at the man behind the desk, then Ming, and finally landing on Loki. "None of these men can help me." I dropped my hand. "Can you?"

"The road is—"

I cut her off. "If one more person tells me about the condition of the road I'm going to scream. Do you hear me, I will scream."

"Yes, madam, I understand."

"So, can you get me a Jeep? Or perhaps find Ming here some tires. Are there no tires in this town, is that really possible?"

"I will see what I can do. Please enjoy a cup of tea in the restaurant while I make some calls." She picked up the phone to show me how serious she was about my request.

"I'll be back in fifteen minutes," I said before turning on my heel and marching into the restaurant, my chin up, eyes slits of anger. Blue walked by my side, his tail low and ears flat to his head.

Loki followed, but kept his distance. I sat down and moments later a waitress arrived with two cups, green leaves on the bottom, and a pot of boiling water. She poured the first cups and then left the pot between us.

"I'm serious," I said to Loki as he sat down next to me. I kept my voice high so that everyone could hear me. "I won't have the time and money I spent getting to this place wasted."

"Of course," he agreed.

We sat in silence, as I stared out the open balcony doors to the rice fields beyond the canal. The women were out there, moving through a different part of the field today. The water reached their calves, the bundle of their skirts around their thighs reminded me of old-fashioned pantaloons.

I kept a scowl on my face. Faking anger always brought that simmering beast to the surface. I was angry that I couldn't get to the tai chi center. I hated yelling at Ming and the hotel staff. I'd worked enough service jobs to know how it felt when a customer acted the way I just had. Lots of people thought they were better than those who served them. Many didn't even think of them fully as people. They would get mad at staff when things went wrong the same way they got mad at their computers when they didn't work. Even when the angry people were at fault, their wrath was directed outwards.

But I also knew from my years of working in coffee shops that it was the loudest, most awful customers who got what they wanted first. Being the quiet, nice customer was good for your karma but not for getting things done. I sipped at the tea. It was hot and perfumed. I kept that scowl on my face, pretending to be angry at the world around me instead of at my own deep failings.

The woman with the red nails came in. "I've worked with Ming to get some extra tires."

I nodded. "Good." Not bothering with a thank you. You wouldn't thank your computer for working the way it was supposed to, would you?

EK

The mood in the Jeep was uncomfortable. I looked out the window, my face relaxed, but still ready to get angry. Ming looked nervous, his eyes kept jumping to the mirror, checking on me.

We traveled the same route we had before, though it was earlier in the day so the light was different, coming from above rather than the west. The mountain's shadows were small, their green surfaces brilliant in the bright midday sun.

Blue laid next to me, his head on my lap. My thigh touched Loki's with every bump. He did not put his arm around me.

Ming slowed down as we neared the rocky section we'd blown our first tire on during our earlier journey. Taking it slowly we made it over the rocks without incident. We continued in silence until Loki asked Ming to turn the radio on. Then we traveled with the familiar chords of pop songs, many of them American with a Chinese singer replacing the likes of Britney Spears and Madonna.

The beats almost matched the bouncing of the Jeep. We were approaching the spot where we'd hit the tacks. I felt Loki tense next to me though his expression stayed mild. Glancing at Ming I saw a line of sweat along his forehead despite the air-conditioning spewing out into the car. I leaned forward, "Remember there are tacks on the road up here," I said. "Be sure to avoid them."

He nodded and drove onto the grass, around where the tacks gleamed in the high sun. I was watching Ming closely, he looked more nervous by the moment. I petted Blue's head. His body bounced with the bumps but he didn't seem to sense any danger. Loki on the other hand was like a hard statue next to me wearing a passive mask. There was something coming. Something soon.

I was wearing my leather jacket and pressed my arm against my side, feeling the heavy pipe there. I didn't think we'd be killed. Just be killed, I mean. Whoever was doing whatever they were doing would want to know who we were, why we wanted to see this tai chi center so badly. We'd shown them that we were not just tourists. That I was not just another rich bitch. But killing me without gaining some knowledge of my purpose would seem stupid.

The left front tire exploded and we veered off the road, smashing into a rock on the side. Blue fell off the seat into the foot well. Loki and I were both wearing seat belts but lurched forward, the straps biting into our chests. I gripped the end of the pipe with my right hand and reached with my other to unlatch my seat belt, staying low, bent over, as if I'd been hurt.

Ming, who'd not been wearing his seat belt, had smashed his face on the steering wheel. He reached up, looking dazed and touched the trickle of blood running from his hairline. Loki leaned over me, pushing me back quickly, so that I didn't know exactly what was happening until he punched Ming hard in the face, knocking him out. Reaching into Ming's jacket Loki came back with a revolver in his hand. He looked out the front window while I looked out the back. There did not seem to be anyone coming toward us.

"They probably have sharpshooters in the rocks there," Loki said, pointing to a pile of boulders that looked like they'd broken loose from the mountain above.

"So, we wait in the car?"

"Yes, I think they will come for us."

"Unless that was just an accident," I said, turning in my seat to look back at the road. I didn't see any tacks but dust was still settling after the crude movements of the vehicle. Blue climbed back onto the seat and looked around. "You okay, boy?"

He leaned into my touch. I felt along his legs and body, not finding any obvious injury. He growled, his nose sniffing at the air. "Gas," Loki said.

I smelled it then. "Yes," I said, looking forward at the crushed bonnet. "Crap."

"I guess we're going out."

"Yes," I agreed.

Loki put the revolver into his pants. "Look dazed," he suggested. "Stay on this side of the Jeep." He was referring to his side, which faced open fields rather than rocks and mountains perfect for hiding in.

He got out first, offering me his hand. I climbed out and Blue leapt to the ground. "We've got to get Ming out," I said. Loki nodded and opened the passenger side, leaning across the seat and grabbing the unconscious man. "I don't think he wanted to betray us," I said.

"Hardly betrayal," Loki said, his voice tight with the effort of hauling the dead weight across the seats. "He never promised us safety. In fact, he practically begged us not to go. If anything—" with one more pull Ming fell out of the car, his feet hitting the dusty road, "we betrayed him."

"How do you figure that?" I asked, watching the rocks beyond the Jeep. There was no movement.

"I just punched him in the face and took his gun."

I nodded. "Good point. But don't you think he was setting us up?"

"That's why I did it, it was only an assumption. We don't know what his plan was. Maybe he wanted to protect us and that's why he brought the gun."

"Is that what you think?"

"I think he has a family and protecting us would be putting them at great risk."

Loki dragged Ming away from the gas-scented Jeep and I followed, out into the open. We were targets now. If they wanted to kill us they could. And still no shots.

Once we were a safe distance from the Jeep Loki laid Ming down. Then I heard the *thwap* of a silenced rifle. The bullet hit the Jeep, rocking it slightly. "Get down," Loki said.

"No, run," I said, grabbing his arm and sprinting into the open field. "They are trying to blow the Jeep."

The explosion came milliseconds after another *thwap*. It knocked us off our feet, flying forward into the rice field. We splashed into the shallow, muddy water. It got into our eyes and mouths, and I came up sputtering. Loki was looking back at the burning Jeep.

Behind it three men were coming out from behind the rocks. "Here we go," I said.

"Yes," Loki agreed, standing up with his hands in the air.

The men yelled, motioning with their weapons for me to rise as well. Blue was by my side, his teeth bared, hackles raised. Brown water splattered his coat, making him look mangy, crazy. One of the men pointed his gun at Blue and I stepped in front of my dog.

The man yelled at me. "He is telling you to move," Loki said.

"Tell him if he wants to kill my dog, he's gonna have to kill me first."

Loki translated and the guy glanced over at the man in the middle.

The one aiming at me was young, the one he looked to was older, maybe in his forties, and apparently in charge. They all wore worn cotton pants and shirts, their black hair shimmering in the bright sun. "Do you speak English?" I asked the older man. He looked at Loki. "Guess not," I said. "Tell him we are here to negotiate the release of our friends."

"I don't think that's a good idea."

"Just do it."

Loki translated and I saw the men's expressions change, they were suddenly unsure. Was it because they were considering our offer or because they had no idea what we were talking about?

The older man spoke, his weapon still facing us. They'd reached Ming at this point and one of the two younger guys bent down and checked for a pulse. I assume that he found one because Ming began to moan slightly. "They want to know who our friends are."

I looked at Loki, Blue still behind me. "What? Tell them our friends were at the tai chi center. Mo-Ping."

Loki translated. The man shook his head. "What? Are they dead?" I asked.

Loki spoke. The man responded. "He wants us to go with them," Loki said.

"Where?"

"Back to the village. They want us to leave."

"Not without Merl, not without Mo-Ping."

Loki translated.

The man raised his gun aggressively and yelled something at Loki. "He says this is not a negotiation."

"Tell him it should be. I'd happily make them all rich men. For their help. If they are just hired guns then let them become mine."

Loki translated. The younger men looked at their boss. I took off my gold bracelet and threw it at the one closest to me. It landed in the dirt at his feet. "It's worth $5000. Tell him."

The man closest to the bracelet spit at it. "I don't think that is going to work," Loki said.

"Why not?"

"No amount of money can protect their families."

"Okay, then we're going to have to neutralize them."

Loki looked over at me. His hands were in the air, as were mine. "How do you propose we do that?"

"They want us to go with them, let's pretend like we are. Then take away their weapons, you know," I smiled. "Get the upper hand."

"You're a dangerous woman, Sydney Rye."

"And you're a survivor, Loki."

He spoke to the men, letting them know we were surrendering. I told Blue to stay behind me as we slowly walked toward the armed men. As I approached, the one closest to me motioned for me to walk in front of him, but I kept going toward him. He motioned again with his rifle, swinging it out to the side, directing me to walk around him.

When he pointed it away from me I leapt for it, grabbing the long barrel, forcing it into the air. The man was surprised, his eyes wide, mouth yelling. I could hear other yelling and then a man screaming. I had both hands on the barrel and the man I was facing had both hands on the stock. I kicked out, taking out his left knee so that he fell, but kept his hands locked on the weapon.

He pulled the trigger and a shot rocketed out, flying into the clear blue sky. I kicked him again, this time in the stomach. He bent forward, but kept his hands on the gun. I jammed it down hard at him, forcing it into his chest. He fell back and I ripped the rifle from his grasp, turning it on him, slipping my finger against the trigger and backing up so I was out of his range.

I glanced around. Blue was shaking the other young man's arm. His rifle was several feet away from him, knocked out of his hand when Blue went for him. Loki and the older man were grappling on the ground. I ran over to where Blue was and picked up the other rifle, then told Blue to release. He hurried to my side.

I pointed the rifles at the two younger men before turning my attention to Loki and the leader struggling on the ground. Blue went in, helping Loki by grabbing the older man by the shoulder, digging his teeth in deep. The man screamed. The rifle was between them, or at least I didn't see it on the ground. I had one in each hand, facing the two unarmed men.

The man Blue had taken down was bleeding pretty badly from his arm. He held it to his chest and lay on his back, not looking like he was planning on doing anything stupid. The other guy, the one I'd disarmed, was sitting up staring at me, at the barrel of his gun, the black hole aimed at his face.

Loki and Blue managed to subdue the older man. Loki sat up, swinging his fist and connecting hard with the guy's face. His head whipped toward me and I saw blood and a tooth fly from his mouth. Loki jumped back, the rifle in his hand, a bruise forming on his left eye.

I called Blue off as Loki pointed the gun at the man on the ground. "You okay?" I asked.

"Yeah," he said, stepping away from the man, who was holding his face with both hands now. "I think I broke his jaw."

"Ask them where their vehicle is."

Ours was still burning on the side of the road, plumes of black smoke floating toward the rocks the men had emerged from. Loki spoke but none of the men answered. "If his jaw is broken he's not going to be able to answer. Ask this one over here," I said, pointing my chin at the guy Blue took down. Loki, keeping his rifle trained on the man at his feet, yelled to the one with the ripped up arm. He didn't answer.

"It can't be far," I said. I looked around at the deserted road, the mountains, the rice paddy with depressions in it where Loki and I had landed.

"I don't know," Loki said. "Can we just leave them here?"

"You think they'll call friends?"

"Wouldn't you?"

"Sure, so I guess we need a straight answer out of one of them. Come here and take this gun," I said. Loki came over and took one of the rifles from me. "Get those two together," I said, referring to the leader and the guy still sitting up, the one who wasn't that hurt, the one who looked like he had some fight left in him.

Loki spoke to the uninjured man, motioning for him to join his leader. The guy didn't move and Loki fired a warning shot, it kicked up the dirt near the man's feet. He threw his hands up, covering his face from the flying bits of rock. Then slowly he stood and moved over to his leader. At Loki's direction he lay down on his stomach next to the other man.

I approached the one Blue had hurt, with Blue by my side. The man looked scared. "Ask him where the car is." I said.

Loki asked again. The man didn't answer.

"Tell him I'll have Blue rip off his fingers."

Loki translated, the man's face drained of what little blood had been left in it. The uninjured man on the ground yelled something, Loki kicked him and he shut up with a groan.

Which reminded me of Ming. I looked over at him. He appeared to still be unconscious but maybe he was faking it. That's probably what I would do in this situation. Looking back at the frightened man in front of me I commanded Blue to growl and approach slowly. The man scooted back, holding his injured arm, still pumping blood through his torn shirt. "Where is your vehicle?" I asked again, moving forward with Blue, as Loki translated.

He went to stand and I fired a warning shot to his left. The man looked on the verge of tears. Something more frightening than a crazed woman and her vicious dog was keeping him silent. He began to cry and I recognized that if he told me where the car was and the other two heard him they'd report it back to whoever was threatening his family. "Okay, Blue," I said. He licked his chops and sat down next to me.

"Ming," I yelled. "You awake?"

He didn't answer. "Watch him," I told Blue, referring to the injured man, then walked over to where Ming was still lying splayed out on the side of the road, close to the burning car. The wind was blowing in the other direction but I could still feel the heat of the fire. Ming had small cuts all over his exposed skin from the explosion. "Ming," I said, tapping him with my foot. Nothing.

"What are you doing?" Loki called, not taking his eyes off his two prisoners.

"Do you think he'd know where the vehicle is? I mean, if we can't find it we're gonna have to walk."

"Walk?" Loki said.

"Yeah, take these three with us and walk."

"Take them with us?"

"It's either that or kill them. We don't have anything to tie them up with."

"I see your point," Loki said.

"Unless Ming here wakes up and tells us where the vehicle is."

"Is he breathing?" Loki asked.

"Yes," I answered, watching the slow and steady rise and fall of Ming's chest. "How hard did you hit him?"

"You can't tell with that kind of thing," Loki said.

I knew what he meant. Some people would be out for minutes. Others hours. It was impossible to say. "We can't leave him here. He might wake up and report what happened."

"Your call," Loki said.

"I don't want to kill them."

"Me either."

"Leave Ming here?"

"Unless you want to make one of these guys carry him."

"Good idea. Get that guy to do it," I said. "It will keep him busy."

Loki spoke to the guy on his stomach. He rose up and glared at Loki as he walked over to Ming. I gave him plenty of room. He hauled Ming onto his shoulder like it wasn't the first time he'd carried an unconscious man.

Loki got the other two moving. I picked up my gold bracelet, slipping it into my pocket, and we started down the road toward the tai chi center.

The two injured men moved about as slow as the one carrying Ming. "How far is it?" I asked Loki.

"I don't know," he said.

"What do you mean you don't know?"

"The map was in the Jeep."

"Are you serious?"

"I think we will come to a small village and then it should be up the hill from there."

"We are going to come to a village first?"

"Yes."

"And how are we are going to explain this?" I asked, pointing at the row of prisoners in front of us.

"This is your plan," Loki said.

"Right, but you didn't mention we'd have to walk through a town."

"What do you want to do about it?"

"I don't know. I wish we'd just found these guys' car." The man carrying Ming stumbled but recovered. "Ask them again what is going on at the tai chi center."

Loki spoke to the men but none of them answered.

"Shit," I said. Blue tapped his nose against my hip and I heard the crunch of tires on the road behind us. Turning around I saw a car in the distance coming toward us, a plume of dust trailing behind it. "You ever carjacked anyone before?" I asked.

CHAPTER THIRTEEN
HIJACKED

Loki looked back at the car. "No," he answered.

The car was not made for this type of road. It was low to the ground, its shocks obviously shot by the way it bounced on the tires. "Doesn't look like an official vehicle," I said.

"No," Loki agreed. "But if I was driving that car I wouldn't get anywhere near us. Not with these weapons and the four men paraded in front of us, most of them bloodied."

"Yes, let's stop. Sit them on the side of the road. Try to look a little more harmless."

"How about you? Have you ever carjacked anyone?" Loki asked me.

"Only in video games," I answered with a smile. "Besides, I'm not going to steal that car. I'm going to buy it," I said, taking off the gold necklace around my neck. Loki yelled to the men to stop. He got them on the side of the road next to a boulder so that he could stand behind it with the gun without being obvious to the passing car. I left my rifle with Loki and had Blue stay with him to help guard the men. Ming was still passed out. He lay on his side next to the three attackers who sat cross-legged.

As the car approached I waved them down. I could make out an older couple through the dusty windshield. They looked suspicious of me.

When the man stopped he didn't put the car in park. Rolling down his window just a little, he spoke to me in Mandarin. I showed him the gold, and pointed to the car.

His wife spoke to him. But he shook his head. I smiled and held the gold chain out. "Eighteen karat," I said.

The woman reached for it but I didn't let her grab it, thinking they'd take off with the car and the gold. That's when one of the young guys, the uninjured one who'd been carrying Ming, decided to make a run for it. He went tearing down the road, back the way we'd come, running past the car. Blue didn't let him get far, he leapt onto his back, taking the man to the ground with a growl. The man screamed. The couple watched and when they turned back to look at me, I smiled. The man began to drive away as fast as the car would go, the dust it kicked up making me cough.

I stepped back and covered my eyes from the grit filling the air. "Well, that didn't work quite the way you planned," Loki said.

"No," I agreed, picking up my rifle from where it lay against the rock. Blue was still growling, the man was still screaming. I turned toward the escaping car, bringing the rifle up to my shoulder. Looking through the magnifier I aimed for the left back tire. My first shot hit the bumper but the second found its mark. The car skidded sideways and came to a stop. The couple did not get out. "Stay here," I told Loki.

"What about Blue?" he asked.

"He'll hold that guy down until I get back."

I jogged down the road, my rifle pointing toward the sky. The sun had dropped to the west, it was probably about 2 pm at this point. My stomach growled. I said a little prayer that they had a spare tire. I slowed to a walk as I approached the vehicle. The couple were turned in their seats, looking at me. I kept my rifle pointing skyward. "I'm not going to hurt you," I yelled, knowing full well they couldn't understand my words but hoping they'd get my tone.

I approached the woman's side. She started to cry, holding onto her husband's arm. He stared at me defiantly. I tried to open her door but it was locked. I made a motion to unlock the door. The husband shook his head. The man's hair was white with age and it swung back and forth with the force of his rejection of my request. I didn't want to point my gun at them but I was doing it. Yelling at them to get out of the car. The husband's face flashed with fear, his wife's fingers dug deeper into his arm. He opened his door and climbed out, hands in the air. I came around the car, holding out the necklace, pointing my gun in the air again. He didn't take it at first. But then his wife was out of the car too. I threw it to her and she caught it, flinching at the contact.

I motioned for them to walk in front of me. We returned to where Loki waited with the passed out Ming, the two injured men, and the one under Blue's jaws. "Ask them what they know about the tai chi center."

"I wouldn't ask them around these men."

"Right, good idea," I said. "Take them back to the car. See if they have a spare tire and ask them for information."

Loki nodded. "But first, let's deal with this situation," I said, motioning at Blue and the man under him. I called Blue off and the man stayed down.

Loki spoke to him and he sat up slowly, touching the back of his neck. The man's hand came back bloody. Red stained the fur around Blue's jaw making him look like some kind of a dangerous beast. Loki got the guy back over to his friends and the passed out Ming. The woman was grabbing her husband's arm again, clutching the necklace between her knobby fingers.

Loki began to walk back toward the car with the elderly couple. I watched the men in front of me. Ming moaned and rolled over, his eyes fluttering against the sun. "Ming, you alive?" I called to him.

His eyes opened and he rolled into a sitting position, holding his jaw. "What happened?" he asked, blinking. Seeing the men in front him, the gun in my hand, the blood on Blue's jaws, his face paled.

"We had an accident," I said. "And then these three guys tried to kidnap us. So we kidnapped them. And now we're forcibly purchasing this couple's car," I used my chin to point down the road.

Ming looked over at them then back at me. "What about my Jeep?"

"Oh, yeah, sorry to tell you but these guys blew it up."

Ming looked at the three men. He did not seem surprised to see them. He said something in Mandarin that I could not understand but it sounded like a curse. "You guys were working together, huh?" I asked.

"They blew up my Jeep. Why would I agree to that? I was just trying to do my job. You're the one who caused this," he said.

"Why? Why can't we go to the tai chi center? Tell me what is happening there and this will all be a lot easier."

"I can't," Ming said, frowning deeply, still rubbing at his jaw.

"Can't or won't?" Ming didn't answer. "Do you know what has happened there?" I demanded. He didn't respond. I looked down the road. It turned out the couple had a spare tire and Loki was watching the man change it. The woman stood a few feet from him. She was talking. Maybe Loki was having better luck. "Ming, I'm going to tell them you told me what is going on."

Ming looked up at me. A bruise was beginning to form on his jaw where Loki punched him. The blood from the wound he sustained in the accident had dried on his face, a red river that ran along his nose and off his chin, staining his shirt. "You want to get me killed?"

"I want to save my friend."

He shook his head. "You cannot save anyone. There is no way."

"Why not?"

"You should have gone home. Now you will never be able to leave."

"How do you figure that?"

"You think you will get away with this? Capturing three policemen?"

"These are policemen?" I asked.

"Yes," he spat.

"Well, they didn't show me any identification," I said.

"You are a fool. This is China. They don't have to show you anything. You can be detained for years without charges. You will be locked up and more than likely executed."

"Do you think that is what happened to my friend?"

Ming stopped talking again. I heard the car start up the road and saw that Loki and the elderly couple were turning around and heading back our way. They pulled up and they all got out, leaving the car running. Loki smiled at me. "I've found something you're going to like," he said, heading toward the trunk. He opened it and pulled out a big pile of rope.

"Excellent," I said. "You any good at tying people up?"

Loki smiled and raised his eyebrows. "Yes," he said, "I'm excellent at it."

"Okay, good," I said, not making eye contact.

"Do you want to leave them behind?" he asked. "Or tie them up and take them with us? We need to take the couple with us," Loki said, his eyes darting to the older couple.

"Okay," I didn't want to ask why in front of Ming but knew that Loki would have his reasons. "I don't think we can fit everyone in the car do you?"

"No, we could put some in the trunk though."

"If we tie them up, gag them, and leave them off the side of the road, far enough not to be easily spotted, what's the chance of them getting found?"

"Pretty slim, I'd say."

"Let's do that. It gives us a little security too."

"What do you mean?"

"Ming says they're cops. If we get into trouble we can use their location as a bargaining chip."

"Police?" Loki said, looking at the men. "What kind?" he asked Ming.

"CCP."

"What does that mean?" I asked.

"Nothing good," Loki answered, his brow furrowing.

"All right, let's get a move on before any other cars come this way."

We moved the men further into the rocks and Loki hog-tied them, their bellies against the dirt, their ankles and wrists bound. "We should not leave them like this for more than a few hours," Loki said.

"Sure," I said. "Hopefully we won't have to."

"What about Ming?" Loki asked.

He stood next to the men, a little unsteady on his feet. "What do you think, Ming? Want to stay with these guys or come with us?"

"Can't you just let me go?" he asked.

"I don't trust you not to release these men and come after us."

"Fine, tie me up then. I'll take my chances here rather than go with you. You're going to die."

"You say that like it's a guarantee. Like you know something."

"If these men came for you, and you didn't go with them, you're dead. You should have left when you had the chance."

"Funny, that's not the first time I've heard something along those lines," I said. "And yet, here I am, still alive."

Ming frowned and laid down. Loki ripped the back of his shirt and shoved it into his mouth before hog tying him like the other men. He gagged them all using pieces of their shirts. The elderly couple watched all this, not saying anything, but not looking particularly scared either.

After double-checking his handiwork Loki led the way back to the car. The older man got behind the wheel, his wife sat next to him, and Loki, Blue, and I climbed into the back. We started down the road again. Loki introduced the couple as Zang Wei and Li Shu. They seemed comfortable with us now. "So, what's going on?" I asked Loki.

"They were headed to the tai chi center."

"Really?"

"Yes, their son is being held there, along with a lot of other political prisoners. The center has been turned into a reeducation center."

"That sounds bad."

"Yes, their son was a teacher there."

"Falun Gong?" I asked.

The woman turned around in her seat, recognizing the words and said something to Loki. "She wants me to tell you that she and her husband are not practitioners. They are not religious. They are communist. But their son is a peaceful man and it is wrong that he is being held."

"He is being held because he is a Falun Gong practitioner?"

"Yes, there are many prisoners at the center. Falun Gong, which as you know is a form of Qigong and is illegal in China. Practitioners are often held without charges brought against them."

"I don't understand," I said. "Qigong is hardly radical. I've seen people practicing in the parks, why isn't Falun Gong allowed when so many others are?"

"You are right that Falun Gong is a peaceful religion. But it is also a powerful religion. And the communist party does not want any powerful, independent forces in their midst. Back in the 90s as it gained popularity, the Communist Party took an interest in the group, eventually arresting some of its leaders. When over a thousand people protested peacefully, the party announced they would release the prisoners. But instead they started a systematic persecution of the religion. Since then tens of thousands of Falun Gong practitioners have been detained. Zang Wei and Li Shu are going to the center because they heard that three lawyers are coming today to try to arrange the release of some of the prisoners. They are going to offer their support. Many of the families of the victims are coming today to do the same."

"So the guards will have their hands full?"

"Yes, but I doubt we will be able to find out if your friend is there."

"What about Mo-Ping?"

The woman turned in her seat again and spoke. "She knows Mo-Ping. She says that she is there."

"All right," I said, nodding my head. "That's one part of the mystery solved." I sat back in my seat. "Doesn't make me feel any better."

"I agree."

"I'm sure that Merl would have come here to try to help her."

"If he was not detained in Shanghai," Loki said.

"I wish there was a way to find out."

"I already checked all my sources and there was no record of a Westerner matching Merl's description having been detained by the police. However, there are many shadows in the legal system and my torch is only so large."

"I know," I said. "Thanks."

We came around a bend and in the far distance I could see a small village at the base of a larger mountain range. It was as if the ground swelled up violently behind the village, producing more monolith-like mountains. The woman began pointing and speaking. "She says that is the village. And that the center is another few miles into the hills. We will be there in about twenty minutes." The road to the village was lined with rice fields, their watery surface glimmering in the sunlight.

"Okay, so let's go over what we know. One," I held up a finger. "Merl arrived in Shanghai a week ago. He went to visit his friend, Sing, the sword maker, and gained entry into the house. He was not seen since and from the rotting food left in the house it appears that no one had been there since Merl went through the door. Leading us to believe that Merl, Sing, his three apprentices and Merl's three dogs went out in a hurry in a different way. Possibly over the rooftops like Sing's grand-daughter, Bai."

Loki nodded.

"Okay, number two," I held up another finger. "We know that Bai was killed on that rooftop three days ago because it happened right in front of us. We have no idea who did the killing or why but we can now safely assume it has something to do with hacking and Falun Gong. According to Dan, Bai was working on releasing information about the prison camps. So let's assume for a moment that Bai was working on exposing this reeducation center, maybe even at the request of her grandfather who was friends with Mo-Ping. Then Merl showed up. Maybe he was arrested along with Sing and his apprentices in Shanghai."

"They left over the roof though. And, according to the cameras, no one appears to have entered the building after Merl."

"That's right, but that doesn't mean the police didn't catch them somehow."

"Perhaps, but taking prisoners over rooftops and down fire escapes?" He shrugged. "Maybe. They usually just take them in a more straightfor-ward way. I mean the police don't have to hide their activities. Lawyers get arrested when trying to do their jobs. It is known in China. And to be honest it is known outside of China to a large degree but there is nothing that can be done about it."

"What do you mean?"

"International pressure does not work. Or at least it has not worked. Peaceful protests do not work. Like I told you, that's how Falun Gong fell under such persecution."

I nodded. "So, if they weren't captured that day, then I think it's safe to assume that Merl and the dogs left Shanghai with Sing, possibly even with the apprentices, and headed this way."

"Where he was then captured."

I shrugged. "Possibly, yes. I mean, I find it hard to believe that he could be captured but it's not impossible."

"Anything is possible," Loki said.

I laughed. "That almost sounds like something a self-help guru would say."

Loki smiled.

I looked out the window, watching the landscape bounce by. "Has anyone tried a violent protest?" I asked. "A prison break?"

"Not that I know of. That is not the Falun Gong way."

"Let's stop in the village. I need to make a phone call and our cells are not getting service."

Loki leaned forward and spoke to the old man who nodded his head.

CHAPTER FOURTEEN
FOLLOWING ORDERS

The village was small and dusty. There were no tourist shops. The street was not busy and there seemed to be a hush over the place, like a secret was being kept here. The car pulled up in front of a phone booth. I locked myself in the stuffy space. The phone took coins and cards. Loki had given me a phone card and I pushed it into the slot before dialing Bobby Maxim's number. He picked up. "Sydney," he said. "Calling to wish me luck?"

"Oh, right, yeah. Good luck on the IPO."

"Thanks, nice of you to call."

I cleared my throat, looking through the scratched Plexiglass of the phone booth at Loki and the couple waiting in the car. Blue's head was stretched out the open window, his nose lifted in the air, sniffing. "That's not the only reason. I may need your help."

"How's that?"

"I'm in China."

"Are you?"

"Yes, and I'm on my way to a reeducation camp deep in the countryside."

"As a prisoner?" his voice sounded serious.

"No," I laughed. "Well, not yet."

"Sydney, this is not a joke."

"I'm sorry, it's Merl. I think he's in a reeducation facility and I want to get him out. Can you help with that?"

"You know where he is?"

"Not for sure, but I should in the next couple of hours."

"I've got some favors I could trade for his release. Depending on what he is being held for."

"I think it's in relation to Falun Gong."

I heard Bobby cover the phone and his voice muffled, speaking to someone else. Then he was back on the line. "Call me when you know where he is for sure. And Sydney?"

"Yeah."

"Don't get caught."

"I won't."

"Where are you now?"

I told him the name of the village and its general location.

"If I have not heard from you in the next twenty-four hours I'm going to come looking for you."

"The woman who swallowed the spider to catch the fly."

"What?"

"Nothing. I just came here looking for Merl. But I don't think he knew at all what he was walking into."

"And you think you do?"

"Not exactly."

"If you had asked my advice earlier I could have helped more."

"You're right. I should have called."

"But you do trust me?"

"Yes," I answered, surprised by how little it felt like a lie.

"Good. We'll talk again once you're sure of where Merl is."

"Because you know people here who can help?"

"I know people everywhere, Sydney. That's why you called me."

We said our goodbyes and I climbed back in the car. The woman pulled out sandwiches as we started to drive again toward the tai chi center. There were only two but she offered one to Loki and me while splitting the other with her husband. It was a pita-type bread filled with fragrant meat and finely chopped vegetables. After devouring my half I was still hungry but knew there was no time to eat.

The road grew narrow and more uneven as we started to climb. However the old car kept going, bouncing and jolting, but steady. There were several houses clustered together on the side of the road and the old man pointed, taking his hand off the wheel for a moment, toward the mountain looming above us. Built into a ledge was a white building, small windows, about four stories. "That's it," Loki told me.

We went around another bend and the building disappeared for a moment, then was in front of us again as we curved with the side of the mountain, making our way up into the sky.

I remembered Merl describing this place to me when we first met years ago. The big wooden platform where he'd seen people in silk pajamas practicing tai chi for the first time, the amazing oval mountains that surrounded it, the peace and sanctuary that he'd found here.

The compound was surrounded by a fence, and a small crowd was gathered at the entrance gate. The original fence appeared to have been low, only about thigh high, but a sturdy-looking chicken wire had been added, making the fence about ten feet tall, barbed wire looped at the top.

Guards, their uniforms dark green, brimmed hats pulled low over their eyes, stood at the gate, rifles that looked a lot like the ones we'd taken off the CCP police earlier clutched in their hands.

The crowd was shabbily dressed, their expressions strained, but they were peaceful. We parked just off the road, a short distance from the center. "How are we going to find out if Merl is in there?" Loki said.

"I don't know. Ask?" Loki raised his brows. "Can't we just ask?"

"No," he said. "We can't just ask."

"It's worth a try."

"Not really."

"Then I guess we need to wait and see what happens."

The couple climbed out of the car, and turning to Loki, Zang Wei asked a question. Loki waved for him to go ahead. The couple, holding hands walked up the road to join the other family members. "They are going to find out if the lawyers have arrived yet."

"Could they ask about Merl?"

"Only if we wanted to risk their lives."

"What if we could arrange the release of their son?"

"We can't."

"I have a connection. I may be able to get him out."

Loki turned to me. "How is that possible? You don't know anyone here."

"I know you," I pointed out.

"Lenox does not know anyone that can pull strings like that."

"I can't tell you who my connection is, but trust me, he has more power than Lenox."

Loki's eyes narrowed. "You are sure?"

"I'm almost positive."

"That is who you called."

"Yes, I told him we were coming here, what we were doing. He said to be careful but if I could be sure of where Merl was, he could arrange to have him released."

"What about Mo-Ping and their son? You're saying you could get them out too."

"I think so." What I wanted to do, of course, was find someone who could draw me a map of the tai chi center, someone who knew the place well. Then, wait until dark and break in, releasing all the prisoners. But would I just be releasing them to be captured again? I couldn't get all those people out of rural China.

A van passed us, its windows tinted, white paint coated in dust. It pulled up in front of the crowd and three men climbed out. "These must be the lawyers," Loki said.

Two of the men were talking to the crowd while a third was speaking to the guards. The guards did not respond, keeping the same stony look on their hardened faces. "What's going on?" I asked.

"You're looking at the same thing as me," Loki said. "I can't hear from here."

"Should we get closer?"

"Not worth the risk. Let's wait."

The crowd began to chant. "What are they saying?"

"They are demanding the release of the prisoners."

The front door of the tai chi center opened and a man came out. He was dressed in a suit, the black material shiny, reflecting silver in the sunlight. He stayed behind the gate talking to the lawyer through the two guards. The lawyer began to yell. The man shook his head. The crowd was becoming more agitated. I heard sirens coming up the hill.

Loki and I shifted in our seats to see three police vehicles. They raced by us, screeching to a halt in front of the crowd, forcing people to press against the fence. Some of the protestors began to run, others yelled at the police as officers piled out of the cars.

The police grabbed the two lawyers closest to them and began to haul them toward the cars. The one talking to the guards was yelling as another cop grabbed him. We watched as the lawyers were all forced into cars, yelling, cursing at the cops.

The crowd circled the police cars, watching and shouting, but not physically intervening. The police got back into the cars and drove off, almost hitting several of the protestors as they tore off back down the road.

"They just arrested the lawyers," I said, trying to digest what I'd just witnessed.

"Yes," Loki answered.

"Is that normal?"

"Normal? No, but it happens."

The crowd was angry, shouting at the guards but not moving toward them. The man in the shiny suit was walking back toward the tai chi center, his jacket flapping in the wind.

Time passed and the crowd simmered down, their anger exhausted, their efforts clearly futile.

EK

The couple returned to the car. They sat for a moment in silence, staring out the front windshield. Then the woman started to cry. She didn't make any noise but tears rolled down her cheeks. Her husband reached out and took her hand. They appeared to have forgotten all about us.

Loki waited a few minutes, then spoke to the man. Soon after, the man started the car and turned us around, heading back down to the village.

"There is a guest house in the village where they can stay," Loki explained. "I offered to pay for their room and rent their car for the rest of the night."

"Good," I said.

After we dropped the couple off at the guest house, where a number of the other families were staying, we drove back up the mountain to the tai chi center, passing the few houses along the way. I looked at the simple cinderblock structures and wondered who lived there. "Farmers," Loki said, seeming to read my mind. "They work the fields below and some work part-time at the tai chi center." He paused. "Or did anyway."

"Where do the guards live?" I asked.

"Probably in the center for now. I doubt this is permanent. They will probably move the prisoners sometime soon, or make some renovations to the space."

"They've already added a lot of barbed wire," I said as the center came back into view. The sun was setting behind the mountain, the sky was turning a deep blue, the first stars just starting to twinkle.

"Yes," Loki said, parking the car down the hill, far enough away from the entrance that we would not be noticed in the dark.

I sat back in the passenger seat, feeling the springs of the cushions through the worn fabric.

"Where do you think the lawyers were taken?" I asked.

Loki shrugged. "The closest police station is by the airport, several hours away."

"Why were they arrested?"

Loki shrugged. "I don't know. They don't necessarily need a reason." He paused for a moment. "There are rules here Sydney, but not everyone has to follow them."

"Like most of the world," I said.

Loki turned to look at me and I glanced in his direction. He was frowning. "This is different," he said.

"There is no just place in the world."

"But in many parts there is law, there is order, there is a system. Australia for example."

"I know that some places are better than others, trust me. But even places where the rule of law seems obvious, a given, even in those places there is corruption—one standard for the powerful, one for everyone else."

"Corruption," Loki said, seeming to roll the word around in his mouth, thinking about it, playing with the syllables.

"It's everywhere."

"Even in Joyful Justice?" he asked.

I thought about Dan and Bobby. How I suspected they'd been working together behind my back. "Yes," I answered. "It is impossible to avoid."

"Because of human nature? Is that what you're saying?"

"Why does corruption exist? I don't know," I said, shrugging. "Perhaps human nature."

"But then is it not also human nature to fight against it."

"To try to create order in a world of chaos," I said with a smile.

Loki laughed. "Yes, I suppose we do do that."

Blue let out a low growl from the back seat and we both turned to look. I heard tires crunching up the road and within a few minutes two sets of headlights appeared. Loki and I both slunk lower in our seats. Two vans drove past us, pulling up in front of the entrance of the tai chi center. An armed man hopped out of the lead van and spoke with the guard at the gate. He then continued down the path to the building's entrance where he went inside. Two more armed men climbed out of the van. They lit up cigarettes. The electric lights shining down on the gate cast long shadows of the vans across the road.

The men finished their cigarettes and were joking with each other, their laughter barely reaching us. The front door to the center opened and the armed man we'd seen leave the van reappeared with three shackled prisoners. They wore white jumpsuits, loose-fitting and stained. The prisoners shuffled down the path, the armed man behind them hurrying them along.

The guard let them out the gate, and the two armed men by the van stepped forward, grabbing the prisoners and pushing them inside. After the guards climbed in, the two vans left heading further up the mountain leaving trails of dirt pluming behind them.

Loki started our car and we followed, having to drive right by the gates on our way. I stayed low in my seat and out of view. Loki kept his gaze facing forward as we passed the entrance. We turned around a bend and didn't see the vans, but the road was winding and there were no turnoffs, so we knew that we were safe maintaining a distance.

We reached the top of a pass and the road sloped down. We still couldn't see the vans ahead of us but their fresh tire marks were obvious in the roadway. The valley below was flat and dark. "There's nothing out there," I said.

"Not that I know of," Loki said.

"Where would they be taking them?" I asked.

"I don't know," Loki said. "But, I don't think it's anywhere good."

We saw the headlights of the vans as they headed into the valley, two spots of light in a sea of darkness. When we reached the valley floor I saw rice paddies on both side of the road. Loki cut our headlights because the road was straight and we could see the van's red taillights in the distance. "Hard to follow them inconspicuously here," I said.

We hit a bump that jarred us and I let out an *oomph*. "It's also hard to drive in complete darkness," Loki said.

"What did you mean," I asked, "when you said they can't be going anywhere good?"

"There are no towns or even villages in this direction," Loki answered me. His hands tightened on the wheel and he chewed on his bottom lip for a moment. "This is probably an execution."

"In the middle of nowhere, in the middle of the night."

"Yes," he answered. "And that might not be all."

CHAPTER FIFTEEN
BLOOD FLOWS

We saw the brake lights glow up ahead and Loki slowed to a stop. The vans pulled off onto the side of the road. We waited, our engine running. The vans were about a hundred feet ahead of us, far enough away that there was no way they could see our unlit car in the dark but close enough that we could see figures climbing out of the lead van. The headlights from the rear vehicle lit the prisoners and guards clearly for a moment as they passed through the bright beams, headed toward the rice paddy.

"Why two vans?" I asked.

"That's what makes me think this is not just a simple execution," Loki said.

"What is it then?"

"Something we need to stop."

He turned off the car and grabbed a rifle out of the back seat, passing it to me before reaching for another. Loki made sure the dome light was set to "off" before opening his door and stepping out into the night. I followed him, opening the back door for Blue, who fell in line with my hip as I hurried to catch up with Loki. In the distance I could see the prisoners and guards were about 15 feet from the vans, still partly illuminated by the headlights. The prisoners were forced onto their knees.

Loki picked up his pace, breaking into a steady jog. I ran alongside him, our rifles held up in front of our chests. We watched as one of the prisoners was pulled away from the others. They blindfolded him. I could see his hands, chains winding off of them, clasped in front of his chest, in a position of prayer or begging. I guessed that he was doing both.

A guard knocked his hands down, exposing his chest. The other two prisoners were huddled together, the two remaining guards standing over them, guns aimed at their heads.

The blindfolded man, his chest exposed, could not see the guard raise his gun. The shot rang out loud in the flat space. The prisoner fell back, his head hitting the ground, his body seeming to disappear into darkness. The guard who shot him and another one picked his body up and began to drag it toward the second van. The back doors opened and we had a clear picture of the interior. There were bright lights that poured out into the night.

Inside was a makeshift operating room with a metal table, tools hanging on the walls, a figure in a white coat wearing a surgical mask. The surgeon jumped out of the van and watched as the two guards hefted the man onto the metal table. They climbed back out and motioned for the doctor to go back in. The white-coated figure stood still, seemingly paralyzed, until one of the guards raised his weapon and yelled something.

We slowed down, less than twenty feet away now, still hidden by the darkness. Loki and I were crouching, making ourselves smaller, Blue stayed to my right, his nose occasionally tapping my hip. I didn't ask what was going on, not wanting to make a sound, but I could guess. Surgery of this nature could only have one purpose.

The van door closed, sinking the night back into darkness, and closing the doctor, the armed guard, and the shot prisoner inside.

Loki looked at me, his eyes shining. "Follow me," he whispered. I nodded.

There were still two guards and two prisoners standing away from the vans. I assumed there was a driver in the medical van and as we moved, single file, down the road, my assumption was proved correct when the driver's door opened and a big, round, figure stepped out. He walked over to the other guards and pulled out a cigarette, the flame of his match lighting his face for a moment. In that brief glimpse I saw that he was sweating, the match he held shook slightly. Whatever was going on in that van was not pleasant.

We were close now, still shrouded by the darkness but about to be within the glow of the red tail lights. The headlights of both vans were still on. We stayed to the right of the road, unable to step off into the rice paddies because of the splashing sound we'd make. Blue was tight to my right knee, the white parts of his coat glimmering softly in the dark night.

None of the guards were looking in our direction. They were on the far side of the vans, on what seemed to be a peninsula out into a rice paddy, a flat, dusty piece of land. Was it created specifically for this, I wondered, or was it just a coincidence, an area left for the farmers to park their cars?

Loki motioned to the surgeon's van, and then started toward it. Blue and I followed. The gun was heavy and reassuring in my hands. My heart rate was slowly picking up the closer we got. Loki looked in the passenger window, then waved for me to look.

There was no passenger seat. The interior space was open to the back, to that table and the prisoner lying on it. The guard was still holding the gun on the doctor who was up to his elbows in the man's chest. Blood was spilling onto the floor. Coming in steady pumps. The prisoner was still alive--they hadn't killed him.

Then the doctor pulled his arms up. He was holding an organ, it was small, brown, and dripping blood. The doctor wore blue surgical gloves and there were spatters of blood on his mask and across the white coat. He was sweating, his brows deeply furrowed as he turned to his left. I could not see where he put the organ but then he was back in the body. I felt bile rising up my throat. The image was so bright, so stark compared to the dark world we stood in. They were dissecting this prisoner, harvesting his organs. I stepped back, not wanting to see any more. I glanced at Loki whose eyes stayed riveted on the scene inside.

I touched his shoulder, and his head pivoted to me. His eyes were cold, filled with an intense emotion. Was it hate? Or anger? A blend of both? Scary in the darkness. I made a gesture that I would go after the men on the other side of the van, and pointed to the interior then at him. He nodded.

Moving slowly, so that my footfalls on the dirt road would not be heard, I circled around to the back of the van, staying just out of the reach of the lights. I paused there. Took a deep breath, peeked around the side of the van, holding that breath, and double-checked that the two guards and the driver were still where we'd left them. They were.

I hid again, taking several even breaths and closing my eyes for a second, finding peace, finding that center where all action came from. Then I stepped out from behind the van, gun out, Blue by my side. The three men were still looking away from the van, their cigarettes held loosely by their sides. I fired the first shot and the guard to the left dropped with an *oof*. The other two turned, I shot the one with his weapon already out first. His body spun and fell onto one of the prisoners who screamed. The sound was loud in the still night. The driver was fumbling at his waist band for his gun when I shot him in the chest. Right in the heart. Dead, dead, dead.

My targets neutralized, I turned around and saw the van doors open, light spilling into the night, blood dripping off the bumper. Loki jumped out, dragging the doctor with him. I didn't have to ask what had happened to the guard. The doctor's mask had slipped and I could see how young he was, not much older than 25. He was babbling. Loki's face was grim, his eyes still held that cold glare when he glanced over at the dead guards. "He says he didn't want to do it, that he did not know why they had brought him here."

"I believe him," I said.

"Thank you," the doctor said in English, his accent thick but words perfectly understandable. "I would never, no doctor. It was not told to me."

"You saw what happened," I said to Loki. "You saw the guard put a gun to his head."

"Yes," Loki agreed with a slight nod, but his grip did not loosen on the man's arm.

The two prisoners were still on their knees, blindfolded. I walked over to them. There was blood on them, splattered across their faces and chests. They'd tried to wipe it off, smearing the droplets into streaks on their cheeks and forehead. They were both young men, their bodies strong. I pulled off the first blindfold and the prisoner blinked, looking up at me. Moving on to the other I pulled off his blindfold. The man flinched at my touch but when he saw me his fear turned to confusion. "Do you speak English?" I asked.

They looked at each other but did not respond. "Loki," I called him over. He came, dragging the doctor with him. "Ask them about Merl," I said.

Loki spoke to the men. They exchanged a glance and then nodded. They looked like they could have been brothers, their hair the same length, cut close to their heads. They shared the same brown skin, tanned by many years in the sun, and dark eyes. The one closer to me spoke. His voice was soft with a layer of desperation under it, as though he was straining to be believed. Loki nodded and then spoke to me. "They know of a man who matches Merl's description. He is being held at the center."

I nodded, swallowing a lump in my throat. Relief was washing through my body, bringing tears to my eyes. "So, he's alive," I said.

"As far as they know."

"What about you, doctor?" I asked, turning to the man Loki still gripped.

He shook his head hard, making his hair flip around his face. "I do not know anything about the prisoners," he said.

"How did you get here then?"

"I was picked up in my office this afternoon. The police said that I was needed. So I came."

"But you've heard about organ harvesting," Loki said, his voice hard, accusatory.

The doctor's eyes widened. "No, I mean, I thought it was made up. I didn't believe," his voice faded.

"Didn't think it could be true," I finished for him looking back at the van. What were we going to do with that body, with those organs? It seemed a waste for them to rot, for the man to have died for nothing.

"He was still alive," the doctor said, his voice cracking. He was shaking his head.

"Where were the organs going?" I asked.

The doctor shook his head, he didn't know.

"They were probably bought," Loki said. "These prisoners match someone wealthy who can afford to pay for their lives."

"It's sickening," I said.

"Yes," Loki agreed.

"What are we going to do with him?" I said, tilting my chin in the doctor's direction. His eyes widened in fear.

"I don't know," Loki said.

"We need these two," I pointed at the prisoners, who were still on their knees, chains tight around their wrists, wrapped around their waists and leading down to ankle restraints. "And a doctor is always useful, but can we trust him?"

The man nodded his head vigorously, "I will tell the police that I don't know what happened. Or I will tell them whatever you want me to tell them. I am at your service. Please don't kill me."

Loki looked at me. "We can use him."

"Yes," I agreed. "I think we can."

CHAPTER SIXTEEN
DECISIONS, DECISIONS

I had hoped that Robert Maxim would be able to get Merl out of the prison using his connections, but I now recognized that was not possible. We were leaving a van with four dead bodies in it on the side of the road. The road was not well-traveled so it was unlikely to be discovered until at least daybreak, however, those organs were obviously headed somewhere and would quickly be missed.

I could try to leave the country, just disappear and trust Bobby to get Merl out now that I knew where he was, but I didn't know how long that would take. And obviously, we didn't have much time. This was not a justice system where the wheels turned slowly, where you were innocent until proven guilty. In this place, at this time, in this exact moment, prisoners' organs were being taken, sold to the highest bidder. There was no time for applying political pull. I was going to have to do this the old-fashioned way.

I found keys on one of the dead guards and uncuffed the prisoners. They helped us pile the three dead men into the surgery van with the other two corpses already in there. I closed the back doors and then went around and climbed into the driver's seat. It had a deep depression from the big man who used to drive it. I wondered how many of these night missions he'd gone out on. The way he'd left the van, his brow sweating and hands shaking as he lit his cigarette, meant either he was new to the duty or it was something you never got used to.

I turned the motor off, the headlights fading into nothing. Taking the keys I climbed back out and slammed the door before locking up the van. I peered in but couldn't see anything. Loki had closed a curtain between the back and the front. But even if it took a while for the bodies to be discovered, there was still someone anxiously waiting for those organs. The doctor had been told nothing. "I asked," he said. "I asked how long I would be gone, for my wife, she likes to know. But they would not tell me."

Loki, Blue, the two freed prisoners, the doctor and I all got into the front van. It had bars on the windows and rows of seats. It didn't have seat belts but there were metal loops on the floor that were used for chaining prisoners in their seats. As we bumped along the road back toward the car I stared at one of the hooks of metal soldered into the floor. I wondered if Merl had been attached to it. I worried if someday I might be.

Loki pulled over in front of our car. Blue and I climbed out, and Loki handed me the keys through the open driver's side window of the van. "We'll park about a half mile up from the center," Loki said.

"I'll be there as soon as I can."

"You're sure your connection will come through?" Loki asked.

"Yes," I answered, hoping my faith in Bobby Maxim was not misplaced.

I got in the car, Blue in the passenger seat, his head almost touching the sagging roof. "Down boy," I told him, pointing at the seat well. He climbed below, so that he was hidden from the outside world, curling himself into as small a ball as he could. The car started with a small putter and the headlights glowed dully, nothing like the high beams of the van in front of us. I turned the car around and started back toward the tai chi center.

The plan was for me to go into the village, drop off the car, and call Bobby. That meant I had to drive by the tai chi center again. Then I had to get back past it again on foot to meet Loki up the hill.

In the meantime, he was going to talk with the prisoners, get them to draw us a map of the center, and come up with a plan to break in, get Merl, and break out.

But first, I had to call Robert Maxim and ask him to arrange a way out of the country. Given the manhunt about to get under way, I couldn't do it without him. I chewed on my lip as we drove over the rutted road, back up the mountain. The landscape was all sharp angles and flat planes. As we approached the tai chi center Loki pulled over. His head-lights faded in my rearview mirror as Blue and I continued.

We came around the bend, and my headlights flashed over the guard by the gate. He shielded his eyes from the light and as I curved around the bend I kept my face turned away so that he would only see my short, dark hair. I watched him in my rearview mirror as I continued down the road. He was under a lamp and I could see his gaze on my car but I didn't see him reach for his radio. It couldn't be so unusual for a car to drive by, and the car would be out of my possession soon. And, given our plan, that guard could well be dead within a few hours and thus unable to tell any authorities about the car, getting Zang Wei and Lei Shu in trouble.

The village had only one street, lined with buildings on both sides with the guest house in the middle. I parked the car nearby, slipping the keys under the driver's seat, and then headed for the pay phone. I could hear loud talking coming from inside the guest house, no doubt the same people who had protested in front of the gates earlier in the day. They were still awake, talking, trying to find a solution, to figure out how to free their loved ones.

I closed myself in the phone booth, getting Blue to squeeze in with me and used Loki's card again to dial Bobby's number. He picked up on the second ring. "I found him," I said.

"Okay, tell me where he is being held."

"No, I mean, there isn't time. He is in too much danger. They all are."

"They?"

"All the prisoners," I swallowed and closed my eyes, seeing the blue gloves holding that brown organ, the fresh blood dripping off of it back onto the body from which it had been stolen. "I need you to arrange safe passage for me, Merl, and at least one other person, possibly two. Plus four dogs."

I heard Bobby snort. "Four dogs? Of course. For the human passengers are they male or female?"

"One of each," I said, thinking of Loki and Mo. "Maybe an elderly man too," I added, remembering Sing.

"Okay," Robert said. "Where do you want to go?"

"Back to the island."

"Well," I could hear a smile in his voice. "You'll have to tell me where it is then."

"Like you don't know."

Bobby laughed. "I don't know everything."

"Dan didn't tell you?" I said, my voice dripping with acid.

"Why would he do that?"

I shook my head. Now was not the time to get into this. "I need a plane and I need it soon."

"How soon?"

"By dawn."

"That is soon," Bobby said, his voice dropping an octave.

"Can you do it?"

"Of course I can. But, like I said, I need to know where you are going."

"Call Dan, he can give you the info."

"Aye, aye, Captain."

I gritted my teeth and wasn't going to say anything but then I heard myself speaking. "See, there, that, you have been talking to Dan. I know it."

Robert laughed. "I don't know what you're talking about. Getting paranoid in your old age, Sydney."

"Whatever, just, just get me out of here," I said, looking around at the quiet street.

"The plane will be waiting for you. Call me when you're on your way. And Sydney?"

"Yeah?"

"Be careful. If you're planning on breaking Merl out of a reeducation camp you'll have to be very careful not to end up in one."

"Wouldn't you save me?" I said, only half joking.

"I'd do my best, but Sydney, let's not forget who you are. If they ever figured out your identity, there would be no saving you. I just want you to understand how much you're risking tonight. Are you sure it's worth it?"

"I'm positive."

"What would you say are your chances of success?"

"I don't know the plan yet so I can't rightly say." I almost laughed.

There was a moment of silence on the other end. "You're joking."

"No, but I'm sure we'll figure it out. You know me, Bobby. I'm a survivor."

"You've been lucky."

"Let's hope my streak continues. I've got to go. Get that plane. Talk to Dan. I'll call you once it's over."

I walked back up the hill, past the dark houses down the road from the tai chi center. The darkness hid me and there were no cars. When I was approaching the center, with its white walls and bright lights, I stayed to the far side of the road. There was a ditch, a rocky eroded area where water obviously flowed down the mountain after a heavy rain. Staying low, Blue behind my left knee, I was out of view of the guard by the gate. Once around the bend and out of sight of the center I straightened back up. It was only another 10 minutes until the van came into view.

The prisoners, Loki, and the doctor were all inside. "Come up with a plan?" I asked as I climbed in, joining them in the back.

Loki nodded. "Yes, to a degree. They are not totally certain of the number of guards but since they lived there prior to it becoming a prison they know the layout well. The authorities turned their bedrooms into cells, the dining hall was still used for dining, and," Loki swallowed, "the practice areas for torture."

"Why?" I asked. "I mean, what kind of information are they trying to get out of them?"

"They want them to confess, Sydney."

"To what?"

"Plotting against the government."

One of the prisoners said something and Loki listened to him before turning to me. "There was an online movement that was gathering evidence of torture and organ harvest of Falun Gong practitioners. They thought the center was involved."

"Was it?" I asked.

"Not these two," Loki said. "But Mo was."

"That makes sense. But is hardly the point right now. Where is Merl?"

"He is in the basement, separate from the other prisoners. We will enter through the front gate. Here is what I'm thinking..." Loki laid out his plan. It sounded as good as any other to me.

"We better hurry," I said, "the faster we get in and out the better."

"Agreed."

"What about the doctor?" I asked.

"We will leave him here," Loki said, "chain him in the van. That way if we are injured he will be here to help, and if everything goes as planned we'll just let him go before leaving."

"Okay."

"Ready?"

I nodded.

EK

I walked alone down the center of the road. Loki, the prisoners and Blue were about ten feet behind, hidden by a boulder. Loki following my movements through the scope of one of the rifles we'd stolen that morning. We had twelve bullets between the two rifles. We also had the four handguns we'd gotten off the guards we'd killed by the van. I had one of those slipped into the back of my waist band. My hands were loose at my sides as I walked toward the center. I wasn't trying to hide my presence or quiet my steps. The plan was to have the man see me. The hope was that he'd want to ask some questions before he shot me.

When the guard noticed me he stepped forward, his hands tensing on his rifle. He yelled something to me. I put my hands up and approached slowly. When he saw that I was a foreigner, his eyebrows shot up and he aimed his weapon at me, yelling. I stopped in my tracks and lowered slowly to my knees. He spoke into the radio on his shoulder and waited for a response before yelling something else to me.

"English," I said back, loud enough for him to hear but quiet enough that it was clear I was not yelling. I was not panicking, I was not a threat. I was just a single woman on a deserted road alone at night.

He opened the gate, approaching me slowly, his knees bent, gun up, muzzle aimed at my chest. I saw the doors to the center open and two more guards came running down the path and through the open gate. The first guard was right in front of me, out of reach, but I knew Loki would have a clear shot. The other two were coming around, as if to grab me.

A shot rang out from behind me and the guard to my left crumpled. Covering my head with my hands I curled into a ball as the man in front of me began to fire over me into the darkness. He wasn't looking at me, neither was the other guard. They were both facing the night, firing over and over again. I reached into the small of my back, removed the handgun and brought it around. I kept my movements slow, invisible to someone staring past me, fearing for their lives.

The gun was in my right hand. I brought it into the curl of my body, hidden from view then passed it under my left arm so that it was aiming at the guard who stood there, firing wildly into the night. I steadied the gun and fired. The guard in front of me saw him fall but didn't realize I was the one who'd shot him. He screamed, spittle shooting out of his mouth, the bright lights over the gate catching it. I sat up and aimed. He didn't have time to lower his weapon before I shot him in the forehead. His eyes stayed on me as he dropped to his knees. They rolled into his head before he tipped over to the side.

That's when I heard the sirens, the wailing of the alarm. Turning toward the tai chi center I stood up and ran through the open gate and sprinted down the path. The door was closing, there was at least one more person in there. I hit it hard with my left shoulder, the gun still tight in my right hand. The door flew open and I fell into the room, landing on the floor, my weapon up and aimed behind the door where a small man in an ill-fitting uniform was tripping backwards from the force of the door knocking him over. I shot him once, it hit his arm and he cried out, grabbing at the injured limb, his eyes wide with fright before I shot him again, this time in the chest. He crumpled to the floor and I whipped my head around, searching the rest of the room.

It was a square, about twenty feet to a side, with a reception desk and a couple of wooden chairs. There was no one else in the room, but I thought it safe to assume there were more on the way.

Loki and the prisoners came in as I was getting up. "We need to turn off the alarm," I said, hurrying to the reception desk. Behind it were several monitors and I saw guards running down halls. "There are more coming," I said.

"Go," Loki told me, leaning over the dead guard behind the door. He stood up and I saw he'd taken the man's gun. "Get Merl, we'll deal with the guards on their way. That way," he pointed with the newly obtained weapon. "The stairs are at the end of the hall."

I followed his directions into an open hall lined with closed doors. Wall sconces lit the narrow space. Only half of them were on. I assumed this portion of the building was mostly unused. At the end of the hall was a door, unlocked. As I pulled it open I heard steps behind me.

Turning and ducking down at the same time I saw a guard coming out of one of the rooms I'd assumed was empty. He was aiming a gun at me, biting his lip, looking nervous and young. I fired, the sound of the gun loud in the narrow hall. The bullet entered his neck. He dropped his gun, reaching both hands to the wound.

He stumbled toward me and then fell, landing on one knee bringing our eyes to the same level before he tipped over onto his side, his last breaths gurgling as blood seeped out of his mouth.

I stood up, returning my attention to the stairs leading to the basement, ignoring the final gasps from the young man behind me, pushing away the thoughts of guilt and fear that tried to pry at my mind. There was no time for that now.

CHAPTER SEVENTEEN
PICKING LOCKS

I descended the stone steps slowly. They curled into darkness, the air growing colder at each stair. Blue was right behind me, the sound of his paw falls reassuring in the damp cold. I pulled out my phone and used the light to navigate further.

The bottom of the steps came suddenly, the hall extending straight ahead was pitch black. I felt along the wall, shining my light, trying to find a switch but there wasn't one. I examined the ceiling and walls and saw no bulbs. There were however, candle holders, but they were empty. The space felt like it was from another time.

Blue pushed past me, his flank rubbing against my leg as he moved forward into the gloom. His nose was in the air, sniffing. I followed him as his pace picked up to a trot, his nose leading the way.

We passed closed wooden doors, their handles coated in dust, until Blue stopped in front of one. Blue pushed his nose into the gap between the door and stone floor, sniffing hard, letting loose a small whine.

Shining my phone light onto the handle I saw that it looked recently used, the dull shine of the metal reflecting back at me. I depressed the lever but it was locked. The door was thick wood, the keyhole centered above the handle. Blue whined again, his feet tapping with impatience on the stone floor, nails clicking. "Merl?" I whispered, my mouth close to the door.

I heard movement, chains jingling. "Sydney?"

His voice was parched, rough, but unmistakably Merl.

"Yes," I said, my throat tight. "It's me. Are you okay?"

The sound of chains moving grew closer until I felt a thud against the door. "I'm alive," he said. "I can't believe you're here."

"You thought I'd let you disappear and not come looking? I'm going to get you out of there."

"Do you have the key?"

"No, but I'll go get it."

"How did you get here?"

"No time now, Merl. I'll be back."

I heard the chains move again, like he was pressing against the door. "It's nice to hear your voice."

"I'll be back," I promised before turning back toward the steps. Blue whined but followed me, his nose tapping my hip. "We need a key," I told him, knowing he couldn't understand but feeling the need to explain why I was leaving our friend chained up in a dark and dismal basement. Was basement even the right word for this place? It was a catacomb.

We went back up the steps. Electric light filled the hall above. The guard I killed lay where I left him, his neck still oozing blood, eyes open, shocked, like he didn't know death was possible. I felt along his belt and patted his pockets but didn't find any keys. I picked up his gun before moving quietly down the hall, back into what had been the lobby and was now the reception room for the detention center. I heard shouts coming from nearby and ducked behind the large desk in the corner. Blue squeezed in next to me and we waited, hearing the people approach. They were yelling, running, their footsteps loud in the quiet center.

I wondered where Loki was. He could pick a lock. A group entered the reception room, their boots landing in unison on the hard stone, making me think they must be guards. Blue's ears perked and I heard it then too, quieter footsteps, coming from the other direction. I peered around the corner of the desk, staying low, sure that the running guards had headed down the hall I'd just left. I saw two people, a man and a woman, both thin, wearing torn silk pajamas, blood crusted in some places.

They moved almost silently, without Blue I never would have noticed them. Their faces were set in stern yet relaxed expressions, their bodies practically floating as they followed the loud men into the hall beyond the reception room. Moments later I heard screaming, a gun shot, bodies falling to the ground. Another gun shot, thuds, flesh against flesh.

They must have been prisoners, released by Loki. But had they won? I sidled up to the doorway and taking a deep breath held it as I looked around the corner, keeping my body as hidden as possible. There had been three guards. They were all on the ground now, their guns scattered.

The former prisoners did not pick up the weapons. Blue growled, and when I glanced down at him, he was staring back into the reception area. I heard more boots coming. The two former prisoners started moving back my way. I ran toward them, coming around the corner fast. They raised their hands, ready for a fight, but quickly realized I was not a guard.

I motioned behind me that more were coming. They ducked into an open doorway and I followed. With my gun up and the door slightly open, we waited. The sounds of boots filled the narrow space outside. There was yelling when they saw the three guards who had been taken down. I heard moaning and realized they hadn't killed them. Peace-loving mother fuckers were going to get themselves killed, I thought unkindly. Principles like theirs were something I could learn from. If I lived long enough, I thought bitterly.

There was more yelling outside. I heard the door to the room next to us get kicked open. They were searching for us, recognizing that the attackers could not have gotten far. Twelve bullets, one pipe, a dog, and two peace-loving, tai chi masters. We had a chance against armed guards but only with the element of surprise.

I motioned to the two prisoners to line up on the wall just out of reach of the door so that when they kicked it open we'd be at the furthest point of their vision without getting hit by the door.

Blue stood next to me. His hackles were up, ready for the fight, to launch himself at the first man through the door. But I laid a hand on his head telling him to wait for my command. He sat, licking his lips, frustrated but obedient. The door flew open and a guard stormed in, I shot him in the back. Cowardly but necessary. There was yelling in the hall and a barrage of bullets flew into the room, passing over the dead man, and splintering the wall beyond him. We were safe standing where we were.

They would have to come in and get us. They sent in two men this time, back to back, facing the sides of the room. Smart. I shot the one facing us before his eyes had a chance to adjust to the dark room. The other spun around but I shot him, crumpling him onto the body of his partner before he'd even discharged one bullet.

A low moan from outside. It was possible I'd gotten all the conscious guards. Though since the prisoners next to me had not taken the weapons of the three they'd knocked out, I couldn't be sure if we were safe yet. There was a shuffling sound, like someone sitting up. They would be disoriented but that didn't mean someone couldn't grab a gun.

But waiting here until the three men became conscious enough to walk into our trap seemed like a bad idea. Who knew how long it would take or if reinforcements would show up? Before I could make a decision the two prisoners slid past me, and the woman peeked into the hall. A small wave of her hand and the man was in the hall, the woman right behind him. I heard a grunt and the sound of metal skittering across the floor.

I stepped out and found the man and woman still standing, a guard at the man's feet who looked freshly laid out, his gun a few feet from his extended left hand.

"Do you know who has the keys?" I asked.

They looked at each other and then back at me. I made a motion like I was opening a door with a key by twisting my fist back and forth. They didn't understand. I did it again, this time more forcefully. "Keys," I said slowly, knowing that saying words people don't understand more slowly does not help, but unable to stop myself. When that didn't work I started to search the knocked-out men in the hall. I found keys on the belt of the second one.

I unclipped them and held them out to the man and woman. They nodded understanding. I pointed toward the basement, asking if they were the right keys for Merl's cell. They raised their shoulders, expressing that they didn't know. Which made sense. As a prisoner in one part of the building why would you know which keys opened cells in the other parts of the prison?

"Loki?" I asked, making a gesture with keys.

They both nodded, I wasn't exactly sure what they were agreeing with, but guessed that someone let them out and it was more than likely Loki.

I decided to try the keys I had and if they didn't work I'd go looking for Loki and his lock pick set. Starting toward the steps, Blue by my side, I noticed that the man and woman were following me. I stopped and pointed at the three unconscious men on the ground. "You can't just leave them there," I said.

Obviously, they didn't understand so I grabbed one of guards under his arms and dragged him into the room with the three dead guards in it, dropping him unceremoniously just inside the door. They got the picture and each grabbed a man, hauling him into the room. We closed the door and I tried the keys until I found one that locked the door.

The three of us then proceeded to Merl's cell, where I announced that I was back. "Not sure I've got the right key though," I said.

"Okay," he said.

"I've got two of the other prisoners with me. Will you be able to walk or do you need help?" I asked, flipping through the keys, trying one after another.

"I'm weak," he said. "Have not eaten in three days."

"What about water?"

"A little."

I found a key that fit. My heartbeat surged. But the key refused to turn. "Dammit," I muttered, continuing to the next key. "Do you speak Mandarin?" I asked Merl.

"A little," he said.

"Ask my companions if there is water nearby."

Merl spoke through the door and the woman answered. "She says there should be some in the kitchen."

"Okay, I think we should try to get some before we leave."

"First let's get the door unlocked Sydney."

I smiled at the fact that even as a half-starved, chained prisoner Merl was offering advice. The last key on the ring didn't open the door and I shoved them into my pocket. "That didn't work," I said. "I'm going to go find Loki, he's got a lock pick set on him."

I looked back down the dark hall toward the stairs. "I'm just not quite sure where he is in the building. But obviously he is letting people out. How many people do you think are imprisoned here?" I asked Merl.

"At least fifty," he said. "That is how many were here when I was brought in. Let me ask."

Merl spoke in Mandarin and the woman answered him. "She's not sure but thinks around seventy now. She was sharing her room with four other women."

"Where did they go?" I asked.

Merl asked. The woman answered. "Shot," Merl said, his voice quiet. "Just now, while they were trying to escape."

"Fuck," I said. "Okay, I'll be back."

Blue and I led the way back up the stairs. I stopped in the hall and picked up two more guns, dropping my almost empty one, surprised at myself for not doing it earlier.

I tried to offer guns to the recently escaped prisoners but they refused them. "Fine," I said, moving forward, gun in each hand, one tucked into my waistband, Blue behind my left knee, the man to my right, the woman to my left. We entered the reception area and the woman pointed toward a door to the left. I followed her through the opening. She led the way upstairs. We came to a hall lined with doors.

I could hear the sounds of people pressing up against the doors, fabric rustling, bodies bumping, whispering. There were a lot of them locked up behind those doors. The woman made the key gesture I'd used earlier. I put a gun under my arm and grabbed them out of my pocket. She took them and started toward the first door.

Gun back in hand I turned to the staircase. Before continuing up I glanced back down the hall. I was pretty certain the stairs were the only way on and off this floor. The man and woman were at the first door, talking through it and trying the keys. "Loki?" I asked.

The man looked up and shrugged. I started up the steps, Blue at my heel. Listening closely I tried to hear if there were boots above. But the volume from below was increasing as I heard the first door open. Excited chatter, as more were free. Yes, I thought, get them all out. The more people running around in here, the more work for the guards who were left. And I had no idea how many that was but I figured we'd find out.

At the top of the steps I paused, listening closely, then turned the corner quickly, extending my guns forward. Nothing but closed doors. The stairs continued up and I followed them until I reached a door. Light coming from underneath told me I was at the roof. The door wasn't locked and I stepped out into the fresh air. The sun was rising.

I could see the whole valley below, the oval mountains jutting into space, the flat planes of the rice fields. Everything was covered in a pink glow, the gauzy light of dawn making it all look soft and harmless.

The roof was black, sunken in places, holding pools of water that reflected the brightening sky above. Opposite was another door. I crossed the space, avoiding the puddles while Blue walked right through them. "Can't help yourself?" I said, looking down at him. He cocked his head. I sighed, knowing it was my fault for not telling him to avoid them.

I opened the door and found another staircase, almost identical to the one we'd come up on the other side. I descended to the top floor, taking it slow, listening closely. There I found a similar yet wholly different scene. It was the same stark white hall, but the doors were all open. I glanced into one and saw bunk beds, unmade. Loki must have been here. But where was he now?

I continued down the steps, and, as I approached the next floor, I heard voices. I stopped and Blue sat on the step above me. There was no way to know if it was prisoners or guards but I guessed that it was prisoners. It sounded like a lot of voices. A loud murmuring, careful in its volume but excited.

I stepped out of the stairwell onto the floor and saw that half the doors were opened and the hall crowded with bodies. About halfway down I saw Loki's black form bent over a door, he got it open and an appreciative sigh was exhaled by those watching. "Loki," I said, pushing through the prisoners. They parted for me, staring after Blue and I as we made our way to Loki.

"Did you find Merl?" he asked, moving onto the next door, as three women came stumbling out of the room he'd just unlocked.

"Yes, I need your help getting his cell open though."

"Where is it?"

"In the basement."

"Okay," he said as the lock he was working on clicked open.

"God you're good at that," I said as he opened the door. Without responding he moved on to the next door. "I found keys on some of the other guards and two escaped prisoners are on the other floors working on getting everyone out. But where will they go?" I asked.

"They have places."

I looked around at the faces watching us. They looked hungry and dirty. "Then why are they all just standing here?" I asked.

Loki looked up at the crowd. "They are probably waiting for everyone to be free."

"They don't kill," I said.

"No."

"Seems like they should."

"Not everyone is like you, Sydney."

"I know that," I said. "But I'm not the one getting rescued, am I?" The lock Loki was working on clicked under his ministrations and he moved on as the crowed moved in to open the door. "Come on," I said, impatient and a little pissed. Like Loki wasn't a killer. I'd seen him shoot a man not thirty minutes ago. There was sweat on his brow as he bent over the next door.

"I must finish this before I come to Merl," Loki said.

"They have the keys, they will get here eventually," I said.

Loki didn't look up from the lock he was working on. I tugged on his elbow but he shook me off. "Give me a little time," he said, an edge of anger in his voice.

"Fine," I said, stepping back. "But we need to get Merl out."

The lock opened and Loki hurried to the next door. There were only four left in the hall and I figured I would let him finish and then drag him to the basement if I had to. It took another fifteen minutes for him to open all the doors.

"Now," I said, taking his arm. "You're coming with me."

EK

Loki moved easily with me through the crowd of recently freed Falun Gong practitioners. They shifted aside, letting us pass, their eyes shining with gratitude. "I hope they get out of here soon," I said.

"They will," Loki promised.

We hurried down the steps, Loki pulling a gun as we reentered the reception area. I heard noise coming from outside and picked up my pace, wondering if police or some kind of backup had arrived. Loki stayed close. We ducked down the next hall, passing the room where we'd locked up the guards, and were in the dark stairwell leading downstairs when I heard the front doors open and heavy boot falls.

"Sounds like backup," I said.

"Yes," Loki agreed.

I pulled out my phone, lighting our way into the cool basement. We reached the bottom and I ran up to Merl's door. Loki was by my side quickly and I held my phone so that it shone onto the lock. Loki pulled out his lock picking kit and went to work. We could hear shouting above. "I doubt they'll come down here first," I said.

"No," Loki said, "but we still have to get out."

The lock clicked once and I felt my heart leap again but Loki didn't immediately open the door. He kept fiddling. "We're almost there, Merl," I said.

"Okay," he said, his voice weak.

Another click and Loki stood up, depressing the latch and opened the door. It was pitch black in the room. I shined my flashlight in and saw Merl on the ground, leaning against the wall. He moved forward and the low light of my phone caught the chains binding his hands, snaking around his waist, and locking to his ankles. His face was dirt-encrusted, his right eye swollen shut. He smiled at me, his lips cracked and a tooth missing. "Oh Merl," I said, dropping to my knees in front of him. I reached out to the chains. They had rubbed his skin raw and bloody.

"I'm okay," he said.

"Loki," I looked up at him. He was already getting new picks out of his pack. He knelt down next to Merl and started to work on the locks at his feet.

Merl's eyes were still bright. His long, curly black hair was loose, falling over his shoulders in knotted strands. His hands were folded together, the fingers interlaced, the nails broken. I heard the lock click and Loki removed it from the chain and reached for the other.

"We're getting out of here," I said. "I've got a plane waiting."

"What about Mo?" he asked.

"We're working on freeing everyone now but the guards' backup just arrived." As if to prove my point we heard gunshots upstairs. Muffled, the blasts sounded like thunder in distant mountains.

I turned to look into the darkness. "I've got three guns," I said. "Loki?"

"One," he said as the second lock clicked open. He pulled it off the chains and began to unravel them. Merl winced as the metal was removed from the wounds the chain links had worn into his skin. More gunshots sounded from above, and yelling.

"We'll be okay," I said as much for myself as the two men with me.

The chains removed, Merl stood to his full height. He was only a couple inches taller than me. I could see that he still had strength in his sinewy arms. That there was still a fire in his eyes.

"Should we wait?" Loki asked. "Until they move further into the prison, they may leave one or two men at the front door but we can take care of that."

"Good idea."

"I need to find Mo," Merl said, his voice still raspy but determined.

I bit my lip, knowing that I was not going to win this argument but guessing that finding Mo in this chaos could be suicide. "Can't we find her after?" I asked.

"She could be killed," Merl said.

"So could we," Loki pointed out.

"You can leave without me," Merl said.

"Shut up, I didn't break in here to free you and then leave you here," I said, annoyed. "Come on Merl, seriously."

He shrugged. "I would understand."

"Shut up," I said, passing one of my guns to Loki and removing the other from my waist band.

Blue stayed close to me as we started back up the steps. Loki followed, Merl bringing up the rear. As we climbed the stairs the noises grew louder, the fighting more obvious. The hallway was empty but I could see people in the reception area. Armed guards in uniforms shooting at unarmed, silk pajama-wearing tai chi practitioners. It was a blood bath. We inched closer to the main room. The scent of blood and gunfire filling the air.

It was as if the prisoners were lining up to be shot down. Crowding into the space, launching themselves at the armed men, just to be killed.

There were seven armed men that I could see. Loki and I made eye contact, our guns both up. "I'll take the left side, you take the right," I suggested. He nodded.

The uniformed men's backs were to us, and the noise from their weapons was so loud that they did not notice our approach until we were standing behind them and had begun firing bullets into them.

I took out two men and was taking aim at two more as they turned their guns around, eyes wide. I got one in the shoulder and he fell back. I missed the other, who fired off a wide shot that hit the ceiling above my head, raining plaster down on me as I fired again, hitting him squarely in the chest.

The man I'd hit in the shoulder was aiming at me, when a woman, small, quick and fearless, launched herself onto his back sending him flying forward, his gun firing wide, then hitting the floor near my feet. The woman kicked the gun away from him, her small form moving at a speed that seemed almost impossible. She was on the man's back, his arms pinned under her knee, his head held down by her hands. The other three guards were dead, taken out by Loki. Merl stumbled forward. "Mo," he said.

The small fury of a woman on the guard's back looked up and, seeing Merl, tears filled her eyes. He crossed the room, leaning on his right leg more than his left, his shoulder on that side also slightly stooped.

Mo, still holding down her victim, watched him approach, a smile growing wider across her face. Another prisoner, a man who obviously knew Mo, touched her shoulder and she stood up, letting him take over pinning the guard.

Merl stopped in front of her and she reached out tentatively, touching his swollen eye. His head was bent toward her. She only came up to the middle of his chest. So small and yet so strong.

Merl stepped closer and she did not back away. I watched them, riveted by their movements. Tears were running down Mo-Ping's cheeks. Merl touched her hip with his good hand and pulled her body against his before lowering his lips to her. She wrapped her hands into his tangled, dirty hair and held him close. Their kiss was at first tentative but quickly turned passionate. Their bodies melded together, their hands gripping onto each other. I turned away, the moment suddenly too intimate to watch.

I looked at Loki who was watching the exit. "More will come," he said. "We have to go now."

"Yes," I agreed.

I crossed the room, walking up behind Merl, and cleared my throat. They continued to kiss. Mo's hands moving down Merl's neck and grasping at his shoulders.

"Merl," I said, my voice low. He didn't notice. "Merl," I said louder. Still no response. I looked over at Loki. He motioned for me to try again. Turning back to Merl I reached out and touched his shoulder. "Merl," I said loudly, giving him a little shake.

He broke the kiss, keeping his arms around Mo, and turned to me.

His eyes were a little glazed, there was a happiness there I'd never seen before. The power of their emotions took my breath away—the fact that even in this insane situation, with blood and pain evident on both their persons, they could be so happy. My heart squeezed. I wanted that kind of happiness, but was terrified of it. Such happiness was dangerous. Because if it was taken from you, it could break you. And I didn't ever want to be broken again.

CHAPTER EIGHTEEN
ESCAPE

The rising sun had cleared the mountains by the time we stepped out into the yard of the tai chi center turned prison camp. Mo Ping had her arm around Merl's waist, supporting him and holding him close. Loki pushed open the gate and stepped through, holding it open for others. The street was quiet. The cars the backup guards had arrived in stood silent in the road.

We walked up the road, headed back to the van, while the freed prisoners dispersed in small groups into the countryside. The dampness of early morning hung in the air. The doctor was where we had left him, shoved between the seats, chained to one of the hooks in the floor. Loki freed him and the doctor stumbled out of the van. Dark circles had formed under his eyes. His white jacket was wrinkled and crusted with dried blood. I wanted to have him take a look at Merl's wounds but didn't think we had time so we just left him there on the side of the road.

Loki took the driver's seat of the van, I got in the passenger seat and Blue fit himself at my feet. He was sprayed with blood, one paw coated with it. I hadn't even noticed earlier.

Merl and Mo climbed gingerly into the back. Merl rested his head against the seat and closed his eyes. Mo Ping held his hand. Loki pulled out onto the deserted road. I looked back at the tai chi center as we drove by it. The building looked quiet. I wondered how long it would take for the army to show up. For them to start to hunt down the prisoners we'd released. Would we make it out of the country in time? Or would our plane be stopped? Would we all end up back in a place like that, or worse?

We continued down the mountain and as the sun drifted toward the top of the world we drove along the rutted road, past the paddy fields, toward our freedom. "Wait," Merl said. "Stop the van."

Loki pulled over. The wind brought the dust that had plumed behind us forward, enveloping the van, making it feel like we were in a brown fog. Merl slid open the van door and climbed out. I followed him as did Mo. Blue stretched, waving his tail and let out a yowl with his yawn. I recognized the spot. It was close to where we'd hit those tacks the first time we tried to get out to the tai chi center. The blackened remains of the Jeep were just down the road. Ming and the police officers we'd left tied up were nearby. I considered freeing them but decided it was too dangerous. I hoped they'd be found but wouldn't risk anything to guarantee it.

Merl whistled, loud and high-pitched. The sound echoed back to us. "What are you doing?" Loki asked.

"My dogs," Merl said. "They should be around here." He whistled again.

Loki looked at me. "I think I saw them," I said. Merl smiled. "That first night we tried to get to the tai chi center. I saw eyes in the rocks, I knew they were animals. I wondered if they were Merl's dogs."

Merl whistled again. Michael, the largest member of Merl's pack, popped up from behind a boulder thirty feet away. Seeing Merl he bolted for him. Lucy, the bitch of Merl's pack, was close behind him. Chula, the youngest and newest member came around the side of the boulder, his tongue hanging out of his head and sprinted after them. They were three streaks of black across the brown ground.

Merl kneeled down and they skidded to a stop, then approached Merl slowly, their tails wagging, ears pinned to their heads. He opened his arms and they all crowded in, curling their bodies, shuddering with pleasure, letting out noises of excitement and contentment. Blue's tail wagged at seeing his friends.

Merl spoke to them softly, telling them how good they were, how happy he was to see them. Mo rested her hand on his shoulder, looking down at the reunion. "So this is where they got you?" I asked.

Merl nodded. "Yes, Sing and I were driving when we blew out a tire. I hit my head on the wheel and Sing broke a couple of ribs I think." Mo's hand tightened on Merl's shoulder. He wasn't looking at me, his eyes still on his dogs, seeming to draw strength from them as he told his story.

"We climbed out. I knew there was a chance this was an attack but my head was fuzzy from the impact. There were five of them." Merl looked up into the rocks, his eyes narrow, seeming to see the men in front of him now. "They had rifles. There were too many of them. We fought but eventually I realized that we didn't have a chance. I sent the dogs away."

I'd done something similar once with Blue. It was in Mexico with Malina, when we'd been kidnapped. Merl had taught me the command "Out." It meant for the dogs to run for cover but not wander far. The three Dobermans would have spent the rest of their lives within a mile or two of this place, waiting for Merl's return.

"We should go," I said.

"Yes," Loki agreed. "We don't have much time."

Merl stood up slowly, his body weak but determined. He caught my gaze with his one good eye. The other was swollen shut. "I failed," he said.

I shook my head. "No, Merl—"

He cut me off, "They shot Sing," Merl said, closing his good eye. A tear snuck from under the lid.

"We can't win them all," I said.

Merl shook his head. "I was foolish. I tried to fight them." The ghost of a smile crossed his lips. "We took out two," Merl said, and I knew the "we" meant him and his dogs. "But there were just too many. I should have been more careful."

Mo Ping pulled at his arm and Merl opened his eyes and looked at her. She shook her head, her eyes glowing up at him. She said something I couldn't understand and Merl nodded slightly before allowing her to lead him to the van.

We all climbed back into the vehicle, the three dogs joining Merl and Mo in the back. I knew I needed to tell them about Bai Sing but I didn't want to pile on the grief at this moment. It could wait.

His pack back together, feeling safe for the first time in a long time, Merl fell asleep, Mo's head resting on his shoulder, her breath as even as his. "They must be so tired," I whispered to Loki.

His eyes flicked to the rearview mirror and he looked at them for a moment, his expression unreadable. "Have you ever loved like that?" I asked. The question had floated through my brain and out of my mouth without a filter. Loki seemed to flinch. "I'm sorry," I said. "It's none of my business. I shouldn't have asked."

Loki's jaw was tight, his eyes squinting against the bright sun of the new day. "I have not," he answered.

"Me either," I said. "Not like that, where it's mutual and..." I looked down at my hands, crusted with dirt and gore, I'd broken a nail at the center, blood welled around it. I didn't know what the word was, how to say what they had that was different than what I'd ever had. Or would ever have. There was innocence to it, a trust I'd never be able to offer.

Loki continued to watch the road, and a long stretch of silence spread between us, punctuated only by the wheezing of the van as we bounced over rocks and the constant hum of the engine. But I felt that he knew what I was talking about. Maybe he didn't have the words either. I didn't think Loki could love either. Not like those two in the back. Faith, I realized then. That's what it was. They had faith. Faith that something good could last.

Tears welled in my eyes, surprising me with their burning. I turned my face, staring out the window at the rice paddies, at the grasses rustling in the wind, the sun sparkling off the muddy water, the blue sky and those unreal mountains. A tear escaped, slipping down my cheek, hanging perilously onto the edge of my jaw before dropping to my shirt.

My phone rang, bringing my attention back to the present. Bobby's voice sounded relaxed. "How did it go?" he asked.

"We're on our way to the airport," I said. "Is the plane waiting?"

"Yes, the first flight will take you to South Korea. I have a member of my team meeting you there. He will bring you up to speed on the rest of the travel plans. You're running later than you expected."

"We had some unforeseen complications."

He cleared his throat. "I've got one of those myself."

"Oh really?"

"Yes, the IPO is going to be fine. There won't be a problem."

"It's in two days, right?"

"Yes, so there isn't time for the news to hit before it happens."

"What news?" I asked, feeling the hairs on the back of my neck raise. Blue pushed his nose into my free hand, his body warm against my legs. I pet his head, listening to Bobby breathe on the other end of the line, across the world, and yet sounding so close.

"There is a whistle-blower."

"A whistle-blower?"

"Yes, and I can't seem to find out who."

We drove through the village where Loki and I had stayed. Tourists still filled the shops or were pulled along in rickshaws, fruit stands bursted with exotic fruits, everything was as we'd left it. "Does it matter? I mean you planned on leaving after the IPO."

"No, it's fine." A waver in his voice, something I'd never heard before.

"You sound unsure."

"It's Declan Doyle."

"What do you mean?" I asked.

"He is blowing the whistle on you, on me, on everything. That we are working together, that I killed Kurt Jessup, everything."

"Everything?" I said, my mind wrapping itself around the massiveness of the lies and secrets about to be exposed.

"Yes."

"I don't care," I said.

Bobby laughed. We were through the village now. I saw a small plane in the distance, making a final approach to the airport. Its wings glinted in the noon day sun. "Well, I guess it will be fine. Except, of course, for the people in your life who are not related to Joyful Justice. Like your mother."

Her face popped into my mind and I pushed it away, swiped it from my vision, smearing her image into a color palette. "I don't care," I said.

"Cold."

"Frozen."

"What about the fact that the myth of you killing your brother's murderer was the inspiration for Joyful Justice. You don't think exposing that lie will change anything?"

"I've never admitted to killing him."

Loki looked over at me and then back at the road.

Bobby laughed. "We can talk about it tomorrow."

"Fine, I'm almost at the airport. Can you have a doctor meet us when we land?" I asked.

"Sure," Robert said. "Have a safe flight."

Merl stirred as we pulled next to the small landing strip. Our jet was waiting. The flight attendant stood at the top of the steps, her eyes shining with the pleasure of serving us. Then her gaze ran over Merl and Mo in their prison rags, the three Doberman Pinschers, the blood on Loki and me, Blue's red-splotched fur, and her face fell, the color draining.

I pretended not to notice. This small plane just had to get its motley passengers out of Chinese air space. Once in South Korea we could get back to the island without much trouble. Loki saw us onto the plane and then started to take his leave.

"You're not coming with us?" I asked.

Loki looked surprised. "My life is here," he said.

"But," I looked over at the flight attendant. "Give us a moment please." She nodded and hurried to the back of the plane, busying herself with coffee cups. "Aren't you in danger? You think it's safe to stay in China?"

"I think it is safe enough."

"But what about Ming and the police? Won't they come after you? Won't they figure out you were involved in what happened at the prison camp?"

192

"I will be back in Shanghai by this evening. I have protection there. Do not worry about me," he smiled and took my hand. "Call me next time you visit the city. It would be my pleasure to host you again."

I laughed. "You're serious."

"Entirely."

"Okay, good luck," I said.

He nodded, squeezing my hand before turning to Merl. They shook hands briefly, Merl thanked him again for his help. "I wish you safe travels," he said, shaking Mo's hand in turn. Then he left. I crossed to the window and watched him climb back into the van. I hoped he was right, that he would be safe but I was frightened for him. How could I not be?

"Please take your seats," the flight attendant announced over the PA system. "We are taking off momentarily."

I sat down in one of the big leather chairs and put on my seat belt, watching through the window as Loki drove away, dust pluming from behind the van.

We landed in South Korea hours later. A man met us at the plane. He introduced himself as "Agent Fields, I'm a friend of Robert Maxim's." He was about six feet tall, wearing a dark suit with a bright blue tie and dark sunglasses. Looking Merl up and down he continued, "I have a house waiting and a doctor on call." He drove a Mercedes, black and shiny with tan leather interior and tinted windows. The license plate had a diplomatic tag on it.

The house was large, owned by an "associate of Mr. Maxim's." The doctor had white hair, an understanding smile and a black bag right out of the 1950s. After bandaging Merl's wounds and giving him antibiotics he left, accepting no payment. "When do we leave?" I asked Agent Fields.

"Two hours," he said. "There is food if you're hungry." We were all starving and devoured the provided meal without a word passing among us.

CHAPTER NINETEEN
REDUX

I slept most of the way back to the island. Merl and Mo talked in low whispers and the rise and fall of their voices lulled me into a deep rest. I didn't wake until we touched down on the runway. I sat up, reaching out into space at the jolt and found Blue waiting. He leaned against my leg and looked up at me, the devotion in his eyes almost unreasonable. "Hey boy," I said, leaning over and kissing the top of his head. He closed his eyes and sighed appreciatively.

Dan was waiting for us as we disembarked. Merl and Dan embraced, their hug tight. Merl introduced Mo and Dan shook her hand. "It's a pleasure to meet you," he said.

"Thank you for having me, for helping us."

Dan nodded. "Of course. Come on, you must all be hungry," Dan said, putting his arm around me in greeting, squeezing my shoulder. "Good to see you," he said as we walked to the Jeep. Blue pushed up against Dan. "You too, boy," he said, letting me go to pet Blue before getting in the Jeep.

I felt like I was living in a loop. How many days had it been since I first landed on the island? Since I accused Dan of betraying me to Bobby Maxim. And here, I'd just used that connection to get myself out of a very tight jam. I counted in my head—nine days had passed. It felt like longer.

"Did Mitchel make it back?" I asked as I got into the passenger side. Blue hopped up into the seat well, just fitting in at my feet.

Dan nodded his head. "The kid too, with his mom." He looked over at me. "He's got potential. And a burning desire, which is half the battle really."

"That's great. What about his mom?"

Dan smiled. "She can't really believe she is here. Started crying when she saw her room." There was something in Dan's eyes as he looked at me, a look too close to admiration, and I turned away. "She is helping out in the kitchen," Dan said.

Merl and Mo settled into the back seat with his three dogs and we started toward the volcano.

"Have you talked to Bobby?" I asked, pushing my hair behind my ears, trying to keep it under control as the breeze whipped it around my head.

"Yeah, he called. Set up a meeting for tonight."

"Did he say what it was about?"

"Doyle."

"Yeah, what do you think?"

Merl leaned forward between the seats. "What's going on?"

Dan glanced at Mo in the rearview mirror. "Let's talk about it later."

Merl nodded, understanding it was council business.

After a brief but filling meal and a quick shower I met with Dan and Merl in Dan's office overlooking the control center below. Merl's hair was pulled back into its customary ponytail, reaching down his back to his waist. He'd shaved and the wounds on his wrists and ankles were freshly bandaged. He was looking down at the floor below when I walked in. "Amazing, isn't it?" he said, glancing over his shoulder at me, smiling.

"Yes," I agreed. "Incredible."

Dan was sitting on his couch. "The rest of the council will be online in about," he checked his watch, "two hours."

"What's going on?" Merl asked. "What did I miss?"

"We've been in a holding pattern until the IPO goes through. We've continued surveillance and any missions that didn't involve Fortress Global clients, but we're ready to move starting tomorrow." I felt a thrill run up my spine thinking about the seven missions set to go off the following day. I'd read all the files the last time I was here and was looking forward to watching them go down.

"The new news," Dan continued, "is that Declan Doyle—" Dan looked at Merl making sure he knew whom we were talking about.

"The New York detective turned homeland security officer who knows that Sydney is actually Joy Humbolt and has been chasing her for years."

"Right, he is whistle-blowing," I said.

"What does that mean?" Merl asked.

"According to what Robert told me he is going public about Bobby and Joyful Justice, about Sydney being Joy, and we're not sure what else. He claims to have evidence. Video footage from Costa Rica."

"When he tried to capture Sydney and Robert?"

"Right."

"But that was an illegal mission."

"Exactly, he's trying to blow up the U.S government, Fortress Global, and Sydney/Joyful Justice all at once."

"How?" Merl asked, sitting down in one of the chairs facing the couch where Dan and I both sat.

"An interview on the TV show *Deadline.*"

"What about the rest of us?" Merl asked. "Does he know about the other council members?"

"I don't think so," Dan said. "We've been incredibly careful. Mulberry I'd say is the only other member in danger of being outed."

"He's at the training camp still?"

"Yes."

"When can I get back there?"

"Whenever you want. I'm guessing Mo will be going with you?"

"Yes, she will be an invaluable member of the team."

"I'm sure she will."

"What about her friends?" I asked. "All those other people in the prison camp?"

"She is going to stay in touch with them. I convinced her that we could do more for them abroad than if we stayed," Merl said.

"Do they want out of the country? Should we try to get them to safety?" Dan asked.

"They want to fight the persecution. Mo didn't want to leave," Merl answered.

"I'm glad she did," I said.

Merl smiled. "Me too. But back to this Declan situation. What's the downside for us?"

"Well, Sydney is going to be a wanted woman again making it much harder for her to move around," Dan said.

"That's going to suck," I admitted.

"Her mother is probably going to get surrounded by press. Hugh too. It's going to ruin their lives."

"Hugh will be fine," I said, referring to my brother's boyfriend at the time of his murder. He knew about Joyful Justice and supported it. As a celebrity chef he also knew how to deal with the press.

"What about your mother?" Dan asked.

"I don't care about her."

"Okay," he said, his voice rising at the end of the word, almost like he didn't believe me. Or didn't approve. I ignored any undertones and stared him down.

"What's our other option? Kill him?" I said, holding Dan's gaze. "I'm not interested in that. I don't think he's a bad man. He just thinks I'm evil and what we're doing is wrong. If we killed everyone who thought that we'd be very busy. We need to keep our eyes on the prize, on fighting for justice where we can."

"You're not going to be able to leave this island," Merl said. "You'll go crazy."

"That's not entirely true," I said. "I mean, come on, I can go to our training camp, any one of Lenox's boats," I smiled, joking but not really. "What can I do about it?"

Dan ran his hand through his hair. "And what about Robert?"

"Oh, yeah, he's fucked," I said.

"I mean, don't you think he is going to kill Declan?"

"Did he say that?" I asked Dan.

"No," he shook his head. "But he's ruthless, Sydney, you know that. Robert Maxim is not going to be okay with staying out of the world. He's kept a very low profile for a man in his position and I don't think he's going to let one whistle-blower destroy that for him."

I sat back on the couch, running my hands over the pattern of the fabric, thinking. "You're right," I said. "He'll try to kill him."

"Try?" Dan said. "Since when does Bobby Maxim 'try'? He *will* kill him."

"Where is the interview taking place? Do we know?"

"Robert didn't say but I'm sure he knows."

"If Robert wants to kill him I'm not sure there is anything we can do to stop him," I said. Merl and Dan both nodded, their expressions thoughtful. "All right, well, let's talk to Robert and see what he has to say before we try to make any decisions."

Both men nodded their agreement. Standing up I walked over to the wall of glass that looked down onto the control room below. I thought about the seven missions Joyful Justice planned to unleash the following day. The capture of the chemical plant in the Amazon. We'd warned them to stop dumping dangerous chemicals and they hadn't, so we were shutting the place down. Permanently. The head of a human trafficking ring, a man who thought of himself as a king, was getting kidnapped. It wouldn't destroy his network but it would be a punishing blow. Once we had him in our grasp we'd figure out how to dismantle his empire.

The offshore accounts of several CEOs who'd refused to curb their policies in ways that we had instructed (two dumping cancer-causing chemicals into water sources and one turning a blind eye to slave practices in his manufacturing) were being emptied and distributed amongst their victims. The captain of a fleet of ships used to transport immigrants from Africa to Europe was being relieved of his vessels.

The people below me--typing on their keyboards, talking on their headsets, watching aerial footage that played on the big screen--were all ready for tomorrow. The people we were going after all thought Fortress

Global had taken care of their problems. They'd know soon enough that wasn't true.

I hoped that awakening would happen when our team members came crashing through the door and not Declan Doyle being interviewed on TV. If they found out before we struck that Robert Maxim betrayed them, it would take away our element of surprise. Robert Maxim would end up with a price on his head. As would I. But did that mean we should stop Declan from going public? Did I really have a choice? There was no controlling Robert Maxim.

EK

Two hours later Dan had set up the monitors on his desk to face us Merl and me on the couch. There were three screens. Lenox and Anita appeared on one, the screen split between their two feeds. Mulberry was on another and Robert on the last. Mulberry brought the meeting to order. He looked tan and healthy, Costa Rica seemed to suit him. His jaw showed a slight stubble and he appeared rested, the lines around his eyes less noticeable than the last time I'd seen him.

I recognized the room he was sitting in, it was Merl's dojo. Light poured in through the large tinted windows, weapons gleamed on the wall behind him. "Robert, tell us what you've learned," Mulberry said, crossing his thick arms and leaning back into his chair.

Robert was wearing a crisp white shirt and yellow tie that brought out the green in his eyes. His hair was dark with silver at his temples. The wall behind him was blank white, leaving nothing on the screen to indicate where he was. "As I've told Sydney, Dan, and Mulberry, Declan Doyle is scheduled to give an interview on the TV show *Deadline* tomorrow night during which he will reveal Sydney's true identity, her relationship to Joyful Justice, and my own involvement."

Lenox and Anita both frowned at this news. "I have not heard this," Anita said, her British accent sounded clipped and angry. "And I have contacts there."

Robert smiled, almost condescending. "Clearly, they are not as good as mine."

Anita blushed. Her long dark hair was pulled back and she wore tortoise shell glasses that brought out the warm brown tones in her skin. Her eyes, large, dark and almond shaped, appeared even bigger through the lenses. Her bright green top, silk and fitted, shimmered in the light. A breeze played with tendrils of hair that had escaped her ponytail. She frowned deeply, her lips shiny and pink with gloss. "Or yours are mistaken," she said, her voice icy.

Robert sat back in his chair. "Feel free to contact your people. But I'm telling you it's going to happen."

Lenox, his dark skin lit by a light to the side, sat in a leather chair. Behind him was a bookshelf, the volumes leather bound with gold lettering. Like a law library. "Is there anything we can do to stop it?" Lenox asked.

Robert smiled. "Of course, but I'm not sure you're going to like it."

Mulberry broke in, "Robert, you can tell us what you propose but this is a decision for the council, a group you are not a member of."

"Of course," Robert said, magnanimous. "I totally understand. I would never deem to tell you what to do."

"So what's your idea?" I asked.

"Easy, we kill Declan," Robert said. "He's become a liability. One that needs immediate disposal."

"What about the footage he has?" I asked. "Of you and me in Costa Rica, what do you know about it?"

"Apparently it's off body cameras from his men. There are lots of angles, lots of ways to see us working together, escaping in your helicopter."

"So, even with Declan dead, what about the footage?"

"Well, obviously Homeland Security does not want this getting out. They would never release the footage. In fact, I'm sure they are doing everything in their power to get it back. Declan is keeping it on his person. On a thumb drive."

"If this is in fact happening," Anita broke in, "*Deadline* would have a copy. No way would they go live with an interview without having seen the footage in question and obtained their own copy."

"Well, I guess they decided to make an exception," Robert said. "From what I understand Declan insisted. Very few people know about this. They are keeping it very quiet because of the danger." Robert smiled, his expression cruel. "Obviously, they didn't want us or Homeland Security finding out."

"Any other questions?" Mulberry asked.

"I'd like to say something before I go," Robert said. Mulberry nodded. "I understand that you make the decisions for Joyful Justice but since this directly affects me I need you to know that I'm not going to just let it happen. If you want to take care of it, fine, but I already have things in motion to," he paused, looking dead into the camera, "deal with this. My telling you was an act of goodwill. Not a plea for help."

"I always assumed as much," I said.

Robert hung up and Mulberry raised his eyebrows. "Who wants to go first?"

"I don't think it's true," Anita said. "There are too many things that don't make sense. Not having copies of the footage, my sources not hearing even a whisper about it."

"Maybe Robert just wants to kill Declan," Mulberry suggested.

"Then why come to us at all?" I asked. "It's not like he doesn't know how to make someone disappear."

"Why come to us with it if he plans on taking care of it himself?" Mulberry said.

"Courtesy, like he said."

Mulberry shook his head. "Courtesy," he muttered.

Lenox broke in. "The damage is substantial to Homeland Security. Perhaps we should inform them and see if they can get it shut down."

Mulberry nodded. "I could make some phone calls. I know a few people over there."

"I don't know," I said. "Seems to me it implicates you. I mean why would you know about it? You and Declan were never friends. Why would you have that information? If this stuff does come out you are the only other member of this council likely to get linked to Joyful Justice."

"I could let them know," Dan said. "I have a connection."

"Who?" Mulberry asked.

"A friend, he got caught hacking into...well, let's just say that as a part of his plea bargain he has to work for Homeland Security until they tell him otherwise."

"Good," Mulberry said. "You contact him, and Anita, you reach out to your contacts, find out if you can substantiate any of this. Let's reconvene in," he looked down at his watch. "an hour. Sound good to everyone?"

It was agreed and we got off the line. Dan went over to his computer and I grabbed my phone to place a call. Merl stood up, "I'll be back in an hour." His three dogs rose with him. They followed him out the door and I watched them until they disappeared down the spiral staircase while I listened to the phone ring.

"Sydney," Robert said when he picked up. "You want to know about my plan."

"Just so we don't end up stepping on each other's toes," I said. "It would be terrible to have our assassins kill each other instead of the man in question."

Robert laughed. "Yes, that would be a real shame."

"So, is that your plan? Killing him?"

"Sweet and simple."

"When?"

"That I don't know for sure. I have a professional on it. They are on deadline though. And this one doesn't miss deadlines. What is your merry band of revolutionaries doing about it?"

"A number of things."

"Checking out my story."

"Obviously."

"Dan is reaching out to his contact at Homeland Security." I didn't say anything. "Anything else?"

"I'm not at liberty to say."

"Oh come now Sydney, I know your games."

"Sometimes I make moves you don't expect."

He laughed. "Yes, and that's why I enjoy you so much." He paused and I could almost hear him thinking. "Don't try to stop me," he said, his voice low.

"Why would I do that?"

"Some idea about right and wrong."

"That would be some crazy idea," I said.

"Sydney, I don't want to live on the run for the rest of my life. And neither do you. Never showing your face anywhere outside of your little Joyful Justice camps, that's no life for you."

He was right, the idea of never going on another mission made my throat squeeze and my heart pound. Like I was locked in a coffin and could hear clumps of dirt hitting the lid. "I don't want that," I said. "But Declan Doyle is a good man."

"He is a traitor."

"A traitor?"

"Yes, he is betraying his government -"

I cut him off. "I thought the American government was a reflection of its people. And I'm pretty sure this isn't betraying them. This is informing them of their nation breaking sovereignty laws and exposing us for the criminal vigilantes we are."

"I thought you were a revolutionary."

"I know what I am, Robert. And it's nothing noble."

"But surely nothing as petty as a criminal." I heard a voice in the background. "I have to go," Robert said. "We'll talk again soon."

An hour later the Joyful Justice council reconvened. Anita started. "My contact confirmed there is a special episode tomorrow night, it's been on lockdown. Very few people have the details, including my source."

Mulberry frowned. "I guess we can assume that Robert is telling the truth then."

"What reason would he have to lie?" I asked.

"Who knows?" Mulberry said. "You seem to have the most insight into him these days."

I ignored his comment and turned to Dan. "Did you talk to your friend?"

"Yeah, he is looking into it. Hasn't heard anything about that mission, let alone footage leaking."

"Well," I said. "Bobby is moving forward with taking Declan out. I don't think there is anything we can do about it."

"We could warn Declan," Dan suggested.

"I'm sure he knows that his life is in danger," Mulberry said. "And reaching out to him feels foolish."

"I don't know," I said. "If we give him a heads up it might put us in his good graces. Let him know we're not totally without scruples."

"I'm fine with Sydney calling him," Lenox said.

"Oh, I didn't mean that I should call him. Just like an anonymous note. Couldn't you send him something untraceable?" I asked Dan.

He shrugged. "We have no idea where he is. Do you even have an email address for him? I'm not sure I could find a phone number. He must be hiding under some pretty thick cover."

"I think it's better coming from you," Lenox said, addressing me.

"Why?"

"You're the obsession."

"What do you mean?"

"From what I understand, and correct me if I'm wrong, he's been chasing you for years. Even before Joyful Justice he was convinced you were still alive and had been trying to find you."

"So, why feed that fire?" I said. "Let him get a note. It will have the same effect. Which, I'll admit, I don't think is going to be much. This is the kind of thing that Robert is very good at."

"Killing men who are about to tell his secrets," Mulberry said.

"It sounds like the point is moot anyway, right Dan? How could we even get hold of him?"

"It's possible I could get some kind of contact information from my guy at Homeland Security."

Mulberry spoke. "Dan, why don't you see what kind of contact information you can gather, then we can decide about contacting him." A murmur of agreement rose from the group.

I turned to Anita. "What do you think the impact will be?"

She raised her eyebrows. "Huge. Multi-pronged. There is the issue of your identity, which will change the way you move around in the world. The fact that Joyful Justice is working with Fortress Global is not going to look good for either organization. Also, the missions set to move forward will be more exposed. It will be obvious to anyone paying attention that we waited till after the IPO. It will look like we're manipulating the stock market. Not a popular move."

"Aren't we?" I asked.

Anita's eyes narrowed. "It's not the primary objective. You're the one who wanted to delay."

"I'm not arguing that," I said. "We're doing it for the resources and knowledge that Robert Maxim provides. Not to mention the additional funds."

"Yes, it's a deal with the devil, but a good one."

"Should we move forward earlier?"

"No," Mulberry said. "Everything is in place. It's not safe to change it now."

"Clearly, it would be better for us if this did not air," Lenox said.

"Decidedly yes," Anita said. "Much better."

"I'm not comfortable with killing a good man for our convenience," Dan said.

"None of us are," Anita said. "But convenience may not be the right word here. It jeopardizes everything. It will be very hard to regain trust, to rebuild our brand. It could end Joyful Justice."

"That's a little dramatic don't you think?" I asked.

Mulberry broke in. "How do we know Robert doesn't want this?"

"Why would he want this, his reputation will be destroyed."

"Sure, but he's about to get stinking rich. The guy can fake his own death and go live on a beach somewhere, having destroyed Joyful Justice as his final act."

"And his own company?"

"Not necessarily," Mulberry said, leaning forward. "He could say he was acting alone, that Fortress Global's management didn't know anything about it, which is true."

"He started the company. It will be destroyed if they learn he was working with us," I said. "It doesn't make sense. I think we just need to sit back and see how this plays out."

Everyone was staring at me, a little surprised. Dan spoke first. "I think that's the first time I've ever heard you suggest that action not be taken."

"Maybe I'm learning," I said.

Merl spoke for the first time. "I agree with Sydney. Warning Declan puts us in danger and will very unlikely be news to him plus, how do we even get a hold of him? The man knows Robert Maxim, he knows his life is in danger. I'm sure he is taking serious precautions. We've agreed that this council does not want to order his murder ourselves. So we wait. Our missions will continue as they would before."

Anita spoke. "What if we lose people because of this? What if some of the members who are going out on these missions balk because of the revelations?"

"That's not going to happen," Merl said. "All the people going out to fight are fighting for their own communities. They came to us, remember? They have more to gain from these missions than we do."

Anita nodded. "I guess you're right. Let's see what happens and then we'll figure out our next move."

With that decided Mulberry moved on to going over the missions for the following day. I listened but there was no role for me in any of them. They'd all been planned before I joined the council. "The live feeds will be running for all the missions," Dan explained. "You've all got your log in information?" The group confirmed they did.

"Is there anything else?" Mulberry asked.

There wasn't and so we got off the line, agreeing to talk after the missions were over. Fortress Global's stock would hit the market at 11:30 pm our time tonight, 9:30 am New York time. With Declan's interview that evening and our missions the next day, it was going to be a busy forty-eight hours.

CHAPTER TWENTY
MISSION IMPOSSIBLE

Dan, Merl, and I were in his office again that evening watching as the stock market opened in New York. Robert Maxim rang the opening bell, smiling at the crowd of traders on the floor below him. He looked rested and unconcerned, wearing a tailored suit and green tie. He shook hands with the men around him. All white, all with that same self-satisfied look, Masters of the Universe.

Fortress Global stock started out strong and continued to sell well. After a half hour Merl excused himself and I left with him. Dan stayed up, he was always a night owl, his best ideas coming to him long after the sun set and hours before it rose again. Merl and I walked through the control room. There were a couple people at desks, their faces pale in the blue glow of their screens. The giant screen that stretched along the front wall was dark.

"How is Mo doing?" I asked. "Has she been in contact with her friends?"

"Yes, they all escaped, they are staying in a safe house north of the prison camp. There are no roads to it and they are pretty sure the government is not aware of its existence."

"What are they going to do?"

"They are trying to figure that out now."

"It seems like an intractable problem."

"Yes, like so many others."

We rode in the elevator in silence. Our dogs were at our feet, sitting patiently, watching for our next move.

"Want to run in the morning?" I asked.

Merl smiled. "I would love that."

"*Deadline* will be on at 10 am. Meet at 8?"

"Perfect." Merl was on the 3rd floor and got off there, turning toward his room, his pace picking up as he headed down the hall. He's excited to see her, I thought.

The doors closed and Blue and I rose to the fifth floor. We walked down to our room. The same one we stayed at a week ago, right next to Dan's. I let us in and turned on the light. I was tired but also felt a nervous energy coursing through me.

I drank a big glass of water and stared out into the dark sea. It was a cloudy night and the sky and ocean were barely distinguishable from each other. The mountainside was just another tone of black. I sat down on the couch and rested my head against the back. Blue hopped up next to me and laid down, placing his head on my lap.

I woke up with the sun just starting to cast its light onto the day. It had not yet risen over the horizon, but the soft gray tones announcing its arrival filled the room. Blue lifted his head when I shifted and stood. He followed me into the bedroom where I peeled off my clothing and climbed under the cool sheets. Closing my eyes I fell right back to sleep.

My phone woke me. "Ready for our run?" Merl asked. The curtains in my room were pulled closed, but a streak of sunlight shot from between them.

"Yeah, give me ten minutes."

I hung up the phone, brushed my teeth, dressed quickly in my jogging clothing, and headed downstairs, Blue tapping his nose against my hip, enthusiastic about the run to come. Merl was waiting for me in the lobby with his three dogs. Their black coats gleamed, sleek and dangerous looking. Merl's hair was tied up into a bun at the back of his head. He wore sweatpants and a tight black T-shirt. His forearms were peppered with bruises, his wrists wrapped in gauze. His eye was looking much better though, the swelling way down, the color fading from deep purple to a serpentine green.

I led him through the underground passages to the path I'd taken my first time here. We ran side by side on the shaded path, our dogs behind us, Blue and Lucy followed by Chula and Michael. Merl set an even pace and I stuck with him. He'd taught me to love running. To love exercise and the power it gave me over my mind and body. We reached the end of the shaded path and continued around the side of the volcano, the ocean on our left, the steep hillside rising up on our right. As the path narrowed I let Merl pull ahead and fell in line behind him.

The wind played with Merl's hair, pulling strands of it free from the band that held it in place. I watched his shoulder blades rise and fall as his arms pumped with each step. "It's about thirty miles around so we should turn back once up here," I said. There was a widening of the path in front of us, where a bench was placed against the hillside.

Merl slowed to a walk as we approached it. We did tricep presses on the bench, then pushups, and finally sit-ups, our feet entangled, holding each other in place. Our dogs sat patiently, watching us.

Before returning to the compound we sat on the bench, facing the ocean, sipping water. "There is something I have to tell you," I said. Merl looked over at me. "Sing's granddaughter." Merl's eyes narrowed. "She was killed." His entire body tensed. A vein in his neck bulged. "I'm sorry."

He broke from my gaze and turned back to the sea. "How?" he asked, his voice raspy with emotion.

"She was shot. A sharpshooter. We were on the roof of Sing's building in Shanghai. They must have been waiting for her." Merl nodded. "I'm sorry," I said again.

"So much loss," he said.

"Did you know her well?"

"I only met her once. When I went to Sing's she was there with him. Together they explained to me about what had happened to Mo Ping, how Bai and her friends were trying to help. She led us over the roofs. She thought the CCP was watching the front door." He looked down at the bandages on his wrists for a moment and then back over at me. "I should have called you. Asked for help."

I shook my head. "You didn't know."

"When they hit our car."

"On your way to the tai chi center?"

Merl nodded. "I hit my head so hard." He looked over at Lucy on the ground. "Lucy knew I was out of it. She kept nudging me, got us out of the car. When those men grabbed me, I fought, the dogs fought. But when I heard the gunshot and I saw Sing fall, it was like a part of me went with him. I knew that they'd won, that there were too many of them and I gave up."

"You did the right thing."

"Did I?" Merl said with a small laugh. "I think I could have killed them all."

"What do you mean?"

He looked at me, there was something in his eyes I'd never seen before. "I was scared Sydney, not of dying, of the rage. The rage I felt at seeing Sing fall. I wanted to kill them all, to disembowel them, to make them suffer. To—" he looked out to the ocean again. "I don't even know, I felt like an animal." He shook his head. "No, not an animal. Like a man. Animals don't seek revenge, they don't want to torture each other. I wanted to hurt them. Really hurt them."

I nodded, understanding.

"And I could have," Merl continued, not looking at me, his eyes focused on the distant horizon. "In my mind, I saw the moves I needed to make, the way to use my pack to kill them all."

"Why didn't you?"

He shook his head. "I didn't want to."

"Because of what it would mean about you?"

He nodded. "I don't want to kill because of rage and hate, Sydney." Merl looked over at me and there was a softness in his gaze, the calm and humanity I was used to seeing there.

"Then you did the right thing."

"How many more people died because of my decision?"

I shook my head. "I don't know."

Merl led on the way back. I enjoyed the even pace, the fact that the speed at which I ran was not something I needed to think about. I liked to jog and sprint but only because I could never settle into the steady rhythm that Merl set. He was an important presence in my life. I felt gratitude that I'd been able to get him back. And fear that I might lose him.

EK

My cell phone was ringing when I stepped out of the shower. I grabbed a towel and dried off quickly, but by the time I got back to my room the phone had stopped. It was an unknown number. My hair dripped onto my shoulders as I held the phone looking down at the missed call message. Then it started to ring again. I swiped it to answer. "Hello?"

"Sydney, it's Declan."

I felt my throat tighten with fear. My eyes jumped to the window. The sun was shining, the sea was calm, small white clouds hovered at the horizon looking innocent and picturesque. "Hello," I said, keeping my voice even.

"We need to talk."

"Isn't that what we are doing?"

He laughed. The sound was at once familiar and foreign. We'd been something to each other once. Something intimate and fun. Now the connection felt even stronger. We were prey and predator. But I had a feeling we both thought we were the predators. "I'm guessing you've heard about *Deadline*."

"Yes," I said. "A desperate move."

"I knew that Robert would try to stop me." I didn't say anything, letting the silence well between us. I felt water trickling off my shoulders. Blue tapped his nose to my hip. I looked down at him. His one blue eye and one brown held my gaze. "I'm expecting that you'll also be sending someone after me."

"No," I said.

"No?"

"I don't want to kill you. As you know, I had my chance not that long ago."

"That was before I threatened to reveal you for what you truly are."

"And what's that?"

"A patsy."

"You don't know what you're talking about," I bluffed.

"I know you didn't kill Kurt Jessup. Don't you think that little detail, the very root of Joyful Justice's pride in you, will affect it? That it wasn't James Humbolt's sister but a powerful and ruthless business mogul who provided justice. Seems to go against everything you stand for."

"Joy Humbolt is dead," I said. "Anyone who has turned her into a hero deserves the disappointment they find when their faith in her is shattered."

"You really believe that?"

"Yes." I felt rooted to the floor. His voice was the only sound. This conversation the most important I'd ever had. "You can reveal whatever you want about me. I'm not afraid of the truth."

"What about the rest of your membership?"

"We can't be built on mistrust."

"And here I was calling to make you a deal."

"For what?"

"You."

"And in exchange?"

"I'll keep my mouth shut."

"I'd be worried about it being shut for you."

He laughed again, that deep rumble I would never forget. It seemed to fill the room, to fill my mind. He had the upper hand. I might be far away, in the middle of an ocean, surrounded by friends, but he had me. Wherever he was, Declan Doyle was holding me in place. "Do you know who he sent after me?"

"No."

"Well, they're dead now."

"You think he'll stop?"

"You can stop him."

"Stop talking in riddles. Tell me what you want."

"Turn yourself in to me."

I laughed. "Why would I do that?"

"So that I don't destroy Joyful Justice."

"You overestimate yourself. And you overestimate me. I'm not the most important thing about Joyful Justice. It's the people who have created it. The men and women who are rising up to take down those who oppress them, poison them, treat them like they're less than human. Don't you see that? Joyful Justice is bigger than any individual. Taking me in to custody wouldn't do a thing to hurt it."

"You're making my point for me. Don't you see, Joy?"

"My name is Sydney Rye."

"Don't you see," he repeated, an edge to his voice, the trace of frustration, "my revealing your connection to Bobby Maxim, to Fortress Global, the information I have, is much more damaging than you turning yourself in to me."

"Why would you want me then? Wouldn't it be better to destroy Joyful Justice than one 'patsy' behind it?"

"You need to pay for your crimes."

"And what about you," I said, stepping forward, bypassing the bed and pacing toward the window, my feet suddenly free, anger rising in my chest. "You broke the law coming after us in Costa Rica. Why am I so much worse than you? Why are you so fucking great?"

"I'm on the right side."

"Says you."

"Turn yourself in or I'll talk."

I didn't answer.

"Think about it. I'll call you back in twenty minutes."

He hung up. I looked down at the phone. My hand was shaking. I threw the phone across the room—it hit the carpeting and slid up against the molding. I didn't know what to do. Blue touched my hip and I looked down at him. I couldn't turn myself in. What about Blue? I'd have to leave him behind. Leave him with Merl. It suddenly dawned on me that I was already planning my surrender, I was figuring out how to get away without telling anyone. How to disappear, to let Declan Doyle take me. Joyful Justice was bigger than me. Declan Doyle was right.

When he called back I was dressed, my phone in my hand, sitting on the floor with my back against the bed, looking out the window at the big blue sky. Blue lay next to me, his head in my lap. "I'll meet you in two weeks," I said. "I need that long to get my affairs in order."

"One week."

"This isn't a negotiation."

"I agree. Meet me in Tokyo airport in one week or the deal is off."

"Two weeks."

"One."

"Two."

"Let's split the difference."

"No."

"Fine."

I hung up the phone and placed it on the carpeting next to me. Blue was looking up at me. "It's okay, boy," I said. "Everything is going to be okay."

EK

A half hour later Merl, Dan and I were sitting in Dan's office. "Any news?" Merl asked Dan.

"Anita's source called and said something is up, but they weren't sure what."

"You think Declan is dead?" Merl asked.

"Been monitoring the police scanner in New York and have not heard anything." He shrugged. "But I'd imagine anyone working for Robert Maxim would know how to make a body disappear and a missing persons report couldn't be filed for at least forty-eight hours."

Merl glanced at his watch. "We'll know soon enough." He looked worried.

"I think it's going to be okay," I said. Merl smiled at me.

The credits for *Deadline* started. An in-depth news program, its opening sequence showed a ticking clock, clips of police cars racing, bombs exploding, a woman clutching her chest and crying, all the modern atrocities cut into one second segments and flashed on the screen while theme music played.

The host, a middle-aged woman with a flawless forehead, tight skin under her eyes, and blond hair blow-dried into a crown around her face looked straight into the camera. She wore a fitted red suit and sat on a tall stool, her ankles crossed, feet resting on the stool's lower rung. "The interview we planned on airing tonight has been post-poned." She didn't look worried by this fact, just a little apologetic. "We have put together a fascinating program of the biggest stories so far this year..."

"I guess that answers that," I said.

"Does it?" Merl asked.

"What do you mean?"

"We don't know what happened to Declan Doyle."

"And I don't think we have to care," I said, standing up. "Not really. Whatever happened is between Robert Maxim and Declan Doyle."

"You're okay with what Maxim did?" Merl asked.

"I don't know what he did," I said.

"Isn't Maxim dangerous to have in our lives?"

"Dangerous and helpful. Let's not forget that you and Mo are here now because of his intervention."

Dan spoke up. "He has a lot of connections. He can do things we can't yet."

"Yet, exactly," I said. "But with his help we'll be able to."

"With his help will we start killing men like Declan Doyle?" Merl asked.

"I don't think so," I said. "But it's a risk we are taking. Now I'm going to go rest before the missions begin."

EK

I laid down on my bed, the curtains pulled, my eyes closed. Tears welled and pooled, then slipped down my cheeks, curling around my ears before soaking into the pillow under my head. My phone rang and I sat up, wiping at my face.

It was Robert Maxim. "You watched, I presume?"

"Yes."

"Bobby to the rescue again."

"Something like that."

"What do you mean?" He sounded almost insulted.

"Nothing."

"I made it easy for you, Sydney. If I hadn't, if I'd said I was going to let him spill his guts…" He laughed, low and light, almost a chuckle. "Oh, I suppose that's the wrong term to use now, isn't it?"

"Gross."

"Yes, it is 'gross' isn't it?" His voice was suddenly hard. "This business you're in. It's disgusting, Sydney. When are you going to get over that?"

"Fuck off."

"You want to feel, oh yes, I forget sometimes how much you feel. You cover it up so well. But really, I do love that about you. All your sweet little emotions. They drive you so fast and so far."

"What do you want Bobby"?

"I was calling expecting you'd want to thank me."

"For what?"

"For solving another one of your problems. How is Merl by the way, and his sweetheart, what's her name again, Mo something?"

"They're fine, thank you."

"Ah, you're welcome."

"Don't you want to thank me?"

"Of course, for what exactly?"

"For holding off on our missions until your company went public this morning. Congratulations, by the way."

"Yes, thank you. I do appreciate your cooperation. Of course, I'm also paying for it."

"Are you celebrating tonight?"

He laughed. "I'm fleeing," he said, and I could almost see the smile on his face, the twinkle in his eye.

"Want to get out of the states before your clients blow up?"

"Yes, that's part of it, of course."

"Where you headed?"

"I'll call you when I get there. Maybe you'll join me. We have so much to discuss."

"Wire the money by next week, or I'll be hunting you."

He laughed again. "I would so enjoy that Sydney."

"I know, Bobby. I know you would. But since you've given your word I expect there'll be no need."

"Of course not. I am a man of honor."

EK

The first mission, the takeover of a chemical plant in the upper Amazon, was set to start in a less than an hour when I walked into the control center. Consuelo Rojas, the woman in charge, the one who'd brought the case to Joyful Justice in the first place, was seated at a desk in the center of the control room. She wore a headset with a microphone curling around to her mouth.

Consuelo's eyes concentrated on the small screen in front of her as she spoke into the mike. She was in her early thirties, short brown hair cut into a bob that she'd placed pins in to keep away from her face as she leaned over the computer equipment in front of her. I watched her for a moment, too far away to hear her voice as she communicated with her team, but close enough to see the expression of determination set into the lines of her face. Consuelo didn't look worried. She looked ready.

She had come from her village six months earlier to train with Dan while the leader of the raid, her cousin, Elvira Diaz, and the other members of the assault team had been in Costa Rica training with Merl. I'd never met Elvira but I had a passing acquaintance with some of the others. Our language barrier had kept us apart, but all members of Joyful Justice shared a burning desire for exacting justice. It was what drove us to these extremes.

The control room was filled with excited expectation. Tension filled the air and voices rose and fell. All of the desks were full. The missions were separated by a few hours each. We expected to find our targets prepared but overly confident. Even though they had been warned, they all thought Fortress Global had stopped us in our tracks. The head of each organization had received a packet of information and a list of demands from Joyful Justice. None had complied. Now they would find out what we could do.

The large screen that filled the far wall of the control room was split into ten different scenes, one for each helmet cam of our team members. They were moving through the jungle, the images jerking with each step. Most the images were of the backs of the fighters, their guns coming in and out of view. The video quality was not great but it was better than seeing nothing. I concentrated on the leader's view, watching the narrow space between the plants that were being maneuvered through. Leaves brushed up against the lens. It was night and the scene was doused in the eerie green of night vision technology.

A building came into view, the lights on the exterior bright white in the night vision.

A word from Consuelo and the electricity was cut, plunging the building into darkness. Its cement walls brightened again almost immediately in the leader's night-vision feed. The team began to move forward. The leader spoke in Spanish, informing Consuelo of each movement, each step of the operation as it progressed.

I'd read the dossier on the leader, Elvira Diaz, before coming down to the control room. A twenty-three year old woman from the village hardest hit by the toxic dumping. Most of her family, including her younger brother and sister, had died. As her voice came over the speakers around the room, quiet and breathless, I recognized the fearless tone, the confidence she felt in how right she was to be doing what she was doing. When you were that right, it felt like nothing could go wrong.

Dan and Merl stood on either side of me. We were in the back of the room, not vital to this mission, merely the people who had the idea that it was possible to fight back against the big guys. While Joyful Justice had provided valuable assistance through training and funding, our most important contribution was to fuel the power of belief that drove those men and women up to the doors of the chemical plant poisoning their lives.

The assault team knew the layout and location of guards, and several of the night employees were on our side. The guns our warriors carried were loaded with darts filled with a powerful and immediate sedative that left the victim paralyzed for twelve hours. In the grainy footage I watched the leader head for the front door with two people behind her. The rest of the team broke into groups of twos and threes and split off, headed to other entrances.

It wasn't a large structure. Only about five thousand square feet. It stood at the top of a hill, about 50 feet above a tributary to a river that provided water for drinking and irrigation to the villages along it. The plant had been dumping dangerous chemicals into that stream for over five years. Lawsuits, protests, and every other legal means had been attempted to no avail. Now it was our turn.

The teams all reached their doors and placed explosives on the hinges and handles before scurrying back into the night. The explosions all happened at once, bright pulses of green on our screens. My heartbeat picked up as our crews ran in, smoke clearing as they advanced quickly. Gunshots in the left corner of the big screen drew my eye. Our team returned fire. The smoke was thick, a neon green fog, something out of a nightmare, a hallucination.

One of our people was hit, and a teammate was soon facing her. The girl's face was half obscured by her night vision goggles. But I could see a blackened hole in her flak jacket. The woman's lips were set in a painful grimace. But she nodded her head to convey that she was okay, that the bullet didn't penetrate.

The other small teams had taken out the men guarding their entrances. They were all moving through the building, rounding up the few employees working at that hour. The cleaners were working for Joyful Justice. There were six of them, all women who'd lost children to the poisoned river that flowed through their village.

"All clear," came over the speakers. A cry of joy went up in the control room. Consuelo was smiling, still sitting down as people slapped her on the back. Dan cheered next to me and moved forward to congratulate Consuelo.

Blue and the other dogs were standing, their tails wagging at the excitement in the room. Merl put his arm around me and smiled. "Fantastic," he said. "I'm so proud of them."

"Me too," I said quietly. We had been clear that if the dumping didn't stop, if the chemicals were not cleaned up, we'd do it ourselves. And so we planned to. We had hired an expert who was working to gather the equipment and personnel necessary to clean up the river, put things back to how they were or as best we could. It would be impossible to make the community whole but we planned to do all we could. And meanwhile, no more chemicals would flow from the plant.

Missions like this, expensive and complicated, were at the heart of Joyful Justice. Never before had an organization attempted this level of interference on so many fronts. I'd always worried about its viability. But as I stood there watching the celebration in the room I knew that it could work. My part wasn't what I had envisioned though. I wouldn't be blowing doors off hinges, killing evil-doers, leading troops into battle. I was going to turn myself in to keep this going.

The mood quieted before the next mission. Next up was kidnapping the head of a human trafficking ring. This would be difficult because his security was intense. We were not his only enemies. He had competition after all. The man lived in a villa, surrounded by olive trees, in a wealthy community in southern Italy. The screen was split up into twelve sections this time. The lead on our end, replacing Consuelo in the center of the control room, was a man named Harrison Gordon. He was not directly related to the case but had experience in leading groups over satellite, having worked with SEAL teams for twenty years.

Leading this group on the ground was a friend of mine, Tanya. She'd been involved in the very first Joyful Justice attack back in Miami and was someone I spent a lot of time with while at our training camp in Costa Rica. Originally from Moldavia Tanya was a gorgeous blonde, an archetypal Slavic beauty. She had come to the United States following that same old dream of opportunity. But when she arrived on those hallowed shores she was forced into prostitution. With Joyful Justice's help Tanya freed herself and the other women being held with her.

Tonight she was cutting through the darkness, her team behind her, weaving through the olive trees. The gnarled trees were not much taller than Tanya. Half her crew was coming up the other side of the villa. They were surrounding it. The house was lit up, a glowing mansion bathed in eerie green light as seen through the night-vision images. I could see three guards pacing on the wide veranda that surrounded the structure.

The trafficker had upped his security since our warning. I'd suggested that the warnings were a mistake, that it was better just to go in guns blazing, but this was before I was on the council and my approach was considered too brash. We were fighting for justice and needed to give people the chance to correct the error of their ways before bursting into their homes and ripping them from their beds.

The lights in the mansion went out. I could hear Tanya's voice. "Power down, moving forward."

The nanny was one of ours, she'd informed us about the security. The power going out was her signal to get the children to a safe place. Hopefully, nowhere near their father. She felt that he'd fight, would rather die than be taken.

Our team was once again armed with dart guns, sophisticated automatic weapons that could fire almost as fast as a machine gun. But they also had pistols with real bullets on their hips, just in case.

"At perimeter," Tanya said.

Harrison gave her the go ahead.

"Move, stage two," she told her team.

I watched as the twelve screens jerked forward. Tanya was near the veranda, gun up to her eye, shot fired. A man on the veranda, wearing a white suit that blazed in the night-vision effect, grabbed for his neck before dropping to his knees. Another man ran over and began to fire in Tanya's direction. The muzzle of his gun lit up with each bullet's expulsion. He fell, the gun arching up, one final burst exploding from the muzzle.

On another camera I saw a team entering through the back door. A man was waiting, gun up. He fired, blasting white light into the camera. It went out. The video from the trailing team member showed the group's leader dropping to the ground, revealing the shooter in front. Our team member started shooting, and the man grabbed for his stomach, sunk to his knees and tipped over.

The first camera was still out, the screen blank. The second camera tracked from the fallen man to the team member on the ground. A hand extended into the picture, turning over the injured body, bulky in its flak jacket. I could see the face of a young man in a blackened helmet. A hand unbuckled the helmet and lifted it, removing the night vision goggles at the same time. There was a welt on the young man's forehead that leaked blood but didn't look like a bullet hole. The hand lifted the damaged helmet, turning it over. The bullet had dented the helmet and knocked the wearer unconscious, but had not penetrated. The fallen team member was alive, and I could now see his chest moving under the flak jacket.

I let out a breath I didn't know I was holding. Harrison ordered the injured man left where he was. They'd come back for him. They needed to keep moving.

Without hesitation the helmet was replaced for what protection it still provided, and the camera continued down the dark hallway, lit by the night-vision lens into a green and ghostly world.

My eyes flicked to the other cameras to see fighting happening all over the place. I couldn't keep it straight. I looked over at Harrison. He was calm, his body still but his lips going, giving them the information and encouragement they needed as they moved throughout the house, taking out the guards. Finally, Tanya was at the ring leader's office. The house had been cleared except for this room. By Harrison's calculations he was in there with four gunmen.

Tanya placed explosives on the hinges and handles of the ornate double doors. It was a replay of what had happened only hours before but on a different continent.

Tanya and her team backed up, slipping around a corner. The blast shook the house, dust rained from the ceiling, the night vision camera catching it like freshly falling snow. Smoke billowed. Our team had masks and they moved into the blinding smoke quickly and efficiently.

The office doors were blackened and off their hinges, blown into the room. One lay across a couch, a man's legs sticking out from underneath. The other door, what was left of it, was in pieces scattered around the room. Gunfire exploded, white flashes in the smoke. Our team fired back. Moments later there was silence. They approached the knocked out guards, taking time to investigate each face until they found the leader, our target. He was sprawled behind his desk with a dart lodged in his cheek. Arms lifted him and then they were all moving through the house.

Three broke off and picked up the injured team member. He was starting to wake up, his eyes fluttering, looking like white orbs.

Helicopters waited on the lawn and when all were on board another cheer went up inside the control room. Harrison pulled off his headset and embraced his assistant next to him. The room crowded around him in celebration. Another successful mission. Another bad guy taken down.

Dan hugged me, lifting me off the floor. I smiled at him. "This is all going so well," I said.

"You almost make that sound like a bad thing," he grinned at me. "Relax, Sydney. It's going well because we trained for this, because we are super-prepared."

"You're right," I smiled. "I'm very proud of everyone."

Dan hugged me again before going to congratulate Harrison. It was his first mission working for us. I pushed through the crowd, following Dan until we reached Harrison. "Great job," Dan said, holding out his hand.

Harrison shook it, his smile happy but tired. "Couldn't have gone smoother," he said.

Dan turned to see me standing next to him. "Have you met Sydney?" he asked.

"Not yet," Harrison said, extending his hand.

"Congratulations," I said, shaking his hand. "You did a great job."

"Couldn't have done it without this amazing equipment and crew," he said, smiling.

"We're lucky to have someone with your experience."

"Feels good to be here," he said before his attention was swamped by the others waiting to congratulate him.

Dan and I moved back through the crowd and up into his office. Merl joined us soon after. He was smiling. "Good day so far."

"Very good," Dan said.

"No casualties on our side and none we know of on the others. Though that guy under the door might be in some trouble," he said with a frown.

"Hopefully he'll make a full recovery and think twice before going against Joyful Justice again," Dan said with a smile.

"Or engaging in any wrongdoing," I said with a small laugh.

Dan sat down at his desk and woke up his computer. "We're almost done hacking into the accounts, too," Dan said, referencing the bank accounts of two CEOs we were stealing from.

"So, just the ships left," I said.

"Yes," Merl answered me. "We won't have live feed from that but there will be video footage."

I nodded. "Sounds good."

"We'll have a meeting of the council tomorrow?" I said. "To go over everything."

"Yup," Dan answered, absorbed in his computer screen.

EK

I watched the footage of the ships alone in my room later that night. Dan invited me to watch it with him in the main room but I begged off. Not ready for another celebration.

Blue sat next to me on the couch, his head towering above mine. I hit play on the TV. The screen showed a single shot, from a distance, of a quiet and dark marina. It was home to seven large boats, their paint chipping, their holds big enough for thirty but used for a hundred people. It was estimated that over 10,000 people had died on ships like these during illegal crossings to southern Europe.

I understood desperation. The willingness to risk life and limb for the promise of something better. Or at least something different. I'd never been a refugee and could only imagine the untenable circumstances that found them climbing onto those rusting ships. They put themselves and their families at risk to the open sea, the cruelty of heartless smugglers, and the distinct possibility of being caught and returned to the place they'd risked everything to flee.

But I knew about risking everything. I'd resent someone taking that option away from me. Yet that's what we were doing here. Blowing up these ships was another mission I didn't take part in planning. I understood that the man who owned them and the crews who operated them were reprehensible and deserved to lose their livelihood, but it seemed that we were cutting off a way out for desperate people. Even if it was a bad way, it was something.

The first ship blew. Even without sound I still jerked with surprise. The next one went. And down the row. A fiery, black-smoke-pouring catastrophe. I leaned toward the screen, filled with bright orange, deep red, pitch black, shocks of blue, and almost felt the heat of the flames on my skin. It was a hellscape.

I thought of my mother then. Her gray eyes so like mine and my brother's. She believed in hell. She thought her gay son James was there, roasting in flames like the ones on the screen. And that I was headed there as well. What she didn't know is I was creating hell right here on earth.

This is who we were. Creating infernal mayhem for our enemies. Eventually, there would be hell to pay. What kind of hell? I wondered. In my case, I'd know the answer in two weeks.

Turn the page to read an excerpt from
Girl with the Gun, **Sydney Rye Mysteries Book 8, or purchase it now**

and continue reading Sydney's next adventure:
emilykimelman.com/GG

Sign up for my newsletter and stay up to date on new releases, free books, and giveaways:
emilykimelman.com/News

Join my Facebook group, *Emily Kimelman's Insatiable Readers,* **to stay up to date on sales and releases, have exclusive giveaways, and hang out with your fellow book addicts:** emilykimelman.com/EKIR.

SNEAK PEEK

GIRL WITH THE GUN, SYDNEY RYE MYSTERIES
BOOK 8

Suds slipped down my body and gathered at my ankles before traveling in a flotilla to the drain. The white, iridescent bubbles jiggled as droplets of water crashed around them. They popped one by one, the mass sinking into the pipe as each individual bubble lost tension and let go.

Letting go is an art.

And I am not an artist.

I'm a killer.

It's not for pleasure, though there is some of that. Lady Justice is tantamount to my god. I serve her single-mindedly, but there is no blindfold. I am prejudice, human—so human.

Would the world be safer with me under lock and key? One less terrorist wreaking havoc. Or more dangerous? One less soldier fighting for justice.

Blue barked. I looked through the fogged glass seeing nothing but gray shapes in the mist. Blue barked again and I turned the water off and opened the shower door, a cloud of steam coming with me into the room.

Another bark, a "hello," a "there is someone here," a "someone we trust" bark. Grabbing a towel off the rack I left the bathroom; making wet prints on the carpeting as I padded through the bedroom into the living room. Blue sat by the door, his large tail swishing back and forth.

He barked again, turning to look at me, his mismatched eyes bright with excitement. He pushed his large head against my hip, urging me toward the door with a soft whine.

Mulberry stood in the hallway, his broad shoulders taking up the width of the doorway. He wore a subdued yellow and green plaid shirt that brought out the same colors in his eyes. Black stubble glittering with copper, gold, and silver covered his jaw.

Blue pushed past me and wriggled his body against Mulberry's legs. The former New York detective broke his gaze from mine and looked down at my dog. He ruffled Blue's head. "Hey, boy."

"I wasn't expecting you."

Mulberry looked up at me, his hand still on Blue. "That's the first thing you say?"

"Hi."

He smiled and gave off a little laugh. "I figured I'd stop by and see you. We left things a little …"

"I thought I was pretty clear."

"I'm not sure it's entirely up to you to decide."

"I'm not sure about having this conversation in a towel."

Mulberry raised an eyebrow. "I don't think you need it."

"Come on in; I'll get dressed."

He followed me into the living room, clicking the door into place.

I dressed in a pair of dark, indigo jeans and a white T-shirt, one of the few I had without any stains. Blue's tail wagged and his tongue lolled out. "Don't look so excited," I told Blue before returning to the living room.

Mulberry waited on the couch. "You want a drink?"

"Sure."

I crossed to the small kitchenette and grabbed us each a bottle of sparkling water; cracking one open, it released that fizzing sound.

Mulberry came up behind me and placed his hand on my hip. I turned to him and opened my mouth to protest, but he shook his head.

He stepped closer so that our bodies brushed. His face was right above mine, his chin angled down, as I stared at his collarbones.

He fisted the short locks at the base of my skull and pulled gently so that my chin rose and our lips touched. His kiss was achingly familiar and electrifyingly new. The smell of him brought back memories I was afraid to face.

The pain of my brother's murder lanced through me; the paleness of his skin, the vivid red of his blood as he died—the gaping wound his loss left in me.

Everybody I love ends up dead. And not some gentle kiss into the night. They leave this world in violence and suffering; they end in misery.

I couldn't watch Mulberry die.

Was the pain of loving him and denying him worse than the ache I feared?

Mulberry's hand squeezed my hip, pressing our bodies together. His heart thumped so hard that I felt it against my breasts. Light danced behind my closed lids. My hands ran over his strong shoulders, caressing the corded muscles, before curving around his neck, intertwining and pulling at him.

Everything about it felt right, except for the consequences.

Mulberry's hands slipped under my shirt and he groaned against my mouth as the rough callouses of his fingers found my bare flesh.

"Stop thinking so much." His lips moved against my neck.

"I'm trying to be smart."

He laughed, his breath hot against my shoulder. "You've never been good at that."

"Hey."

"You're all instinct." A shiver ran from his lips over my skin. "You're overthinking this thing." I closed my eyes and relished the way we fit, the familiarity and the danger, the tugging of my heart toward him. This love wasn't a controllable force. "Stop trying to keep us all safe, Sydney."

"I have to."

He brought his head up, his steady gaze held mine. "You have to keep yourself safe."

"I'm—"

His eyes narrowed as my voice failed me. He shook his head and smiled a lazy, sexy grin. "You're not going to prison. Only a fool would waste an asset like you."

"What?" Fear spiked through me. "How do you know?" Blue was whining. "Just a minute, Mulberry." I shook him and he just kept up that grin, that all knowing, glinting-eyed smile.

Blue's whine pitched up.

"Stop!" I yelled, rolling over, my sheets tangled around me.

I stared across the expanse of the king-sized bed at Blue, who stood next to it, a soft whine pulling me fully out of the dream. The height of a Great Dane, with the coat of a wolf and the long, regal snout of a Collie, Blue had one blue eye and one brown. His eyebrows were raised and pushed together, creating a crease at the top of his long snout. He was worried about me.

I relaxed into the pillows, staring up at the ceiling. Just me and Blue were in the room. Mulberry was thousands of miles away.

My dreams were getting more vivid. The soft rumble of thunder sent a shiver of panic through me.

I didn't look at the window, not wanting to see that the sky was blue and the Pacific Ocean placid. Not wanting confirmation that my mind was tricking me, again. That I was broken, delusional. Crazy.

I threw off the blankets. Blue pranced happily and licked at my bare knee as I crossed the room to my chest of drawers and pulled out jogging clothes. Blue swung his tail, tapping his feet with excitement.

I shook my head, trying to dispel the unease that throbbed in my body.

I didn't bother with a leash for Blue. Here on the island, it wasn't necessary. I took the elevator down to the ground level and made my way through the warren of passages that led to the outside. Pushing through the final door, the sun glared into my eyes and I squinted against it.

Would this be one of the last times I saw the sun? Would Declan Doyle lock me in a cell without windows? I looked down at Blue and my chest tightened. How could I leave him?

Blue stayed at my hip as I walked along the dirt path. It wound around the volcano. The trail was over thirty miles long so I usually just jogged out for five miles and then back.

I broke into an easy run, my limbs warming up. The day wasn't hot yet, just very warm, the air moist and salty. As we came out from under the tree covering, the Pacific Ocean glittered in front of us. Blue touched his nose to my hip. Did he know how beautiful it was? Even in his black-and-white vision, was the ocean awe-inspiring?

I picked up my pace and the trail curled around the mountainside, the volcano rising to my right, and an almost sheer cliff of black, volcanic rock that ended in the Pacific Ocean to my left. Waves slapped against the rocks, spraying white foam.

The island was the headquarters of Joyful Justice, the vigilante network named after my birth name, Joy Humbolt.

Dan Burke, our head of operations, purchased the island from the estate of a billionaire. A prepper, paranoid about the fate of the world, he'd designed and constructed a safe haven that could house almost a hundred people, inside the inactive volcano.

Now, the basement levels were used for our headquarters, and the top floors were housing. This was where all of the missions for Joyful Justice were planned and led from.

Most of the people who lived and worked here didn't know I was the inspiration for the organization. I faked Joy's death years ago, hoping to end the fascination with her, but all I did was make her a martyr. Now, Declan Doyle, a former New York Police detective and current Homeland Security asshat was blackmailing me, threatening to reveal my true identity and other secrets about my past.

I picked up my pace, my feet pounding against the soft, dirt path, my breath long and steady, my muscles beginning to burn. Blue sprinted ahead of me, looking back over his shoulder, his tongue lolling out, his smile infectious. The pure delight he experienced on a run was half the reason I did it. The other half was to steady my mind and keep myself sane. Too bad it wasn't working the way that it used to.

My trainer, Merl, taught me to run when he first met me. When I was sprinting, my lungs fighting for air, my muscles on fire, there was no room in my head for questions or fear. It was just me in my body, racing.

Blue barked and I picked up my pace, legs flying, extending to their full length. We came around a bend; the wind whipping off the ocean kicked my hair around my face so that it stung my cheeks. Blue barked and I slowed. Someone was coming in the opposite direction.

Merl's three Dobermans came charging down the path with him close behind. He wore his long, tightly curled, black hair up in a bun. Mirrored aviators sat on his nose.

We both came to a stop as the dogs greeted each other. The path was narrow here and a frisson of fear jostled me as the dogs pranced around each other. Of course, they could handle it; they knew where the edge was. They knew how far to push it. I wish I shared their insights.

"Good morning," Merl said. I returned the greeting, the "good" sticking in my throat. "You okay?" Merl took off his glasses. His big brown eyes framed by thick lashes caught my gaze.

"Sure, yeah. I just didn't sleep well."

Merl nodded slowly. "You sure? You've been kind of off lately."

I looked away from him. The wounds on Merl's wrist had healed, leaving fat, red scars. He'd recently been imprisoned himself, taken hostage in China while trying to rescue his love, Mo Ping. I'd saved him —the way that he had always saved me.

Could he help me now? Was there any help for me?

"How is Mo Ping?" I asked, changing the subject, looking out to the sea, hiding from him.

"She's good. Are you?" Merl reached out and touched my forearm, trying to get me to look at him. I kept my gaze averted. "Are you seeing things again?"

Merl knew what it was to love from afar; he'd spent years pining after Mo Ping before admitting his feelings. I could tell him about Mulberry. That was safe. "I dreamed about Mulberry last night."

Merl nodded, his lips set with empathy.

"Why don't you go to Costa Rica? Go see him." Mulberry was at our training camp deep in the Central American jungle half-way around the world. Merl was headed back there soon himself. If I hadn't promised to meet Declan Doyle in Tokyo so that he could lock me up in exchange for keeping my secrets, I'd have that option.

"Maybe I will," I lied.

"You could use a break. You've been going nonstop."

I nodded and looked over at him. Merl smiled, raising his eyebrows, trying to remind me that we were friends, that I could trust him.

"I'll see you at the council meeting today." I started to move past him.

"Sure, sounds good."

I picked up my pace again, just a gentle run. Blue tapping his nose rhythmically against my hip. Mulberry's kiss flirted through my mind and his words resounded inside my skull.

An asset? I stopped running, my feet freezing to the ground. Of course! I might not know when thunder was real, but I was an asset. Declan would be a fool to lock me up and throw away the key. There were things I could do that no one else on the planet could, connections I had that no one else did, and that made me way too important to disappear. I turned around and ran back toward Merl, his dogs alerting him to my approach. Merl turned and cocked his head in question.

I was out of breath when I reached him. "Merl, there is something I've got to tell you."

EK

We sat in Dan's office, five stories underground, overlooking the headquarters of Joyful Justice. Through the interior window, I could see the wall of screens and banks of desks facing it. There were no active missions at the moment, but the screens displayed several aerial shots, places we were watching, reconnaissance missions.

I had just finished telling them about the deal I had made with Declan Doyle. Doyle was a New York City cop when I first met him and was now an important operative for Homeland Security. He was the only person in authority who knew my secrets—that Sydney Rye was Joy Humbolt; that Joy the Martyr was thus still alive; and that it was Bobby Maxim, not Joy, who killed the mayor of New York City—the celebrated act that had made Joy an inspiration to so many.

Maxim had tried unsuccessfully to assassinate Doyle. Now Doyle was threatening to expose the truth about Joy/Sydney, destroying the mythology at the core of Joyful Justice, if I didn't turn myself in to him and go to prison for my various crimes.

"So, you're telling me that Declan Doyle isn't dead," Dan said. His sun-bleached hair was long, and he pushed it out of his eyes as he sat forward, his back to his desk that was covered in computer monitors. Merl and I sat on the black, leather couch, facing him. Our dogs lounged around the office, Blue by my feet, his eyes closed and breath even.

"That's right. He killed the assassin Robert Maxim sent after him and then made his offer to me."

Dan sat back in his chair; it creaked under his weight. He was over six feet tall, and pure wiry muscle. He led a stand-up paddleboard group four days a week, his way of getting the "computer nerds" out of the basement. His light-green eyes seemed even brighter against the dark tan of his skin.

"And you waited a week to tell us this?" Dan raised his eyebrows. A host of accusations were in that one sentence: you don't trust us, you're not a team player, you don't love me.

"It just occurred to me that he's not going to lock me up."

"I agree with her," Merl said. "I'm sure that Homeland Security wants something from her. Otherwise, there would be no reason to keep it secret. They'd want to announce her capture."

"So? What do you want to do?" Dan asked.

I was surprised he wasn't giving me more shit. Then again, maybe he'd finally realized what I was capable of. Or, more to the point, not capable of.

Dan and I had spent about six months together enjoying something very similar to love. Living in a small bungalow in Goa, India, he tended a garden and smoked hash while I read paperback novels. We shared a deep intimacy during that time, something I'd never had before, or since. The memory of his touch gave me strength. Dan was gentle and firm, strong and vulnerable: a wonderful man. It was the simplest my life had been since my brother's murder. The most peaceful. But, I couldn't live that way. There was no simple happiness for me. Unfortunately for Dan.

"I think we should let her go, and see how it plays out," Merl said. "You can track her, stay in touch. I don't think having a working relationship with Homeland Security is a terrible idea."

Dan shook his head. "No, it's a great idea." He turned to his computer for a moment. "I'll put a tracking beacon in Blue's collar." Blue raised his head at the sound of his name. "I've been working on something new that will allow me not only to track you, but also pick up on any communication devices near you and patch into them. So even if they take your cell, which I'm sure they will, we'll still be able to communicate."

"Wait, what? How is that possible?"

Dan looked over his shoulder at me and grinned. He was making fun of me and I smiled back, because I liked it when he teased. "Do you really want me to try and explain it to you?"

I shook my head. "I don't need to know the details of your genius, Dan. Just how I can use the damn thing."

He laughed. "Basically," he turned back around, crossing his foot over his thigh, "the beacon will allow me to patch into any cell phone or other form of communication device near you. So you're holding a walkie-talkie, I can cut in. You're with someone who has a cell phone, I can call you on it. Or just patch into the line."

"That's pretty cool."

"Actually," he grinned. "It's revolutionary."

"A revolutionary idea for a revolutionary. That works."

Merl's eyebrows conferred above his nose. "Sydney, I want to ask you something and I want you to be really honest with me." Lightning sizzled at the edge of my vision. I knew what he was going to ask and I knew that I would lie. "Are you seeing things?"

The lightning leapt across my vision and danced on the ceiling. I smiled. "Don't worry, I'm all good."

Continue reading *The Girl with the Gun*: emilykimelman.com/GG

EK

Sign up for my newsletter and stay up to date on new releases, free books, and giveaways:
emilykimelman.com/News

Join my Facebook group, *Emily Kimelman's Insatiable Readers,* **to stay up to date on sales and releases, have exclusive giveaways, and hang out with your fellow book addicts:** emilykimelman.com/EKIR.

AUTHOR'S NOTE

Thank you for reading *Shadow Harvest*. I'm excited that you made it here to my "note". I'm guessing that means that you enjoyed my story. If so, would you please write a review for *Shadow Harvest*? You have no idea how much it warms my heart to get a new review. And this isn't just for me, mind you. Think of all the people out there who need reviews to make decisions. The children who need to be told this book is not for them. And the people about to go away on vacation who could have so much fun reading this on the plane. Consider it an act of kindness to me, to the children, to humanity.

Let people know what you thought about *Shadow Harvest* on your favorite ebook retailer.

Thank you,

Emily

ACKNOWLEDGEMENTS

None of my books are possible without the help of so many people.

My best friend, Mette Hansen-Karademir, is the first person to read my stories and helps me to form them into what you all read. I don't know what I would do without her guidance.

My father, Donald Kimelman, helps my prose sing.

Autumn Whitehurst created the illustration for my cover and I think you'll all agree it's pretty awesome.

My husband, Sean, puts up with my mood swings, makes me dinner, tells me I'm wonderful, and generally takes care of me, understanding that sometimes my head is in Sydney Rye's world instead of our own.

ABOUT THE AUTHOR

I write because I love to read...but I have specific tastes. I love to spend time in fictional worlds where justice is exacted with a vengeance. Give me raw stories with a protagonist who feels like a friend, heroic pets, plots that come together with a BANG, and long series so the adventure can continue. If you got this far in my book then I'm assuming you feel the same…

Sign up for my newsletter and
never miss a new release or sale:
emilykimelman.com/News

Join my Facebook group, *Emily Kimelman's Insatiable Readers,* to stay up to date on sales and releases, have exclusive giveaways, and hang out with your fellow book addicts: emilykimelman.com/EKIR.

If you've read my work and want to get in touch please do! I loves hearing from readers.
www.emilykimelman.com
emily@emilykimelman.com

facebook.com/EmilyKimelman
instagram.com/emilykimelman

EMILY'S BOOKSHELF

Visit www.emilykimelman.com to purchase your next adventure.

EMILY KIMELMAN
MYSTERIES & THRILLERS

Sydney Rye Mysteries

Unleashed

Death in the Dark

Insatiable

Strings of Glass

Devil's Breath

Inviting Fire

Shadow Harvest

Girl with the Gun

In Sheep's Clothing

Flock of Wolves

Betray the Lie

Savage Grace

Blind Vigilance

Fatal Breach

Undefeated

Relentless

Brutal Mercy

Starstruck Thrillers

A Spy Is Born

EMILY REED

URBAN FANTASY

Kiss Chronicles

Lost Secret

Dark Secret

Stolen Secret

Buried Secret

Date TBA

Lost Wolf Legends

Butterfly Bones

Date TBA

Made in the USA
Middletown, DE
04 October 2024

61855085R00149